# LET ME TELL YOU A STORY

"You'll really want to believe it's all a pack of lies. The fact of the matter is you'll lose any respect you may have had for me when you hear the next."

"I don't know if I want to hear this . . ."

"I want you to."

# Sometimes They Bite

## 18 MURDEROUS TALES

---

# Sometimes They Bite

## LAWRENCE BLOCK

AVON BOOKS ◆ NEW YORK

AVON BOOKS
A division of
The Hearst Corporation
1350 Avenue of the Americas
New York, New York 10019

First Avon Books Printing: October 1992

AVON TRADEMARK REG. U.S. PAT. OFF. AND IN OTHER COUNTRIES, MARCA
REGISTRADA, HECHO EN CANADA

Printed in Canada

UNV   10   9   8   7   6   5   4   3

# ACKNOWLEDGMENTS

THE AUTHOR WISHES to acknowledge with gratitude the magazines in which these stories made their initial appearance. "And Miles to Go Before I Sleep" (originally published as "Life After Life"), "Collecting Ackermans", "The Dettweiler Solution", "Funny You Should Ask" (originally "A Pair of Recycled Jeans"), "Like a Dog in the Street", "Nothing Short of Highway Robbery", "One Thousand Dollars a Word", "Out the Window", "Sometimes They Bite", "Strangers on a Handball Court", "This Crazy Business of Ours" and "When This Man Dies" were first published in Alfred Hitchcock's Mystery Magazine. "A Bad Night for Burglars" (originally "Gentleman's Agreement"), "The Ehrengraf Defense" (originally "The Ehrengraf Method"), "The Ehrengraf Obligation" and "Going Through the Motions" first appeared in Ellery Queen's Mystery Magazine. "Like a Thief in the Night" was first published in Cosmopolitan.

For Mim and Hi and Lucy and Jerry with nepotic affection

# CONTENTS

# INTRODUCTION

SHORT STORIES ARE a labor of love. The magazine market for fiction has dried up, while the rates publishers pay have remained at pre-inflationary levels. I know a chap who makes a living writing nothing but short fiction, but I also know two men and a woman who make their living walking other people's dogs, and they at least don't have to worry about coming up with new ideas all the time.

It was not ever thus. There was a time when magazines provided us with the greater portion of our fictional amusement and diversion. The top markets paid high prices to top writers, while lesser markets served as an invaluable training ground for beginners. Television and mass-market paperback books changed all this, probably forever. The short story, like virtue, has become its own reward, and the only reason to sit down and write one is the personal satisfaction.

And isn't that reason enough? Novels are work, and plenty of it, and there are stretches in most of them that are about as much fun for the writer as trench warfare. A short story, on the other hand, can be held complete in the mind and written in a single session. I wouldn't suggest for a moment that it's easier to write saleable short stories than novels— it's probably the other way around—but it's a good deal less exhausting, and it's often more fun. The excitement of the idea, the initial burst of enthusiasm, is enough to see one through to the completion of the task.

11

I suspect these stories ought to be allowed to speak for themselves, but perhaps a few lines on the origins of some of them might be of interest. Most were written between books, or when a work in progress had ground to a halt. Some were produced in transit, with the typewriter propped on a motel desk and the author confronted by his own unshaven reflection in the mirror that always hangs above those desks.

The title story, *Sometimes They Bite*, was written at the Hatteras Island Motel in Rodanthe, North Carolina. I spent a month there one autumn, living entirely on what I caught fishing off the pier. It was in Rodanthe that I asked a shopkeeper about her source for recycled blue jeans, and a few days later, at a motel in Wilmington, North Carolina, *Funny You Should Ask* rolled out of the typewriter.

*Nothing Short of Highway Robbery* was also written on the road, and grew out of a galling incident. A stop for gas somewhere in Arizona led inexorably to a one hundred seventy-five dollar tab for various repairs,. and to this day I don't know whether I made a wise investment in preventive maintenance or got myself rather deftly conned. I pulled out of that service station steaming like an overheated Studebaker, and before I was five miles down the road the plot of the story had fixed itself in my mind. I wrote it the following morning in Roswell, New Mexico, hoping only to cover the repair bill with the proceeds. A subsequent television sale was frosting on the cupcake.

When I lived in New Brunswick, New Jersey, my cross-the-street neighbors were Bob and Helene Ferguson. Bob's dad ran the local animal shelter, which had to close because of an incident of vandalism similar to that described in *The Gentle Way*—but in the story I was able to bring matters to a more satisfactory conclusion.

I've included two stories about Martin Ehrengraf, the natty little criminal lawyer whose clients always turn out to be innocent. The late Fred Dannay, who bought the Ehrengraf stories for Ellery Queen's Mystery Magazine, saw Ehrengraf as a direct descendant of Randolph Mason, a similarly criminous lawyer created by Melville Davisson Post. I had never read the Post stories but am happy to continue the tradition. Mason ultimately reformed and became a force for good; Ehrengraf, I feel confident, will never undergo this sort of spiritual transformation. But I could be wrong.

Two other series characters appear in this collection: Bernie Rhodenbarr in *Like a Thief in the Night* and Matthew Scudder in *Out the Window.* The Rhodenbarr story is atypical in that he's not the viewpoint character, but I trust Bernie's friends and admirers will enjoy seeing him from another angle. (The title character in *A Bad Night for Burglars*, written before Bernie's debut in *Burglars Can't Be Choosers*, was probably a prototype for Bernie.)

Perhaps the best reason to include an introduction to this collection is that it provides me with the opportunity to thank Eleanor Sullivan, who bought and published so many of these stories in the first place. It is greatly to her credit that she accepted *One Thousand Dollars a Word*, a distressingly accurate portrayal of the economics of the short story game. And my thanks go too to publisher Don Fine and editor Arnold Ehrlich, who have enabled me to present these brief fictions in permanent form.

Some years ago Fredric Brown ended an introduction to a volume of short stories with the hope that the reader might get as much pleasure from them as he had derived from cashing the checks they had brought him. I can do better than that. I hope you enjoy reading them as much as I enjoy writing them.

—Lawrence Block

# SOMETIMES
# THEY
# BITE

MOWBRAY HAD BEEN fishing the lake for better than two hours before he encountered the heavy-set man. The lake was supposed to be full of largemouth bass and that was what he was after. He was using spinning gear, working a variety of plugs and spoons and jigs and plastic worms in all of the spots where a lunker largemouth was likely to be biding his time. He was a good fisherman, adept at dropping his lure right where he wanted it, just alongside a weedbed or at the edge of subsurface structure. And the lures he was using were ideal for late fall bass. He had everything going for him, he thought, but a fish on the end of his line.

He would fish a particular spot for a while, then move off to his right a little ways, as much for something to do as because he expected the bass to be more cooperative in another location. He was gradually working his way around the western rim of the lake when he stepped from behind some brush into a clearing and saw the other man no more than a dozen yards away.

The man was tall, several inches taller than Mowbray, very broad in the shoulders and trim in the hips and at the waist. He wore a fairly new pair of blue jeans and a poplin windbreaker over a navy flannel shirt. His boots looked identical to Mowbray's, and Mowbray guessed they'd been purchased from the same mail-order outfit in Maine. His gear was a baitcasting outfit, and Mowbray followed his line out with his eyes and saw a red bobber sitting on the water's surface some thirty yards out.

The man's chestnut hair was just barely touched with gray. He had a neatly trimmed moustache and the shadowy beard of someone who had arisen early in the morning. The skin on his hands and face suggested he spent much of his time out of doors. He was certainly around Mowbray's age, which was forty-four, but he was in much better shape than Mowbray was, in better shape, truth to tell, than Mowbray had ever been. Mowbray at once admired and envied him.

The man had nodded at Mowbray's approach, and Mowbray nodded in return, not speaking first because he was the invader. Then the man said,. "Afternoon. Having any luck?"

"Not a nibble."

"Been fishing long?"

"A couple of hours," Mowbray said. "Must have worked my way halfway around the lake, as much to keep moving as anything else. If there's a largemouth in the whole lake you couldn't prove it by me."

The man chuckled. "Oh, there's bass here, all right. It's a fine lake for bass, and a whole lot of other fish as well."

"Maybe I'm using the wrong lures."

The big man shook his head. "Doubtful. They'll bite anything when their dander is up. I think a largemouth would hit a shoelace if he was in the mood, and when he's sulky he wouldn't take your bait if you threw it in the water with no hook or line attached to it. That's just the way they are. Sometimes they bite and sometimes they don't."

"That's the truth." He nodded in the direction of the floating red bobber. "I don't suppose you're after bass yourself?"

"Not rigged up like this. No, I've been trying to get myself a couple of crappies." He pointed over his shoulder with his thumb, indicating where a campfire was laid. "I've got the skillet and the oil, I've got the meal to roll 'em in and I've got the fire all laid just waiting for the match. Now all I need is the fish."

"No luck?"

"No more than you're having."

"Which isn't a whole lot," Mowbray said. "You from around here?"

"No. Been through here a good many times, however. I've fished this lake now and again and had good luck more often than not."

"Well," Mowbray said. The man's company was invigorating, but there was a strict code of etiquette governing meetings of this nature. "I think I'll head on around the next bend. It's probably pointless but I'd like to get a plug in the water."

"You never can tell if it's pointless, can you? Any minute the wind can change or the temperature can drop a few degrees and the fish can change their behavior completely. That's what keeps us coming out here year after year, I'd say. The wonderful unpredictability of the whole affair. Say, don't go and take a hike on my account."

"Are you sure?"

The big man nodded, hitched at his trousers. "You can wet a line here as good as further down the bank. Your casting for bass won't make a lot of difference as to whether or not a crappie or a sunnie takes a shine to the shiner on my hook. And, to tell you the truth, I'd be just as glad for the company."

"So would I," Mowbray said, gratefully. "If you're sure you don't mind."

"I wouldn't have said boo if I did."

Mowbray set his aluminum tackle box on the ground, knelt beside it and rigged his line. He tied on a spoon plug, then got to his feet and dug out a pack of cigarettes from the breast pocket of his corduroy shirt. He said, "Smoke?"

"Gave 'em up a while back. But thanks all the same."

Mowbray smoked his cigarette about halfway down, then dropped the butt and ground it underfoot. He stepped to the water's edge, took a minute or so to read the surface of the lake then cast his plug a good distance out. For the next fifteen minutes or so the two men fished in companionable silence. Mowbray had no strikes but expected none and was resigned to it. He was enjoying himself just the same.

"Nibble," the big man announced. A minute or two went by and he began reeling in. "And a nibble's the extent of it," he said. "I'd better check and see if he left me anything."

The minnow had been bitten neatly in two. The big man had hooked him through the lips and now his tail was missing. His fingers very deft, the man slipped the shiner off the hook and substituted a live one from his bait pail. Seconds later the new minnow was in the water and the red bobber floated on the surface.

"I wonder what did that," Mowbray said.

"Hard to say. Crawdad, most likely. Something ornery."

"I was thinking that a nibble was a good sign, might mean the fish were going to start playing along with us. But if it's just a crawdad I don't suppose it means very much."

"I wouldn't think so."

"I was wondering," Mowbray said. "You'd think if there's bass in this lake you'd be after them instead of crappies."

"I suppose most people figure that way."

"None of my business, of course."

"Oh, that's all right. Hardly a sensitive subject. Happens I like the taste of little panfish better than the larger fish. I'm not a sport fisherman at heart, I'm afraid. I get a kick out of catching 'em, but my main interest is how they're going to taste when I've fried 'em up in the pan. A meat fisherman is what they call my kind, and the sporting fraternity mostly says the phrase with a certain amount of contempt." He exposed large white teeth in a sudden grin. "If they fished as often as I do, they'd probably lose some of their taste for the sporting aspect of it. I fish more days than I don't, you see. I retired ten years ago, had a retail business and sold it not too long after my wife died. We were never able to have any children so there was just myself and I wound up with enough capital to keep me without working if I didn't mind living simply. And I not only don't mind it, I prefer it."

"You're young to be retired."

"I'm fifty-five. I was forty-five when I retired, which may be on the young side, but I was ready for it."

"You look at least ten years younger than you are."

18

"If that's a fact, I guess retirement agrees with me. Anyway, all I really do is travel around and fish for my supper. And I'd rather catch small fish. I did the other kind of fishing and tired of it in no time at all. The way I see it, I never want to catch more fish than I intend to eat. If I kill something, it goes in that copper skillet over there. Or else I shouldn't have killed it in the first place."

Mowbray was silent for a moment, unsure what to say. Finally he said, "Well, I guess I just haven't evolved to that stage yet. I have to admit I still get a kick out of fishing, whether I eat what I catch or not. I usually eat them but that's not the most important part of it to me. But then I don't go out every other day like yourself. A couple times a year is as much as I can manage."

"Look at us talking," the man said, "and here you're not catching bass while I'm busy not catching crappie. We might as well announce that we're fishing for whales for all the difference it makes."

A little while later Mowbray retrieved his line and changed lures again, then lit another cigarette. The sun was almost gone. It had vanished behind the tree line and was probably close to the horizon by now. The air was definitely growing cooler. Another hour or so would be the extent of his fishing for the day. Then it would be time to head back to the motel and some cocktails and a steak and baked potato at the restaurant down the road. And then an evening of bourbon and water in front of the motel room's television set, lying on the bed with his feet up and the glass at his elbow and a cigarette burning in the ashtray.

The whole picture was so attractive that he was almost willing to skip the last hour's fishing. But the pleasure of the first sip of the first martini would lose nothing for being deferred an hour, and the pleasure of the big man's company was worth another hour of his time.

And then, a little while later, the big man said, "I have an unusual question to ask you."

"Ask away."

"Have you ever killed a man?"

It *was* an unusual question, and Mowbray took a few extra

seconds to think it over. "Well," he said at length, "I guess I have. The odds are pretty good that I have."

"You killed someone without knowing it?"

"That must have sounded odd. You see, I was in the artillery in Korea. Heavy weapons. We never saw what we were shooting at and never knew just what our shells were doing. I was in action for better than a year, stuffing shells down the throat of one big mother of a gun, and I'd hate to think that in all that time we never hit what we aimed at. So I must have killed men, but I don't suppose that's what you're driving at."

"I mean up close. And not in the service, that's a different proposition entirely."

"Never."

"I was in the service myself. An earlier war than yours, and I was on a supply ship and never heard a shot fired in anger. But about four years ago I killed a man." His hand dropped briefly to the sheath knife at his belt. "With this."

Mowbray didn't know what to say. He busied himself taking up the slack in his line and waited for the man to continue.

"I was fishing," the big man said. "All by myself, which is my usual custom. Saltwater though, not fresh like this. I was over in North Carolina on the Outer Banks. Know the place?" Mowbray shook his head. "A chain of barrier islands a good distance out from the mainland. Very remote. Damn fine fishing and not much else. A lot of people fish off the piers or go out on boats, but I was surfcasting. You can do about as well that way as often as not, and that way I figured to build a fire right there on the beach and cook my catch and eat it on the spot. I'd gathered up the driftwood and laid the fire before I wet a line, same as I did today. That's my usual custom. I had done the same thing the day before and I caught myself half a dozen Norfolk spot in no time at all, almost before I could properly say I'd been out fishing. But this particular day I didn't have any luck at all in three hours, which shows that saltwater fish are as unpredictable as the freshwater kind. You done much saltwater fishing?"

"Hardly any."

"I enjoy it about as much as freshwater, and I enjoyed that

20

day on the Banks even without getting a nibble. The sun was warm and there was a light breeze blowing off the ocean and you couldn't have asked for a better day. The next best thing to fishing and catching fish is fishing and not catching 'em, which is a thought we can both console ourselves with after today's run of luck."

"I'll have to remember that one."

"Well, I was having a good enough time even if it looked as though I'd wind up buying my dinner, and then I sensed a fellow coming up behind me. He must have come over the dunes because he was never in my field of vision. I knew he was there— just an instinct, I suppose—and I sent my eyes as far around as they'd go without moving my head, and he wasn't in sight." The big man paused, sighed. "You know," he said, "if the offer still holds, I believe I'll have one of those cigarettes of yours after all."

"You're welcome to one," Mowbray said, "but I hate to start you off on the habit again. Are you sure you want one?"

The wide grin came again. "I quit smoking about the same time I quit work. I may have had a dozen cigarettes since then, spaced over the ten-year span. Not enough to call a habit."

"Then I can't feel guilty about it." Mowbray shook the pack until a cigarette popped up, then extended it to his companion. After the man helped himself Mowbray took one as well, and lit them both with his lighter.

"Nothing like an interval of a year or so between cigarettes to improve their taste," the big man said. He inhaled a lungful of smoke, pursed his lips to expel it in a stream. "I'll tell you," he said, "I really want to tell you this story if you don't mind hearing it. It's one I don't tell often, but I feel a need to get it out from time to time. It may not leave you thinking very highly of me but we're strangers, never saw each other before and as likely will never see each other again. Do you mind listening?"

Mowbray was frankly fascinated and admitted as much.

"Well, there I was knowing I had someone standing behind me. And certain he was up to no good, because no one comes up behind you quiet like that and stands there out of sight with

21

the intention of doing you a favor. I was holding onto my rod, and before I turned around I propped it in the sand butt end down, the way people will do when they're fishing on a beach. Then I waited a minute, and then I turned around as if not expecting to find anyone there, and there he was, of course.

"He was a young fellow, probably no more than twenty-five. But he wasn't a hippie. No beard, and his hair was no longer than yours or mine. It did look greasy, though, and he didn't look too clean in general. Wore a light blue T-shirt and a pair of white duck pants. Funny how I remember what he wore but I can see him clear as day in my mind. Thin lips, sort of a wedge-shaped head, eyes that didn't line up quite right with each other, as though they had minds of their own. Some active pimples and the scars of old ones. He wasn't a prize.

"He had a gun in his hand. What you'd call a belly gun, a little .32-calibre Smith & Wesson with a two-inch barrel. Not good for a single damned thing but killing men at close range, which I'd say is all he ever wanted it for. Of course I didn't know the maker or calibre at the time. I'm not much for guns myself.

"He must have been standing less than two yards away from me. I wouldn't say it took too much instinct to have known he was there, not as close as he was."

The man drew deeply on the cigarette. His eyes narrowed in recollection, and Mowbray saw a short vertical line appear, running from the middle of his forehead almost to the bridge of his nose. Then he blew out smoke and his face relaxed and the line was gone.

"Well, we were all alone on that beach," the man continued. "No one within sight in either direction, no boats in close offshore, no one around to lend a helping hand. Just this young fellow with a gun in his hand and me with my hands empty. I began to regret sticking the rod in the sand. I'd done it to have both hands free, but I thought it might be useful to swing at him and try whipping the gun out of his hand.

"He said, 'All right, old man. Take your wallet out of your pocket nice and easy.' He was a Northerner, going by his accent, but the younger people don't have too much of an accent wherever they're from. Television, I suppose, is the cause of it. Makes the whole world smaller.

"Now I looked at those eyes, and at the way he was holding that gun, and I knew he wasn't going to take the wallet and wave bye-bye at me. He was going to kill me. In fact, if I hadn't turned around when I did he might well have shot me in the back. Unless he was the sort who liked to watch a person's face when he did it. There are people like that, I understand."

Mowbray felt a chill. The man's voice was so matter-of-fact, while his words were the stuff nightmares are made of.

"Well, I went into my pocket with my left hand. There was no wallet there. It was in the glove compartment of my car, parked off the road in back of the sand dunes. But I reached in my pocket to keep his eyes on my left hand, and then I brought the hand out empty and went for the gun with it, and at the same time I was bringing my knife out of the sheath with my right hand. I dropped my shoulder and came in low, and either I must have moved quick or all the drugs he'd taken over the years had slowed him some, but I swung that gun hand of his up and sent the gun sailing, and at the same time I got my knife into him and laid him wide open."

He drew the knife from its sheath. It was a filleting knife, with a natural wood handle and a thin, slightly curved blade about seven inches long. "This was the knife," he said. "It's a Rapala, made in Finland, and you can't beat it for being stainless steel and yet taking and holding an edge. I use it for filleting and everything else connected with fishing. But you've probably got one just like it yourself."

Mowbray shook his head. "I use a folding knife," he said.

"You ought to get one of these. Can't beat 'em. And they're handy when company comes calling, believe me. I'll tell you, I opened this youngster up the way you open a fish to clean him. Came in low in the abdomen and swept up clear to the bottom of the rib cage, and you'd have thought you were cutting butter as easy as it was." He slid the knife easily back into its sheath.

Mowbray felt a chill. The other man had finished his cigarette, and Mowbray put out his own and immediately selected a fresh

23

one from his pack. He started to return the pack to his pocket, then thought to offer it to the other man.

"Not just now. Try me in nine or ten months, though."

"I'll do that."

The man grinned his wide grin. Then his face went quickly serious. "Well, that young fellow fell down," he said. "Fell right on his back and lay there all opened up. He was moaning and bleeding and I don't know what else. I don't recall his words, his speech was disjointed, but what he wanted was for me to get him to a doctor.

"Now the nearest doctor was in Manteo. I happened to know this, and I was near Rodanthe which is a good twenty miles from Manteo if not more. I saw how he was cut and I couldn't imagine his living through a half-hour ride in a car. In fact if there'd been a doctor six feet away from us I seriously doubt he could have done the boy any good. I'm no doctor myself, but I have to say it was pretty clear to me that boy was dying.

"And if I tried to get him to a doctor, I'd be ruining the interior of my car for all practical purposes, and making a lot of trouble for myself in the bargain. I didn't expect anybody would seriously try to pin a murder charge on me. It stood to reason that fellow had a criminal record that would reach clear to the mainland and back, and I've never had worse than a traffic ticket and few enough of those. And the gun had his prints on it and none of my own. But I'd have to answer a few million questions and hang around for at least a week and doubtless longer for a coroner's inquest, and it all amounted to a lot of aggravation for no purpose, since he was dying anyway.

"And I'll tell you something else. It wouldn't have been worth the trouble even to save him, because what in the world was he but a robbing, murdering snake? Why, if they stitched him up he'd be on the street again as soon as he was healthy and he'd kill someone else in no appreciable time at all. No, I didn't mind the idea of him dying." His eyes engaged Mowbray's. "What would you have done?"

Mowbray thought about it. "I don't know," he said. "I honestly can't say. Same as you, probably."

24

"He was in horrible pain. I saw him lying there, and I looked around again to assure myself we were alone, and we were. I thought that I could grab my pole and frying pan and my few other bits of gear and be in my car in two or three minutes, not leaving a thing behind that could be traced to me. I'd camped out the night before in a tent and sleeping bag and wasn't registered in any motel or campground. In other words I could be away from the Outer Banks entirely in half an hour, with nothing to connect me to the area, much less to the man on the sand. I hadn't even bought gas with a credit card. I was free and clear if I just got up and left. All I had to do was leave this young fellow to a horribly slow and painful death." His eyes locked with Mowbray's again, with an intensity that was difficult to bear. "Or," he said, his voice lower and softer, "or I could make things easier for him."

"Oh."

"Yes. And that's just what I did. I took and slipped the knife right into his heart. He went instantly. The life slipped right out of his eyes and the tension out of his face and he was gone. And that made it murder."

"Yes, of course."

"Of course," the man echoed. "It might have been an act of mercy, but legally it transformed an act of self-defense into an unquestionable act of criminal homicide." He breathed deeply. "Think I was wrong to do it?"

"No," Mowbray said.

"Do the same thing yourself?"

"I honestly don't know. I hope I would, if the alternative was leaving him to suffer."

"Well, it's what I did. So I've not only killed a man, I've literally murdered a man. I left him under about a foot of sand at the edge of the dunes. I don't know when the body was discovered. I'm sure it didn't take too long. Those sands shift back and forth all the time. There was no identification on him, but the police could have labeled him from his prints, because an upstanding young man like him would have had his prints on file. Nothing on his person at all except for about fifty dollars in cash, which destroys the theory that he was robbing me in order to provide himself with that night's dinner." His face relaxed in a half-smile. "I took the money," he said. "Didn't see as he had any need for it, and I doubted he had much of a real claim to it, as far as that goes."

"So you not only killed a man but made a profit on it."

"I did at that. Well, I left the Banks that evening. Drove on inland a good distance, put up for the night in a motel just outside of Fayetteville. I never did look back, never did find out if and when they found him. It'd be on the books as an unsolved homicide if they did. Oh, and I took his gun and flung it halfway to Bermuda. And he didn't have a car for me to worry about. I suppose he thumbed a ride or came on foot, or else he parked too far away to matter." Another smile. "Now you know my secret," he said.

"Maybe you ought to leave out place names," Mowbray said.

"Why do that?"

"You don't want to give that much information to a stranger."

"You may be right, but I can only tell a story in my own way. I know what's going through your mind right now."

"You do?"

"Want me to tell you? You're wondering if what I told you is true or not. You figure if it happened I probably wouldn't tell you, and yet it sounds pretty believable in itself. And you halfway hope it's the truth and halfway hope it isn't. Am I close?"

"Very close," Mowbray admitted.

"Well, I'll tell you something that'll tip the balance. You'll really want to believe it's all a pack of lies." He lowered his eyes. "The fact of the matter is you'll lose any respect you may have had for me when you hear the next."

"Then why tell me?"

"Because I feel the need."

"I don't know if I want to hear this," Mowbray said.

"I want you to. No fish and it's getting dark and you're probably anxious to get back to wherever you're staying and have a drink and a meal. Well, this won't take long." He had been reeling in his line. Now the operation was concluded, and he set the rod

26

deliberately on the grass at his feet. Straightening up, he said, "I told you before about my attitude toward fish. Not killing what I'm not going to eat. And there this young man was, all laid open, internal organs exposed—"

"Stop."

"I don't know what you'd call it, curiosity or compulsion or some primitive streak. I couldn't say. But what I did, I cut off a small piece of his liver before I buried him. Then after he was under the sand I lit my cookfire and—well, no need to go into detail."

Thank God for that, Mowbray thought. For small favors. He looked at his hands. The left one was trembling. The right, the one gripping his spinning rod, was white at the knuckles, and the tips of his fingers ached from gripping the butt of the rod so tightly.

"Murder, cannibalism and robbing the dead. That's quite a string for a man who never got worse than a traffic ticket. And all three in considerably less than an hour."

"Please," Mowbray said. His voice was thin and high-pitched. "Please don't tell me any more."

"Nothing more to tell."

Mowbray took a deep breath, held it. This man was either lying or telling the truth, Mowbray thought, and in either case he was quite obviously an extremely unusual person. At the very least.

"You shouldn't tell that story to strangers," he said after a moment. "True or false, you shouldn't tell it."

"I now and then feel the need."

"Of course, it's all to the good that I *am* a stranger. After all, I don't know anything about you, not even your name."

"It's Tolliver."

"Or where you live, or—"

"Wallace P. Tolliver. I was in the retail hardware business in Oak Falls, Missouri. That's not far from Joplin."

"Don't tell me anything more," Mowbray said desperately. "I wish you hadn't told me what you did."

"I had to," the big man said. The smile flashed again. "I've told that story three times before today. You're the fourth man ever to hear it."

Mowbray said nothing.

"Three times. Always to strangers who happen to turn up while I'm fishing. Always on long lazy afternoons, those afternoons when the fish just don't bite no matter what you do."

Mowbray began to do several things. He began to step backward, and he began to release his tight hold on his fishing rod, and he began to extend his left arm protectively in front of him.

But the filleting knife had already cleared its sheath.

# THE EHRENGRAF DEFENSE

"AND YOU ARE Mrs. Culhane," Martin Ehrengraf said. "Do sit down, yes, I think you will find that chair comfortable. And please pardon the disarray. It is the natural condition of my office. Chaos stimulates me. Order stifles me. It is absurd, is it not, but so then is life itself, eh?"

Dorothy Culhane sat, nodded. She studied the small, trimly built man who remained standing behind his extremely disorderly desk. Her eyes took in the narrow moustache, the thin lips, the deeply set dark eyes. If the man liked clutter in his surroundings, he certainly made up for it in his grooming and attire. He wore a starched white shirt, a perfectly tailored dove gray three-button suit, a narrow dark blue necktie.

Oh, but she did not want to think about neckties—

"Of course you are Clark Culhane's mother," Ehrengraf said. "I had it that you had already retained an attorney."

"Alan Farrell."

"A good man," Ehrengraf said. "An excellent reputation."

"I dismissed him this morning."

"Ah."

Mrs. Culhane took a deep breath. "He wanted Clark to plead guilty," she said. "Temporary insanity, something of the sort.

29

He wanted my son to admit to killing that girl."

"And you did not wish him to do this."

"My son is innocent!" The words came in a rush, uncontrollably. She calmed herself. "My son is innocent," she repeated, levelly now. "He could never kill anyone. He can't admit to a crime he never committed in the first place."

"And when you said as much to Farrell—"

"He told me he was doubtful of his ability to conduct a successful defense based on a plea of innocent." She drew herself up. "So I decided to find someone who could."

"And you came to me."

"Yes."

The little lawyer had seated himself. Now he was doodling idly on a lined yellow scratch pad. "Do you know much about me, Mrs. Culhane?"

"Not very much. It's said that your methods are unorthodox—"

"Indeed."

"But that you get results."

"Results. Indeed, results." Martin Ehrengraf made a tent of his fingertips and, for the first time since she had entered his office, a smile bloomed briefly on his thin lips. "Indeed I get results. I *must* get results, my dear Mrs. Culhane, or else I do not get my dinner. And while my slimness might indicate otherwise, it is my custom to eat very well indeed. You see, I do something which no other criminal lawyer does, at least not to my knowledge. You have heard what this is?"

"I understand you operate on a contingency basis."

"A contingency basis." Ehrengraf was nodding emphatically. "Yes, that is precisely what I do. I operate on a contingency basis. My fees are high, Mrs. Culhane. They are extremely high. But they are due and payable only in the event that my efforts are crowned with success. If a client of mine is found guilty, then my work on his behalf costs him nothing."

The lawyer got to his feet again, stepped out from behind his desk. Light glinted on his highly polished black shoes. "This is common enough in negligence cases. The attorney gets a share in the settlement. If he loses he gets nothing. How much greater is his incentive to perform to the best of his ability, eh? But why limit this practice to negligence suits? Why not have all lawyers paid in this fashion? And doctors, for that matter. If the operation's a failure, why not let the doctor absorb some of the loss, eh? But such an arrangement would be a long time coming, I am afraid. Yet I have found it workable in my practice. And my clients have been pleased by the results."

"If you can get Clark acquitted—"

"Acquitted?" Ehrengraf rubbed his hands together. "Mrs. Culhane, in my most notable successes it is not even a question of acquittal. It is rather a matter of the case never even coming to trial. New evidence is discovered, the actual miscreant confesses or is brought to justice, and one way or another charges against my client are dropped. Courtroom pyrotechnics, wizardry in cross-examination—ah, I prefer to leave that to the Perry Masons of the world. It is not unfair to say, Mrs. Culhane, that I am more the detective than the lawyer. What is the saying? 'The best defense is a good offense.' Or perhaps it is the other way around, the best offense being a good defense, but it hardly matters. It is a saying in warfare and in the game of chess, I believe, and neither serves as the ideal metaphor for what concerns us. And what does concern us, Mrs. Culhane—" and he leaned toward her and the dark eyes flashed "—what concerns us is saving your son's life and securing his freedom and preserving his reputation. Yes?"

"Yes. Yes, of course."

"The evidence against your son is considerable, Mrs. Culhane. The dead girl, Althea Patton, was his former fiancée. It is said that she jilted him—"

"He broke the engagement."

"I don't doubt that for a moment, but the prosecution would have it otherwise. This Patton girl was strangled. Around her throat was found a necktie."

Mrs. Culhane's eyes went involuntarily to the lawyer's own blue tie, then slipped away.

"A particular necktie, Mrs. Culhane. A necktie made exclusively for and worn exclusively by members of the Caedmon Society at Oxford University. Your son attended Dartmouth, Mrs. Culhane, and after graduation he spent a year in advanced study in England."

"Yes."

"At Oxford University."

"Yes."

"Where he became a member of the Caedmon Society."

"Yes."

Ehrengraf breathed in through clenched teeth. "He owned a necktie of the Caedmon Society. He appears to be the only member of the society residing in this city and would thus presumably be the only person to own such a tie. He cannot produce that tie, nor can he provide a satisfactory alibi for the night in question."

"Someone must have stolen his tie."

"The murderer, of course."

"To frame him."

"Of course," Ehrengraf said soothingly. "There could be no other explanation, could there?" He breathed in, he breathed out, he set his chin decisively. "I will undertake your son's defense," he announced. "And on my usual terms."

"Oh, thank heavens."

"My fee will be seventy-five thousand dollars. That is a great deal of money, Mrs. Culhane, although you might very well have ended up paying Mr. Farrell that much or more by the time you'd gone through the tortuous processes of trial and appeal and so on, and after he'd presented an itemized accounting of his expenses. My fee includes any and all expenses which I might incur. No matter how much time and effort and money I spend on your son's behalf, the cost to you will be limited to the figure I named. And none of that will be payable unless your son is freed. Does that meet with your approval?"

She hardly had to hesitate but made herself take a moment before replying. "Yes," she said. "Yes, of course. The terms are satisfactory."

"Another point. If, ten minutes from now, the district attorney should decide of his own accord to drop all charges against your son, you nevertheless owe me seventy-five thousand dollars. Even though I should have done nothing to earn it."

"I don't see—"

The thin lips smiled. The dark eyes did not participate in the smile. "It is my policy, Mrs. Culhane. Most of my work, as I have said, is more the work of a detective than the work of a lawyer. I operate largely behind the scenes and in the shadows. Perhaps I set currents in motion. Often when the smoke clears it is hard to prove to what extent my client's victory is the fruit of my labor. Thus I do not attempt to prove anything of the sort. I merely share in the victory by collecting my fee in full whether I seem to have earned it or not. You understand?"

It did seem reasonable, even if the explanation was the slightest bit hazy. Perhaps the little man dabbled in bribery, perhaps he knew the right strings to pull but could scarcely disclose them after the fact. Well, it hardly mattered. All that mattered was Clark's freedom, Clark's good name.

"Yes," she said. "Yes, I understand. When Clark is released you'll be paid in full."

"Very good."

She frowned. "In the meantime you'll want a retainer, won't you? An advance of some sort?"

"You have a dollar?" She looked in her purse, drew out a dollar bill. "Give it to me, Mrs. Culhane. Very good, very good. An advance of one dollar against a fee of seventy-five thousand dollars. And I assure you, my dear Mrs. Culhane, that should this case not resolve itself in unqualified success I shall even return this dollar to you." The smile, and this time there was a twinkle in the eyes. "But that will not happen, Mrs. Culhane, because I do not intend to fail."

It was a little more than a month later when Dorothy Culhane made her second visit to Martin Ehrengraf's office. This time the little lawyer's suit was a navy blue pinstripe, his necktie maroon with a subdued below-the-knot design. His starched white shirt might have been the same one she had seen on her earlier visit. The shoes, black wing tips, were as highly polished as the other pair he'd been wearing.

His expression was changed slightly. There was something that might have been sorrow in the deep-set eyes, a look that suggested a continuing disappointment with human nature.

"It would seem quite clear," Ehrengraf said now. "Your son has been released. All charges have been dropped. He is a free man, free even to the extent that no shadow of suspicion hangs over him in the public mind."

"Yes," Mrs. Culhane said, "and that's wonderful, and I couldn't be happier about it. Of course it's terrible about the girls, I hate to think that Clark's happiness and my own happiness stem from their tragedy, or I suppose it's tragedies, isn't it, but all the same I feel—"

"Mrs. Culhane."

She bit off her words, let her eyes meet his.

"Mrs. Culhane, it's quite cut and dried, is it not? You owe me seventy-five thousand dollars."

"But—"

"We discussed this, Mrs. Culhane. I'm sure you recall our discussion. We went over the matter at length. Upon the successful resolution of this matter you were to pay me my fee, seventy-five thousand dollars. Less, of course, the sum of one dollar already paid over to me as a retainer."

"But—"

"Even if I did nothing. Even if the district attorney elected to drop charges before you'd even departed from these premises. That, I believe, was the example I gave at the time."

"Yes."

"And you agreed to those terms."

"Yes, but—"

"But what, Mrs. Culhane?"

She took a deep breath, set herself bravely. "Three girls," she said. "Strangled, all of them, just like Althea Patton. All of them the same physical type, slender blondes with high foreheads and prominent front teeth, two of them here in town and one across the river in Montclair, and around each of their throats—"

"A necktie."

"The same necktie."

"A necktie of the Caedmon Society of Oxford University."

"Yes." She drew another breath. "So it was obvious that there's a maniac at large," she went on, "And the last killing was in Montclair, so maybe he's leaving the area, and my God, I hope so, it's terrifying, the idea of a man just killing girls at random because they remind him of his mother—"

"I beg your pardon?"

"That's what somebody was saying on television last night. A psychiatrist. It was just a theory."

"Yes," Ehrengraf said. "Theories are interesting, aren't they? Speculation, guesswork, hypotheses, all very interesting."

"But the point is—"

"Yes?"

"I know what we agreed, Mr. Ehrengraf. I know all that. But on the other hand you made one visit to Clark in prison, that was just one brief visit, and then as far as I can see you did nothing at all, and just because the madman happened to strike again and kill the other girls in exactly the same manner and even use the same tie, well, you have to admit that seventy-five thousand dollars sounds like quite a windfall for you."

"A windfall."

"So I was discussing this with my own attorney—he's not a criminal lawyer, he handles my personal affairs—and he suggested that you might accept a reduced fee by way of settlement."

"He suggested this, eh?"

She avoided the man's eyes. "Yes, he did suggest it, and I must say it seems reasonable to me. Of course I would be glad to reimburse you for any expenses you incurred, although I can't honestly say that you could have run up much in the way of expenses, and he suggested that I might give you a fee on top of that of five thousand dollars, but I *am* grateful, Mr. Ehrengraf, and I'd be willing to make that ten thousand dollars, and you have to admit that's not a trifle, don't you? I have money, I'm comfortably set up financially, but no one can afford to pay out seventy-five thousand dollars for nothing at all, and—"

"Human beings," Ehrengraf said, and closed his eyes. "And the rich are the worst of all," he added, opening his eyes, fixing them upon Dorothy Culhane. "It is an unfortunate fact of life that only the rich can afford to pay high fees. Thus I must make my living acting on their behalf. The poor, they do not agree to an arrangement when they are desperate and go back on their word when they are in more reassuring circumstances."

"It's not so much that I'd go back on my word," Mrs. Culhane said. "It's just that—"

"Mrs. Culhane."

"Yes?"

"I am going to tell you something which I doubt will have any effect upon you, but at least I shall have tried. The best thing you could do, right at this moment, would be to take out your checkbook and write out a check to me for payment in full. You will probably not do this, and you will ultimately regret it."

"Is that... are you threatening me?"

A flicker of a smile. "Certainly not. I have given you not a threat but a prediction. You see, if you do not pay my fee, what I shall do is tell you something else which will lead you to pay me my fee after all."

"I don't understand."

"No," Martin Ehrengraf said. "No, I don't suppose you do. Mrs. Culhane, you spoke of expenses. You doubted I could have incurred significant expenses on your son's behalf. There are many things I could say, Mrs. Culhane, but I think it might be best for me to confine myself to a brisk accounting of a small portion of my expenses."

"I don't—"

"Please, my dear lady. Expenses. If I were listing my expenses, dear lady, I would begin by jotting down my train fare to New York City. Then taxi fare to Kennedy Airport, which comes to twenty dollars with tip and bridge tolls, isn't that exorbitant?"

"Mr. Ehrengraf—"

"*Please.* Then airfare to London and back. I always fly first class, it's an indulgence, but since I pay my own expenses out of my own pocket I feel I have the right to indulge myself. Next

36

a rental car hired from Heathrow Airport and driven to Oxford and back. The price of gasoline is high enough over here, Mrs. Culhane, but in England they call it petrol and they charge the earth for it."

She stared at him. His hands were folded atop his disorderly desk and he went on talking in the calmest possible tone of voice and she felt her jaw dropping but could not seem to raise it back into place.

"In Oxford I had to visit five gentlemen's clothiers, Mrs. Culhane. One shop had no Caedmon Society cravats in stock at the moment. I purchased one necktie from each of the other shops. I felt it really wouldn't do to buy more than one tie in any one shop. A man prefers not to call attention to himself unnecessarily. The Caedmon Society necktie, Mrs. Culhane, is not unattractive. A navy blue field with a half-inch stripe of royal blue and two narrower flanking stripes, one of gold and the other of a rather bright green. I don't care for regimental stripes myself, Mrs. Culhane, preferring as I do a more subdued style in neckwear, but the Caedmon tie is a handsome one all the same."

"My God."

"There were other expenses, Mrs. Culhane, but as I pay them myself I don't honestly think there's any need for me to recount them to you, do you?"

"My God. Dear God in heaven."

"Indeed. It would have been better all around, as I said a few moments ago, had you decided to pay my fee without hearing what you've just heard. Ignorance in this case would have been, if not bliss, at least a good deal closer to bliss than what you're undoubtedly feeling at the moment."

"Clark didn't kill that girl."

"Of course he didn't, Mrs. Culhane. Of course he didn't. I'm sure some rotter stole his tie and framed him. But that would have been an enormous chore to prove and all a lawyer could have done was persuade a jury that there was room for doubt, and poor Clark would have had a cloud over him all the days of his life. Of course you and I know he's innocent—"

"He *is* innocent," she said. "He *is*."

"Of course he is, Mrs. Culhane. The killer was a homicidal maniac striking down young women who remind him of his mother. Or his sister, or God knows whom. You'll want to get out your checkbook, Mrs. Culhane, but don't try to write the check just yet. Your hands are trembling. Just sit there, that's the ticket, and I'll get you a glass of water. Everything's perfectly fine, Mrs. Culhane. That's what you must remember. Everything's perfectly fine and everything will continue to be perfectly fine. Here you are, a couple of ounces of water in a paper cup, just drink it down, there you are, *there* you are."

And when it was time to write out the check her hand did not shake a bit. Pay to the order of Martin H. Ehrengraf, seventy-five thousand dollars, signed Dorothy Rodgers Culhane. Signed with a ball-point pen, no need to blot it dry, and handed across the desk to the impeccably dressed little man.

"Yes, thank you, thank you very much, my dear lady. And here is your dollar, the retainer you gave me. Go ahead and take it, please."

She took the dollar.

"Very good. And you probably won't want to repeat this conversation to anyone. What would be the point?"

"No. No, I won't say anything."

"Of course not."

"Four neckties." He looked at her, raised his eyebrows a fraction of an inch. "You said you bought four of the neckties. There were—there were three girls killed."

"Indeed there were."

"What happened to the fourth necktie?"

"Why, it must be in my bureau drawer, don't you suppose? And perhaps they're all there, Mrs. Culhane. Perhaps all four neckties are in my bureau drawer, still in their original wrappings, and purchasing them was just a waste of time and money on my part. Perhaps that homicidal maniac had neckties of his own and the four in my drawer are just an interesting souvenir and a reminder of what might have been."

"Oh."

"And perhaps I've just told you a story out of the whole cloth, an interesting turn of phrase since we are speaking of silk neckties. Perhaps I never flew to London at all, never motored to Oxford, never purchased a single necktie of the Caedmon Society. Perhaps that was just something I trumped up on the spur of the moment to coax a fee out of you."

"But—"

"Ah, my dear lady," he said, moving to the side of her chair, taking her arm, helping her out of the chair, turning her, steering her toward the door. "We would do well, Mrs. Culhane, to believe that which it most pleases us to believe. I have my fee. You have your son. The police have another line of inquiry to pursue altogether. It would seem we've all come out of this well, wouldn't you say? Put your mind at rest, Mrs. Culhane, dear Mrs. Culhane. There's the elevator down the hall on your left. If you ever need my services you know where I am and how to reach me. And perhaps you'll recommend me to your friends. But discreetly, dear lady. Discreetly. Discretion is everything in matters of this sort."

She walked very carefully down the hall to the elevator and rang the bell and waited. And she did not look back. Not once.

# STRANGERS ON A HANDBALL COURT

WE MET FOR the first time on a handball court in Sheridan Park. It was a Saturday morning in early summer with the sky free of clouds and the sun warm but not yet unbearable. He was alone on the court when I got there and I stood for a few moments watching him warm up, slamming the little ball viciously against the imperturbable backstop.

He didn't look my way, although he must have known I was watching him. When he paused for a moment I said, "A game?"

He looked my way. "Why not?"

I suppose we played for two hours, perhaps a little longer. I've no idea how many games we played. I was several years younger, weighed considerably less and topped him by four or five inches.

He won every game.

When we broke, the sun was high in the sky and considerably hotter than it had been when we started. We had both been sweating freely and we stood together, rubbing our faces and chests with our towels. "Good workout," he said. "There's nothing like it."

"I hope you at least got some decent exercise out of it," I said apologetically. "I certainly didn't make it much of a contest."

"Oh, don't bother yourself about that," he said, and flashed a shark's smile. "Tell you the truth, I like to win. On and off the court. And I certainly got a workout out of you."

I laughed. "As a matter of fact, I managed to work up a thirst. How about a couple of beers? On me, in exchange for the hand-ball lesson."

He grinned. "Why not?"

We didn't talk much until we were settled in a booth at the Hofbrau House. Generations of collegians had carved combinations of Greek letters into the top of our sturdy oak table. I was in the middle of another apology for my athletic inadequacy when he set his stein down atop Zeta Beta Tau and shook a cigarette out of his pack. "Listen," he said, "forget it. What the hell, maybe you're lucky in love."

I let out a bark of mirthless laughter. "If this is luck," I said, "I'd hate to see misfortune."

"Problems?"

"You might say so."

"Well, if it's something you'd rather not talk about—"

I shook my head. "It's not that—it might even do me good to talk about it—but it would bore the daylights out of you. It's hardly an original problem. The world is overflowing these days with men in the very same leaky boat."

"Oh?"

"I've got a girl," I said. "I love her and she loves me. But I'm afraid I'm going to lose her."

He frowned, thinking about it. "You're married," he said.

"No."

"She's married."

I shook my head. "No, we're both single. She wants to get married."

"But you don't want to marry her."

"There's nothing I want more than to marry her and spend the rest of my life with her."

His frown deepened. "Wait a minute," he said. "Let me think. You're both single, you both want to get married, but there's a problem. All I can think of is she's your sister, but I can't believe that's it, especially since you said it's a common problem. I'll tell you, I think my brain's tired from too much time in the sun. What's the problem?"

"I'm divorced."

"So who isn't? I'm divorced and I'm remarried. Unless it's a religious thing. I bet that's what it is."

"No."

"Well, don't keep me guessing, fella. I already gave up once, remember?"

"The problem is my ex-wife," I said. "The judge gave her everything I had but the clothes I was wearing at the time of the trial. With the alimony I have to pay her, I'm living in a furnished room and cooking on a hotplate. I can't afford to get married, and my girl wants to get married—and sooner or later she's going to get tired of spending her time with a guy who can never afford to take her anyplace decent." I shrugged. "Well," I said, "you get the picture."

"Boy, do I get the picture."

"As I said, it's not a very original problem."

"You don't know the half of it." He signaled the waiter for two more beers, and when they arrived he lit another cigarette and took a long swallow of his beer. "It's really something," he said. "Meeting like this. I already told you I got an ex-wife of my own."

"These days almost everybody does."

"That's the truth. I must have had a better lawyer than you did, but I still got burned pretty bad. She got the house, she got the Cadillac and just about everything else she wanted. And now she gets fifty cents out of every dollar I make. She's got no kids, she's got no responsibilities, but she gets fifty cents out of every dollar I earn and the government gets another thirty or forty cents. What does that leave me?"

"Not a whole lot."

"You better believe it. As it happens I make a good living. Even with what she and the government take I manage to live

43

pretty decently. But do you know what it does to me, paying her all that money every month? I hate that woman's guts and she lives like a queen at my expense."

I took a long drink of beer. "I guess our problems aren't all that different."

"And a lot of men can say the same thing. Millions of them. A word of advice, friend. What you should do if you marry your girl friend—"

"I can't marry her."

"But if you go ahead and marry her anyway. Just make sure you do what I did before I married my second wife. It goes against the grain to do it because when you're about to marry someone you're completely in love and you're sure it's going to last forever. But make a prenuptial agreement. Have it all signed and witnessed before the marriage ceremony, and have it specify that if there's a divorce she does not get dime one, she gets zip. You follow me? Get yourself a decent lawyer so he'll draw up something that will stand up, and get her to sign it, which she most likely will because she'll be so starry-eyed about getting married. Then you'll have nothing to worry about. If the marriage is peaches and cream forever, which I hope it is, then you've wasted a couple of hundred dollars on a lawyer and that's no big deal. But if anything goes wrong with the marriage, you're in the catbird seat."

I looked at him for a long moment. "It makes sense," I said.

"That's what I did. Now my second wife and I, we get along pretty good. She's young, she's beautiful, she's good company, I figure I got a pretty good deal. We have our bad times, but they're nothing two people can't live with. And the thing is, she's not tempted by the idea of divorcing me, because she knows what she'll come out with if she does. Zeeee-ro."

"If I ever get married again," I said, "I'll take your advice."

"I hope so."

"But it'll never happen," I said. "Not with my ex-wife bleeding me to death. You know, I'm almost ashamed to say this, but what the hell, we're strangers, we don't really know each other, so I'll admit it. I have fantasies of killing her. Stabbing her, shooting her, tying her to a railroad track and letting a train solve my problem for me."

"Friend, you are not alone. The world is full of men who dream about killing their ex-wives."

"Of course I'd never do it. Because if anything ever happened to that woman, the police would come straight to me."

"Same here. If I ever put my ex in the ground, there'd be a cop knocking on my door before the body was cold. Of course that particular body was *born* cold, if you know what I mean."

"I know what you mean," I said. This time I signaled for more beer, and we fell silent until it was on the table in front of us. Then, in a confessional tone, I said, "I'll tell you something. I would do it. If I weren't afraid of getting caught, I would literally do it. I'd kill her."

"I'd kill mine."

"I mean it. There's no other way out for me. I'm in love and I want to get married and I can't. My back is to the proverbial wall. I'd do it."

He didn't even hesitate. "So would I."

"Really?"

"Sure. You could say it's just money, and that's most of it, but there's more to it than that. I hate that woman. I hate the fact that she's made a complete fool out of me. If I could get away with it, they'd be breaking ground in her cemetery plot any day now." He shook his head. "*Her* cemetery plot," he said bitterly. "It was originally *our* plot, but the judge gave her the whole thing. Not that I have any overwhelming urge to be buried next to her, but it's the principle of the thing."

"If only we could get away with it," I said. And, while the sentence hung in the air like an off-speed curve ball, I reached for my beer.

Of course a light bulb did not actually form above the man's head—that only happens in comic strips—but the expression on his jowly face was so eloquent that I must admit I looked up expecting to see the light bulb. This, clearly, was a man who had just Had An Idea.

He didn't share it immediately. Instead he took a few minutes to work it out in his mind while I worked on my beer. When I saw that he was ready to speak I put my stein down.

"I don't know you," he said.

I allowed that this was true.

"And you don't know me. I don't know your name, even your first name."

"It's—"

He showed me a palm. "Don't tell me. I don't want to know. Don't you see what we are? We're strangers."

"I guess we are."

"We played handball for a couple of hours. But no one even knows we played handball together. We're having a couple of beers together, but only the waiter knows that and he won't remember it, and anyway no one would ever think to ask him. Don't you see the position we're in? We each have someone we want dead. Don't you understand?"

"I'm not sure."

"I saw a movie years ago. Two strangers meet on a train and— I wish I could remember the title."

*"Strangers on a Train?"*

"That sounds about right. Anyway, they get to talking, tell each other their problems and decide to do each other's murder. Do you get my drift?"

"I'm beginning to."

"You've got an ex-wife, and I've got an ex-wife. You said you'd commit murder if you had a chance to get away with it, and *I'd* commit murder if I had a chance to get away with it. And all we have to do to get away with it is switch victims." He leaned forward and dropped his voice to an urgent whisper. There was no one near us, but the occasion seemed to demand low voices. "Nothing could be simpler, friend. *You* kill *my* ex-wife. *I* kill *your* ex-wife. And we're both home free."

My eyes widened. "That's brilliant," I whispered back. "It's absolutely brilliant."

"You'd have thought of it yourself in another minute," he said modestly. "The conversation was headed in that direction."

46

"Just brilliant," I said.

We sat that way for a moment, our elbows on the table, our heads separated by only a few inches, basking in the glow generated by his brilliant idea. Then he said, "One big hurdle. One of us has to go first."

"I'll go first," I offered. "After all, it was your idea. It's only fair that I go first."

"But suppose you went first and I tried to weasel out after you'd done your part?"

"Oh, you wouldn't do that."

"Damn right I wouldn't, friend. But you can't be sure of it, not sure enough to take the short straw voluntarily." He reached into his pocket and produced a shiny quarter. "Call it," he said, tossing it into the air.

"Heads," I said. I always call heads. Just about everyone always calls heads.

The coin landed on the table, spun for a dramatic length of time then came to rest between Sigma Nu and Delta Kappa Epsilon.

Tails.

I managed to see Vivian for a half hour that afternoon. After the usual complement of urgent kisses I said, "I'm hopeful. About us, I mean. About our future."

"Really?"

"Really. I have the feeling things are going to work out."

"Oh, darling," she said.

The following Saturday dawned bright and clear. By arrangement we met on the handball court, but this time we played only half a dozen games before calling it a day. And after we had toweled off and put on shirts, we went to a different bar and had but a single beer apiece.

"Wednesday or Thursday night," he said. "Wednesday I'll be playing poker. It's my regular game and it'll last until two or three in the morning. It always does, and I'll make certain that this is no exception. On Thursday, my wife and I are invited to a dinner party and we'll be playing bridge afterward. That won't last past midnight, so Wednesday would be better—"

"Wednesday's fine with me."

"She lives alone and she's almost always home by ten. As a matter of fact she rarely leaves the house. I don't blame her, it's a beautiful house." He pursed his lips. "But forget that. The earlier in the evening you do the job, the better it is for me— in case doctors really can determine time of death—"

"I'll call the police."

"How's that?"

"After she's dead I'll give the police an anonymous phone call, tip them off. That way they'll discover the body while you're still at the poker game. That lets you out completely."

He nodded approval. "That's damned intelligent," he said. "You know something? I'm thrilled you and I ran into each other. I don't know your name and I don't want to know your name, but I sure like your style. Wednesday night?"

"Wednesday night," I agreed. "You'll hear it on the news Thursday morning, and by then your troubles will be over."

"Fantastic," he said. "Oh, one other thing." He flashed the shark's smile. "If she suffers," he said, "that's perfectly all right with me."

She didn't suffer.

I did it with a knife. I told her I was a burglar and that she wouldn't be hurt if she cooperated. It was not the first lie I ever told in my life. She cooperated, and when her attention was elsewhere I stabbed her in the heart. She died with an expression of extreme puzzlement on her none-too-pretty face, but she didn't suffer, and that's something.

Once she was dead I went on playing the part of the burglar. I ransacked the house, throwing books from their shelves and turning drawers over and generally making a dreadful mess. I found quite a bit of jewelry, which I ultimately put down a sewer, and I found several hundred dollars in cash, which I did not.

After I'd dropped the knife down another sewer and the white cotton gloves down yet a third sewer, I called the police. I said

48

I'd heard sounds of a struggle coming from a particular house, and I supplied the address. I said that two men had rushed from the house and had driven away in a dark car. No, I could not identify the car further. No, I had not seen the license plate. No, I did not care to give my name.

The following day I spoke to Vivian briefly on the telephone. "Things are going well," I said.

"I'm so glad, darling."

"Things are going to work out for us," I said.

"You're wonderful. You know that, don't you? Absolutely wonderful."

On Saturday we played a mere three games of handball. He won the first, as usual, but astonishingly I beat him in the second game, my first victory over him, and I went on to beat him again in the third. It was then that he suggested that we call it a day. Perhaps he simply felt off his game, or wanted to reduce the chances of someone's noticing the two of us together. On the other hand, he had said at our first meeting that he liked to win. Conversely, one might suppose that he didn't like to lose.

Over a couple of beers he said, "Well, you did it. I knew you'd do it and at the same time I couldn't actually believe you would. Know what I mean?"

"I think so."

"The police didn't even hassle me. They checked my alibi, of course—they're not idiots. But they didn't dig too deep because they seemed so certain it was a burglary. I'll tell you something, it was such a perfectly faked burglary that I even began to get the feeling that that was what happened. Just a coincidence, like. You chickened out and a burglar just happened to do the job."

"Maybe that's what happened," I suggested.

He looked at me, then grinned slyly. "You're one hell of a guy," he said. "Cool as a cucumber, aren't you? Tell me something. What was it like, killing her?"

"You'll find out soon enough."

"Hell of a guy. You realize something? You have the advantage over me. You know my name. From the newspapers. And I still don't know yours."

"You'll know it soon enough," I said with a smile. "From the newspapers."

"Fair enough."

I gave him a slip of paper. Like the one he'd given me, it had an address block-printed in pencil. "Wednesday would be ideal," I said. "If you don't mind missing your poker game."

"I wouldn't have to miss it, would I? I'd just get there late. The poker game gives me an excuse to get out of my house, but if I'm an hour late getting there my wife'll never know the difference. And even if she knew I wasn't where I was supposed to be, so what? What's she gonna do, divorce me and cut herself out of my money? Not likely."

"I'll be having dinner with a client," I said. "Then he and I will be going directly to a business meeting. I'll be tied up until fairly late in the evening—eleven o'clock, maybe midnight."

"I'd like to do it around eight," he said. "That's when I normally leave for the poker game. I can do it and be drawing to an inside straight by nine o'clock. How does that sound?"

I allowed that it sounded good to me.

"I guess I'll make it another fake burglary," he said. "Ransack the place, use a knife. Let them think it's the same crazy burglar striking again. Or doesn't that sound good to you?"

"It might tend to link us," I said.

"Oh."

"Maybe you could make it look like a sex crime. Rape and murder. That way the police would never draw any connection between the two killings."

"Brilliant," he said. He really seemed to admire me now that I'd committed a murder and won two games of handball from him.

"You wouldn't actually have to rape her. Just rip her clothing and set the scene properly."

"Is she attractive?" I admitted that she was, after a fashion. "I've always sort of had fantasies about rape," he said, carefully avoiding my eyes as he spoke. "She'll be home at eight o'clock?"

"She'll be home."

"And alone?"

"Absolutely."

He folded the slip of paper, put it into his wallet, dropped bills from his wallet on the table, swallowed what remained of his beer and got to his feet. "It's in the bag," he said. "Your troubles are over."

"Our troubles are over," I told Vivian.

"Oh, darling," she said. "I can hardly believe it. You're the most wonderful man in the world."

"And a sensational handball player," I said.

I left my house Wednesday night at half past seven. I drove a few blocks to a drugstore and bought a couple of magazines, then went to a men's shop next door and looked at sport shirts. The two shirts I liked weren't in stock in my size. The clerk offered to order them for me but I thought it over and told him not to bother. "I like them," I said, "but I'm not absolutely crazy about them."

I returned to my house. My handball partner's car was parked diagonally across the street. I parked my own car in the driveway and used my key to let myself in the front door. From the doorway I cleared my throat, and he spun around to face me, his eyes bulging out of his head.

I pointed to the body on the couch. "Is she dead?"

"Stone dead. She fought and I hit her too hard . . ." He flushed a deep red, then he blinked. "But what are you doing here? Don't you remember how we planned it? I don't understand why you came here tonight of all nights."

"I came here because I live here," I said. "George, I'd love to explain but there's no time. I wish there were time but there isn't."

I took the revolver from my pocket and shot him in the face.

"The police were very understanding," I told Vivian. "They seem to think the shock of his ex-wife's death unbalanced him.

They theorize that he was driving by when he saw me leave my house. Maybe he saw Margaret at the door saying goodbye to me. He parked, perhaps with no clear intention, then went to the door. When she opened the door, he was overcome with desire. By the time I came back and let myself in and shot him it was too late. The damage had been done."

"Poor George."

"And poor Margaret."

She put her hand on mine. "They brought it on themselves," she said. "If George hadn't insisted on that vicious prenuptial agreement we could have had a properly civilized divorce like everybody else."

"And if Margaret had agreed to a properly civilized divorce she'd be alive today."

"We only did what we had to do," Vivian said. "It was a shame about his ex-wife, but I don't suppose there was any way around it."

"At least she didn't suffer."

"That's important," she said. "And you know what they say— you can't break an egg without making omelets."

"That's what they say," I agreed. We embraced, and some moments later we disembraced. "We'll have to give one another rather a wide berth for a month or two," I said. "After all, I killed your husband just as he finished killing my wife. If we should be seen in public, tongues would wag. In a month or so you'll sell your house and leave town. A few weeks after that I'll do the same. Then we can get married and live happily ever after, but in the meantime we'd best be very cautious."

"You're right," she said. "There was a movie like that, except nobody got killed in it. But there were these two people in a small town who were having an affair, and when they met in public they had to pretend they were strangers. I wish I could remember the title."

"*Strangers When We Meet?*"

"That sounds about right."

# LIKE A DOG
# IN THE
# STREET

THE CAPTURE OF the man called Anselmo amounted to the gathering together of innumerable threads, many of them wispy and frail. For almost two years the terrorist had been the target of massive manhunt operations launched by not one but over a dozen nations. The one valid photograph of him, its focus blurred and indistinct, had been reproduced and broadcast throughout the world; his features—the jagged and irregular yellow teeth, the too-small upturned nose, the underslung jaw, the bushy eyebrows grown together into a single thick, dark line—were as familiar to the general public as they were to counterintelligence professionals and Interpol agents.

Bit by bit, little by little, the threads began to link up. In a cafe in a working-class neighborhood in Milan, two men sat sipping espresso laced with anisette. They spoke of an interregional soccer match, and of the possibility of work stoppage by the truck dispatchers. Then their voices dropped, and one spoke quickly and quietly of Anselmo while the other took careful note of every word.

In a suburb of Asunción, a portly gentleman wearing the uniform of a brigadier general in the Paraguayan army shared the front seat of a four-year-old Chevrolet Impala with a slender young man wearing the uniform of a chauffeur. The general

talked while the chauffeur listened. While Anselmo was not mentioned by name, he was the subject of the conversation. At its
conclusion the chauffeur gave the general an envelope containing
currency in the amount of two thousand German marks. Three
hours later the chauffeur—who was not a chauffeur—was on a
plane for Mexico City. The following afternoon the general—
who was not really a general—was dead of what the attending
physician diagnosed as a massive myocardial infarction.

In Paris, in the Ninth Arrondissement, three security officers,
one of them French, entered an apartment which had been under
surveillance for several weeks. It proved to be empty. Surveillance
was continued but no one returned to the apartment during the
course of the following month. A thoroughgoing analysis of various papers and detritus found in the apartment was relayed in
due course to authorities in London and Tel Aviv.

In West Berlin, a man and woman, both in their twenties,
both blond and fair-skinned and blue-eyed and looking enough
alike to be brother and sister, made the acquaintance of a dark-
haired and full-bodied young woman at a cabaret called Justine's.
The three shared a bottle of sparkling Burgundy, then repaired
to a small apartment on the Bergenstrasse where they shared
several marijuana cigarettes, half a bottle of Almspach brandy
and a bed. The blond couple did certain things which the dark-
haired young woman found quite painful, but she gave every
appearance of enjoying the activity. Later, when she appeared to
be asleep, the blond man and woman talked at some length. The
dark-haired young woman, who was in fact awake throughout
this conversation, was still awake later on when the other two
lay sprawled beside her, snoring lustily. She dressed and left
quickly, pausing only long enough to slit their throats with a
kitchen knife. Her flight to Beirut landed shortly before two in
the afternoon, and within an hour after that she was talking with
a middle-aged Armenian gentleman in the back room of a travel
agency.

Bits and pieces. Threads, frail threads, coming together to form
a net...

And throughout it all the man called Anselmo remained as

LIKE A DOG IN THE STREET

active as ever. A Pan Am flight bound for Belgrade blew up in the air over Austria. A telephone call claiming credit for the deed on behalf of the Popular Front for Croatian Autonomy was logged at the airline's New York offices scant minutes before an explosion shredded the jetliner.

A week earlier, rumors had begun drifting around that Anselmo was working with the Croats.

In Jerusalem, less than a quarter of a mile from the Wailing Wall, four gunmen burst into a Sephardic synagogue during morning services. They shot and killed twenty-eight members of the congregation before they themselves were rooted out and shot down by police officers. The dead gunmen proved to be members of a leftist movement aimed at securing the independence of Puerto Rico from the United States. But why should Puerto Rican extremists be mounting a terrorist operation against Israel?

The common denominator was Anselmo.

An embassy in Washington. A police barracks in Strabane, in Northern Ireland. A labor union in Buenos Aires.

Anselmo.

Assassinations. The Spanish ambassador to Sweden shot down in the streets of Stockholm. The sister-in-law of the premier of Iraq. The Research and Development head of a multinational oil company. A British journalist. An Indonesian general. An African head of state.

Anselmo.

Hijacking and kidnapping. Ransom demands. Outrages.

Anselmo. Always Anselmo.

Of course it was not always his hand on the trigger. When the Puerto Rican gunmen shot up the Jerusalem synagogue, Anselmo was playing solitaire in a dimly lit basement room in Pretoria. When a firebomb roasted the Iraqi premier's sister-in-law, Anselmo was flashing a savage yellow smile in Bolivia. It was not Anselmo's hand that forced a dagger between the ribs of General Suprandoro in Jakarta; the hand belonged to a nubile young lady from Thailand, but it was Anselmo who had given her her instructions, Anselmo who had decreed that Suprandoro must die and who had staged and scripted his death.

55

Bits and pieces. A couple of words scrawled on the back of an envelope. A scrap of conversation overheard. Bits, pieces, scraps. Threads, if you will.

Threads braided together can make strong rope. Strands of interwoven rope comprise a net.

When the net dropped around Anselmo, Nahum Grodin held its ends in his knobby hands.

It was early summer. For three days a dry wind had been blowing relentlessly. The town of Al-dhareesh, a small Arab settlement on the West Bank of the Jordan, yielded to the wind as to a conquering army. The women tended their cooking fires. Men sat at small tables in their courtyards sipping cups of sweet black coffee. The yellow dogs that ran through the narrow streets seemed to stay more in the shadows than was their custom, scurrying from doorway to doorway, keeping their distance from passing humans.

"Even the dogs feel it," Nahum Grodin said. His Hebrew bore Russian and Polish overtones. "Look at them. The way they slink around."

"The wind," Gershon Meir said.

"Anselmo."

"The wind," Meir insisted. A sabra, he had the unromantic outlook of the native-born. He was Grodin's immediate subordinate in the counterterror division of Shin Bet, and the older man knew there was no difference in the keenness both felt at the prospect of springing a trap upon Anselmo. But Grodin felt it all in the air while Meir felt nothing but the dry wind off the desert.

"The same wind blows over the whole country," Grodin said. "And yet it's different here. The way those damned yellow dogs stay in the shadows."

"You make too much of the Arabs' mongrel dogs."

"And their children?"

"What children?"

"Aha!" Grodin extended a forefinger. "The dogs keep to the shadows. The children stay in their huts and avoid the streets

56

altogether. Don't tell me, my friend, that the wind is enough to keep children from their play."

"So the townspeople know he's here. They shelter him. That's nothing new."

"A few know he's here. The ones planning the raid across the Jordan, perhaps a handful of others. The rest are like the dogs and the children. They sense something in the air."

Gershon Meir looked at his superior officer. He considered the set of his jaw, the reined excitement that glinted in his pale blue eyes. "Something in the air," he said.

"Yes. You feel something yourself, Gershon. Admit it."

"I feel too damned much caffeine in my blood. That last cup of coffee was a mistake."

"You feel more than caffeine."

Meir shrugged but said nothing.

"He's here, Gershon."

"Yes, I think he is. But we have been so close to him so many times—"

"This time we have him."

"When he's behind bars, that's when I'll say we have him."

"Or when he's dead."

Again the younger man looked at Grodin, a sharp look this time. Grodin's right hand, knuckles swollen with arthritis, rested on the butt of his holstered machine pistol.

"Or when he's dead," Gershon Meir agreed.

Whether it was merely the wind or something special in the air, the man called Anselmo felt it, too. He set down his little cup of coffee—it was sweeter than he liked it—and worried his chin with the tips of his fingers. With no apparent concern he studied the five men in the room with him. They were local Arabs ranging in age from sixteen to twenty-eight. Anselmo had met one of them before in Beirut and knew two of the others by reputation. The remaining two were unequivocally guaranteed by their comrades. Anselmo did not specifically trust them—he had never in his life placed full trust in another human being—but neither did he specifically distrust them. They were village

Arabs, politically unsophisticated and mentally uncomplicated, desperate young men who would perform any act and undertake any risk. Anselmo had known and used just that sort of man throughout the world. He could not have functioned without such men.

Something in the air...

He went to a window, inched the burlap curtain aside with the edge of his palm. He saw nothing remarkable, yet a special perception more reliable than eyesight told him the town was swarming with Israelis. He did not have to see them to be certain of their presence.

He turned, considered his five companions. They were to cross the river that night. By dawn they would have established their position. A school bus loaded with between fifty and sixty retarded childen would slow down before making a left turn at the corner where Anselmo and his men would be posted. It would be child's play—he bared his teeth in a smile at the phrase—child's play to shoot the tires out of the bus. In a matter of minutes all of the Jewish children and their driver would be dead at the side of the road. In a few more minutes Anselmo and the Arabs would have scattered and made good their escape.

A perfect act of terror, mindless, meaningless, unquestionably dramatic. The Jews would retaliate, of course, and of course their retaliation would find the wrong target, and the situation would deteriorate. And in the overall scheme of things—

But was there an overall scheme of things? At times, most often late at night just before his mind slipped over the edge into sleep, then Anselmo could see the outline of some sort of master plan, some way in which all the component parts of terror which he juggled moved together to make a new world. The image of the plan hovered at such times right at the perimeter of his inner vision, trembling at the edge of thought. He could almost see it, as one can almost see God in a haze of opium.

The rest of the time he saw no master plan and had no need to search for one. The existential act of terror, theatrical as thunder, seemed to him to be a perfectly satisfactory end in itself. Let the children bleed at the roadside. Let the plane explode overhead. Let the rifle crack.

Let the world take note.

He turned once more to the window but left the curtain in place, merely testing the texture of the burlap with his fingertips. Out there in the darkness. Troops, police officers. Should he wait in the shadows for them to pass? No, he decided quickly. The village was small and they could search it house by house with little difficulty. He could pass as an Arab—he was garbed as one now—but if he was the man they were looking for they would know him when they saw him.

He could send these five out, sacrifice them to suicidal combat while he made good his own escape. It would be a small sacrifice. They were unimportant, expendable; he was Anselmo. But if the Jews had encircled the town a diversion would have little effect.

He snapped his head back, thrust his chin forward. A sudden gesture. Time was his enemy, only drawing the net tighter around him. The longer he delayed, the greater his vulnerability. Better a bad decision than no decision at all.

"Wait here for me," he told his men, his Arabic low and guttural. "I would see how the wind blows."

He began to open the door, disturbing the rest of a scrawny long-muzzled dog. The animal whined softly and took itself off to the side. Anselmo slipped through the open door and let it close behind him.

The moon overhead was just past fullness. There were no clouds to block it. The dry wind had blown them all away days ago. Anselmo reached through his loose clothing, touched the Walther automatic on his hip, the long-bladed hunting knife in a sheath strapped to his thigh, the smaller knife fastened with tape to the inside of his left forearm. Around his waist an oilcloth money belt rested next to his skin. It held four passports in as many names and a few thousand dollars in the currencies of half a dozen countries. Anselmo could travel readily, crossing borders as another man would cross the street. If only he could first get out of Al-dhareesh.

He moved quickly and sinuously, keeping to the shadows, letting his eyes and ears perform a quick reconnaissance before moving onward. Twice he spotted armed uniformed men and withdrew before he was seen, changing direction, scurrying through a yard and down an alleyway.

They were everywhere.

Just as he caught sight of still another Israeli patrol on a street corner, gunfire broke out a few hundred yards to his left. There was a ragged volley of pistol fire answered by several bursts from what he identified as an Uzi machine pistol. Then silence.

His five men, he thought. Caught in the house or on the street in front of it, and if he'd stayed there he'd have been caught with them. From the sound of it, they hadn't made much trouble. His lip curled and a spot of red danced in his forebrain. He only hoped the five had been shot dead so that they couldn't inform the Jews of his own presence.

As if they had to. As if the bastards didn't already know...

A three-man patrol turned into the street a dozen houses to Anselmo's left. One of the men kicked at the earth as he walked and the dust billowed around his feet in the moonlight. Anselmo cursed the men and the moonlight and circled around the side of a house and slipped away from the men.

But there was no way out. All the streets were blocked. Once Anselmo drew his Walther and took deliberate aim at a pair of uniformed men. They were within easy range and his finger trembled on the trigger. It would be so nice to kill them, but where was the profit in it? Their companions would be on him in an instant.

If you teach a rat to solve mazes, presenting it over a period of months with mazes of increasing difficulty and finally placing it in a maze which is truly unsolvable, the rat will do a curious thing. He will scurry about in an attempt to solve the maze, becoming increasingly inefficient in his efforts, and ultimately he will sit down in a corner and devour his own feet.

There was no way out of Al-dhareesh and the Israelis were closing in, searching the village house by house, moving ever nearer to Anselmo, cutting down his space. He tucked himself into a corner where a four-foot wall of sun-baked earth butted against the wall of a house. He sat on his haunches and pressed himself into the shadows.

Footsteps—

A dog scampered along close to the wall, found Anselmo, whimpered. The same dog he'd disturbed on leaving the house? Not likely, he thought. The town was full of these craven whining beasts. This one poked its nose into Anselmo's side and whimpered again. The sound was one the terrorist did not care for. He laid a hand on the back of the dog's skull, gentling it. The whimpering continued at a slightly lower pitch. With his free hand, Anselmo drew the hunting knife from the sheath on his thigh. While he went on rubbing the back of the dog's head he found the spot between the ribs. The animal had almost ceased to whimper when he sent the blade home, finding the heart directly, making the kill in silence. He wiped the blade in the dog's fur and returned it to its sheath.

A calm descended with the death of the dog. Anselmo licked a finger, held it overhead. Had the wind ceased to blow? It seemed to him that it had. He took a deep breath, released it slowly, got to his feet.

He walked not in the shadows but down the precise middle of the narrow street. When the two men stepped into view ahead of him he did not turn aside or bolt for cover. His hand quivered, itching to reach for the Walther, but the calm which had come upon him enabled him to master this urge.

He threw his hands high overhead. In reasonably good Hebrew he sang out, "I am your prisoner!" And he drew his lips back, exposing his bad teeth in a terrible grin.

Both men trained their guns on him. He had faced guns innumerable times in the past and did not find them intimidating. But one of the men held his Uzi as *if he* was about to fire it. Moonlight glinted on the gun barrel. Anselmo, still grinning, waited for a burst of fire and an explosion in his chest.

It never came.

* * *

The two men sat in folding chairs and watched their prisoner through a one-way mirror. His cell was as small and bare as the room from which they watched him. He sat on a narrow iron bedstead and stroked his chin with the tips of his fingers. Now and then his gaze passed over the mirror.

"You'd swear he can see us," Gershon Meir said.

"He knows we're here."

"I suppose he must. The devil's cool, isn't he? Do you think he'll talk?"

Nahum Grodin shook his head.

"He could tell us a great deal."

"He'll never tell us a thing. Why should he? The man's comfortable. He was comfortable dressed as an Arab and now he's as comfortable dressed as a prisoner."

Anselmo had been disarmed, of course, and relieved of his loose-fitting Arab clothing. Now he wore the standard clothing issued to prisoners—trousers and a short-sleeved shirt of gray denim, cloth slippers. The trousers were of course beltless and the slippers had no laces.

Grodin said, "He could be made to talk. No, *nahr*, I don't mean torture. You watch too many films. Pentothal, if they'd let me use it. Although I suspect his resistance is high. He has such enormous confidence."

"The way he smiled when he surrendered to us."

"Yes."

"For a moment I thought—"

"Yes?"

"That you were going to shoot him, Nahum."

"I very nearly did."

"You suspected a trap? I suppose—"

"No." Grodin interlaced his fingers, cracked his knuckles. Several of the joints throbbed slightly. "No," he said, "I knew it was no trick. The man is a pragmatist. He knew he was trapped. He surrendered to save his skin."

"And you thought to shoot him anyway?"

"I should have done it, Gershon. I should have shot him.

62

Something made me hesitate. And you know the saying. He who hesitates and so forth, and I hesitated and was lost. I was not lost but the opportunity was. I should have shot him at once. Without hesitating, without thinking, without anything but an ounce of pressure on the trigger and a few punctuation marks for the night."

Gershon studied the man they were discussing. He had removed one of the slippers and was was picking at his feet. Gershon wanted to look away but watched, fascinated. "You want him dead," he said.

"Of course."

"We're a progressive nation. We don't put them to death anymore. Life imprisonment's supposed to be punishment enough. You don't agree?"

"No."

"You like the eye-for-eye stuff, huh?"

"'And you shall return eye for eye, tooth for tooth, hand for hand, foot for foot, burning for burning.' It's not a terrible idea, you know. I would not be so quick to dismiss it out of hand."

"Revenge."

"Or retribution, more accurately. You can't have revenge, my friend. Not in this sort of case. The man's crimes are too enormous for his own personal death to balance them out. But that is not why I wish I'd killed him."

"Then I don't understand."

Nahum Grodin aimed a forefinger at the glass. "Look," he said. "What do you see?"

"A piggish lout picking his feet."

"You see a prisoner."

"Of course. I don't understand what you're getting at, Nahum."

"You think you see a prisoner. But he is not our prisoner, Gershon."

"Oh?"

"We are his prisoners."

"I do not follow that at all."

"No?" The older man massaged the knuckle of his right index finger. It was that finger, he thought, which had hesitated upon

63

the trigger of the Uzi. And now it throbbed and ached. Arthritis? Or the punishment it deserved for its hesitation?

"Nahum—"

"We are at his mercy," Grodin said crisply. "He's our captive. His comrades will try to bring about his release. As long as he is our prisoner he is a sword pointed at our throats."

"That's farfetched."

"Do you really think so?" Nahum Grodin sighed. "I wish we were not so civilized as to have abolished capital punishment. And at this particular moment I wish we were a police state and this vermin could be officially described as having been shot while attempting to escape. We could take him outside right now, you and I, and he could attempt to escape."

Gershon shuddered. "We could not do that."

"No," Grodin agreed. "No, we could not do that. But I could have gunned him down when I had the chance. Did you ever see a mad dog? When I was a boy in Lublin, Gershon, I saw one running wild. They don't really foam at the mouth, you know. But I seem to remember that dog having a foamy mouth. And a policeman shot him down. I remember that he held his pistol in both hands, held it out in front of him with both arms fully extended. Do you suppose I actually saw the beast shot down or that the memory is in part composed of what I was told? I could swear I actually saw the act. I can see it now in my mind, the policeman with his legs braced and his two arms held out in front of him. And the dog charging. I wonder if that incident might have had anything to do with this profession I seem to have chosen."

"Do you think it did?"

"I'll leave that to the psychiatrists to decide." Grodin smiled, then let the smile fade. "I should have shot this one down like a dog in the street," he said. "When I had the chance."

"How is he dangerous in a cell?"

"And how long will he remain in that cell?" Grodin sighed. "He is a leader. He has a leader's magnetism. The world is full of lunatics to whom this man is special. They'll demand his release. They'll hijack a plane, kidnap a politician, hold school-children for ransom."

"We have never paid ransom."

"No."

"They've made such demands before. We've never released a terrorist in response to extortion."

"Not yet we haven't."

Both men fell silent. On the other side of the one-way mirror, the man called Anselmo had ceased picking his toes. Now he stripped to his underwear and seated himself on the bare tiled floor of his cell. His fingers interlaced behind his head, he began doing sit-ups. Muscles worked in his flat abdomen and his thin corded thighs as he raised and lowered the upper portion of his body. He exercised rhythmically, pausing after each series of five sit-ups, then springing to his feet after he had completed six such series. Having done so, he paused deliberately to flash his teeth at the one-way mirror.

"Look at that," Gershon Meir said. "Like an animal."

Nahum Grodin's right forefinger resumed aching.

Grodin was right, of course. Revolutionaries throughout the world had very strong reasons for wishing to see Anselmo released from his cell. In various corners of the globe, desperate men plotted desperate acts to achieve this end.

The first attempts were not successful. Less than a week after Anselmo was taken, four men and two women stormed a building in Geneva where high-level international disarmament talks were being conducted. Two of the men were shot, one fatally. One of the women had her arm broken in a struggle with a guard. The rest were captured. In the course of interrogation, Swiss authorities determined that the exercise had had as its object the release of Anselmo. The two women and one of the men were West German anarchists. The other three men, including the one who was shot dead, were Basque separatists.

A matter of days after this incident, guerrillas in Uruguay stopped a limousine carrying the Israeli ambassador to a reception in the heart of Montevideo. Security police were following the ambassador's limousine at the time, and the gun battle which ensued claimed the lives of all seven guerrillas, three security policemen, the ambassador, his chauffeur and four presumably innocent bystanders. While the purpose of the attempted kidnapping was impossible to determine, persistent rumors linked the action to Anselmo.

Within the week, Eritrean revolutionaries succeeded in skyjacking an El Al 747 en route from New York to Tel Aviv. The jet with 144 passengers and crew members was diverted to the capital of an African nation where it overshot the runway, crashed and was consumed in flames. A handful of passengers survived. The remaining passengers, along with all crew members and the eight or ten Eritreans, were all killed.

Palestinians seized another plane, this one an Air France jetliner. The plane was landed successfully in Libya and demands presented which called for the release of Anselmo and a dozen or so other terrorists then held by the Israelis. The demands were rejected out of hand. After several deadlines had come and gone, the terrorists began executing hostages, ultimately blowing up the plane with the remaining hostages aboard. According to some reports, the terrorists were taken into custody by Libyan authorities; according to other reports they were given token reprimands and released.

After the affair in Libya, both sides felt they had managed to establish something. The Israelis felt they had proved conclusively that they would not be blackmailed. The loosely knit group who aimed to free Anselmo felt just as strongly that they had demonstrated their resolve to free him—no matter what risks they were forced to run, no matter how many lives, their own or others, they had to sacrifice.

"If there were two Henry Clays," said the bearer of that name after a bitterly disappointing loss of the presidency, "then one of them would make the other president of the United States of America."

It is unlikely that Anselmo knew the story. He cared nothing for the past, read nothing but current newspapers. But as he exercised in his cell his thoughts often echoed those of Henry Clay.

If there were only two Anselmos, one could surely spring the other from this cursed jail.

But it didn't require a second Anselmo, as it turned out. All it took was a nuclear bomb.

The bomb itself was stolen from a NATO installation forty miles from Antwerp. A theft of this sort is perhaps the most difficult way of obtaining such a weapon. Nuclear technology is such that anyone with a good grounding in college-level science can put together a rudimentary atomic bomb in his own basement workshop, given access to the essential elements. Security precautions being what they are, it is worlds easier to steal the component parts of a bomb than the assembled bomb itself. But in this case it was necessary not merely to have a bomb but to let the world know that one had a bomb. Hence the theft via a daring and dramatic dead-of-night raid. While media publicity was kept to a minimum, people whose job it was to know such things knew overnight that a bomb had been stolen, and that the thieves had in all likelihood been members of the Peridot Gang.

The Peridot Gang was based in Paris, although its membership was international in nature. The gang was organized to practice terrorism in the Anselmo mode. Its politics were of the left, but very little ideology lay beneath the commitment to extremist activism. Security personnel throughout Europe and the Middle East shuddered at the thought of a nuclear device in the hands of the Peridots. Clearly they had not stolen the bomb for the sheer fun of it. Clearly they intended to make use of it, and clearly they were capable of almost any outrage.

Removing the bomb from the Belgian NATO installation had been reasonably difficult. In comparison, disassembling it and smuggling it into the United States, then transporting it into New York City and reassembling it and finally installing it in the interfaith meditation chamber of the United Nations—all of that was simplicity itself.

Once the meditation chamber had been secured, a Peridot

emissary presented a full complement of demands. Several of these had to do with guaranteeing the eventual safety of gang members at the time of their withdrawal from the chamber, the UN building and New York itself. Another, directed at the General Assembly of the United Nations, called for changes in international policy toward insurgent movements and revolutionary organizations. Various individual member nations were called upon to liberate specific political prisoners, including several dozen persons belonging to or allied with the Peridot organization. Specifically, the government of Israel was instructed to grant liberty to the man called Anselmo.

Any attempt to seize the bomb would be met by its detonation. Any effort to evacuate the United Nations building or New York itself would similarly prompt the Peridots to set the bomb off. If all demands were not met within ten days of their publication, the bomb would go off.

Authorities differed in their estimates of the bomb's lethal range. But the lowest estimate of probable deaths was in excess of one million.

Throughout the world, those governments blackmailed by the Peridots faced up to reality. One after the other they made arrangements to do what they could not avoid doing. Whatever their avowed policy toward extortion, however great their reluctance to liberate terrorists, they could not avoid recognizing a fairly simple fact: they had no choice.

Anselmo could not resist a smile when the two men came into the room. How nice, he thought, that it was these two who came to him. They had captured him in the first place, they had attempted to interrogate him time and time again and now they were on hand to make arrangements for his release. It seemed to him that there was something fitting in all of this.

"Well," he said. "I guess I won't be with you much longer, eh?"

"Not much longer," the older man said.

"When do you release me?"

"The day after tomorrow. In the morning. You are to be turned

68

over to Palestinians at the Syrian border. A private jet will fly
you to one of the North African countries, either Algeria or Libya.
I don't have the details. I don't believe they have been finalized
as yet."

"It hardly matters."

The younger of the Israelis, dark-eyed and olive-skinned, cleared
his throat. "You won't want to leave here in prison clothes," he
said. "We can give you what you wore when you were captured
or you may have western dress. It's your choice."

"You are very accommodating," Anselmo told him.

The man's face colored. "The choice is yours."

"It's of no importance to me."

"Then you'll walk out as you walked in."

"It doesn't matter what I wear." He touched his gray denim
clothing. "Just so it's not this." And he favored them with a smile
again.

The older man unclasped a small black bag, drew out a hypodermic needle. Anselmo raised his eyebrows. "Pentothal," the
man said.

"You could have used it before."

"It was against policy."

"And has your policy changed?"

"Obviously."

"A great deal has changed," the younger man added. "A package bill passed the Knesset last evening. There was a special
session called for the purpose. The death penalty has been re-
stored."

"Ah."

"For certain crimes only. Crimes of political terrorism. Any
terrorists captured alive will be brought to trial within three days
after capture. If convicted, sentence will be carried out within
twenty-four hours after it has been pronounced."

"Was there much opposition to this bill?"

"There was considerable debate. But when it came to a vote
the margin was overwhelming for passage."

Anselmo considered this in the abstract. "It seems to me that
it is an intelligent bill," he said at length. "I inspired it, eh?"

"You might say that."

"So you will avoid this sort of situation in the future. But of course there is a loss all the same. No doubt that explains the debate. You will not look good to the rest of the world, executing prisoners so quickly after capture. There will be talk of kangaroo courts, star chamber hearings, that sort of thing." He flashed his teeth. "But what choice did you have? None."

"There's another change that did not require legislation," the older man said. "An unofficial change of policy for troops and police officers. We will have slower reflexes when it comes to noticing that a man is attempting to surrender."

Anselmo laughed aloud at the phrasing. "Slower reflexes! You mean you will shoot first and ask questions later."

"Something along those lines."

"Also an intelligent policy. I shall make my own plans accordingly. But I don't think it will do you very much good, you know."

The man shrugged. The hypodermic needle looked small in his big gnarled hand. "The pentothal," he said. "Will it be necessary to restrain you? Or will you cooperate?"

"Why should I require restraint? We are both professionals, after all. I'll cooperate."

"That simplifies things."

Anselmo extended his arm. The younger man took him by the wrist while the other one readied the needle. "This won't do you any good either," Anselmo said conversationally. "I've had pentothal before. It's not effective on me."

"We'll have to establish that for ourselves."

"As you will."

"At least you'll get a pleasant nap out of it."

"I never have trouble sleeping," Anselmo said. "I sleep like a baby."

He didn't fight the drug but went with the flow as it circulated in his bloodstream. His consciousness went off to the side somewhere. There was orchestral music interwoven with a thunderstorm. The bolts of lightning, vivid against an indigo background, were extraordinarily beautiful.

70

Then he was awake, aware of his surroundings, aware that the two men were speaking but unable to make sense of their conversation. When full acuity returned he gave no sign of it at first, hoping to overhear something of importance, but their conversation held nothing of interest to him. After a few minutes he stirred himself and opened his eyes.

"Well?" he demanded. "Did I tell you any vital secrets?"

The older one shook his head.

"I told you as much."

"So you did. You'll forgive our not taking your word, I hope."

Anselmo laughed aloud. "You have humor, old one. It's almost a pity we're enemies. Tell me your name."

"What does it matter?"

"It doesn't."

"Nahum Grodin."

Anselmo repeated the name aloud. "When you captured me," he said. "In that filthy Arab town."

"Al-dhareesh."

"Al-dhareesh. Yes. When I surrendered, you know, I thought for a long moment that you were going to gun me down. That wind that blew endlessly, and the moon glinting off your pistol and something in the air. Something in the way you were standing. I thought you were going to shoot me."

"I very nearly did."

"Yes, so I thought." Anselmo laughed suddenly. "And now you must wish that you did, eh? Hesitation, that's what kills men, Grodin. Better the wrong choice than no choice at all. You should have shot me."

"Yes."

"Next time you'll know better, Grodin."

"Next time?"

"Oh, there will be a next time for us, old one. And next time you won't hesitate to fire, but then next time I'll know better than to surrender. Eh?"

"I almost shot you."

"I sensed it."

"Like a dog."

"A dog?" Anselmo thought of the dogs in the Arab town, the one he'd disturbed when he opened the door, the whining one he'd killed. His hand remembered the feel of the animal's skull and the brief tremor that passed through the beast when the long knife went home. It was difficult now to recall just why he had knifed the dog. He supposed he must have done it to prevent the animal's whimpering from drawing attention, but was that really the reason? The act itself had been so reflexive that one could scarcely determine its motive.

As if it mattered.

Outside, the sunlight was blinding. Gershon Meir took a pair of sunglasses from his breast pocket and put them on. Nahum Grodin squinted against the light. He never wore sunglasses and didn't mind the glare. And the sun warmed his bones, eased the ache in his joints.

"The day after tomorrow," Gershon Meir said. "I'll be glad to see the last of him."

"Will you?"

"Yes. I hate having to release him but sometimes I think I hate speaking with him even more."

"I know what you mean."

They walked through the streets in a comfortable silence. After a few blocks the younger man said, "I had the oddest feeling earlier. Just for a moment."

"Oh?"

"When you gave him the pentothal. For an instant I was afraid you were going to kill him."

"With pentothal?"

"I thought you might inject an air bubble into a vein. Anything along those lines. It would have been easy enough."

"Perhaps. I don't know that I'd be able to find a vein that easily, actually. I'm hardly a doctor. A subcutaneous injection of pentothal, that's within my capabilities, but I might not be so good at squirting air into a vein. But do you think for a moment I'd be mad enough to kill him?"

"It was a feeling, not a thought."

"I'd delight in killing him," Grodin said. "But I'd hate to wipe out New York in the process."

"They might not detonate the bomb just for Anselmo. They want to get the other prisoners out, and they want their other demands. If you told them Anselmo had died a natural death they might swallow it and pretend to believe it."

"You think we should call their bluff that way?"

"No. They're lunatics. Who knows what they might do?"

"Exactly," Grodin said.

"It was just a feeling, that's all."

And a little further on: "Nahum? It's a curious thing. When you and Anselmo talk I might as well not be in the room."

"I don't take your meaning, Gershon."

"There's a current that runs between the two of you. I feel utterly excluded from the company. The two of you, you seem to understand each other."

"That's interesting. You think I understand Anselmo? I don't begin to understand him. You know, I didn't expect to gain any real information from him while he was under the pentothal. But I did hope to get some insight into what motivated the man. And he gave me nothing. He likes to see blood spill, he likes loud noises. You know what Bakunin said?"

"I don't even know who Bakunin was. A Russian?"

"A Russian. 'The urge to destroy is a creative urge,' that's what he said. Perhaps the context in which he said it mitigates the line somewhat. I wouldn't know. Anselmo is an embodiment of that philosophy. He only wishes to destroy. No. Gershon, I do not understand him."

"But there is a sympathy between the two of you. I'm not putting it well, I know, but there is something."

Grodin did not reply immediately. Finally he said, "The man says we'll meet again. He's wrong."

Yet they might have met again on the day that Anselmo was released. Grodin and his assistant were on hand. They watched from a distance while the terrorist was escorted from his cell to an armored car for transport to the Syrian lines, and Grodin had been assigned to oversee security procedures lest some zealot shoot Anselmo down as he emerged from the prison. They followed the armored car in a vehicle of their own, Meir driving, Grodin at his side. The ceremony at the Syrian border, by means of which custody of Anselmo was transferred from his Israeli guards to a group of Palestinian commandos, was indescribably tense; nevertheless it was concluded without a hitch.

Just before he entered the waiting car, Anselmo turned for a last look across the border. His eyes darted around as if seeking a specific target. Then he thrust out his jaw and drew back his lips, baring his jagged teeth in a final hideous smile. He gave his head a toss and ducked down into the car. The door swung shut. Moments later the car sped toward Damascus.

"Quite a performance," Gershon Meir said.

"He's an actor. Everything is performance for him. His whole life is theater."

"He was looking for you."

"I think not."

"He was looking for someone. For whom else would he look?"

Grodin gave his head an impatient shake. His assistant looked as though he would have liked to continue the conversation, but recognized the gesture and let it drop.

On the long drive back Nahum Grodin leaned back in his seat and closed his eyes. It seemed to him that he dreamed without quite losing consciousness. After perhaps half an hour he opened his blue eyes and straightened up in his seat.

"Where is he now?" he wondered aloud. "Damascus? Or is his plane already in the air?"

"I'd guess he's still on the ground."

"No matter. How do you feel, Gershon? Letting such a one out of our hands? Forget revenge. Think of the ability he has to work with disparate groups of lunatics. He takes partisans of one mad cause and puts them to work on behalf of another equally insane movement. He coordinates the actions of extremists who have nothing else in common. And his touch is like nobody else's. This latest devilment at the United Nations—it is almost impossible to believe that someone other than Anselmo planned

74

it. In fact I would not be surprised to learn that he had hatched the concept some time ago to be held at the ready in the event that he should ever be captured."

"I wonder if that could be true."

"It's not impossible, is it? And we had to let him go."

"We'll never have to do that again."

"No," Grodin agreed. "One good thing's come of this. The new law is not perfect, God knows. Instant trials and speedy hangings are not what democracies ought to aspire to. But it is comforting to know that we will not be in this position again. Gershon?"

"Yes?"

"Stop the car, please. Pull off on the shoulder."

"Is something wrong?"

"No. But there is something I've decided to tell you. Good, and turn off the engine. We'll be here a few moments." Grodin squeezed his eyes shut, put his hand to his forehead. Without opening his eyes he said, "Anselmo said he and I would meet again. I told you the other day that he was wrong."

"I remember."

"He'll never return to Israel, you see. He'll meet his friends, if one calls such people friends, and he'll go wherever he has it in mind to go. And in two weeks or a month or possibly as much as two months he will experience a certain amount of nervousness. He may be mentally depressed, he may grow anxious and irritable. It's quite possible that he'll pay no attention to these signs because they may not be very much out of the ordinary. His life is disorganized, chaotic, enervating, so this state I've discussed may be no departure from the normal course of things."

"I don't understand, Nahum."

"Then after a day or so these symptoms will be more pronounced," Grodin went on. "He may run a fever. His appetite will wane. He'll grow quite nervous. He may talk a great deal, might even become something of a chatterbox. You recall that he said he sleeps like a baby. Well, he may experience insomnia.

"Then after a couple of days things will take a turn for the worse." Grodin took a pinseal billfold from his pocket, drew out an unfolded sheet of paper. "Here's a description from a medical encyclopedia. 'The agitation of the sufferer now becomes greatly increased and the countenance now exhibits anxiety and terror. There is marked embarrassment of the breathing, but the most striking and terrible features of this stage are the effects produced by attempts to swallow fluids. The patient suffers from thirst and desires eagerly to drink, but on making the effort is seized with a violent suffocative paroxysm which continues for several seconds and is succeeded by a feeling of intense alarm and distress. Indeed the very thought of drinking suffices to bring on a choking paroxysm, as does also the sound of running water.

"'The patient is extremely sensitive to any kind of external impression—a bright light, a loud noise, a breath of cool air—anything of this sort may bring on a seizure. There also occur general convulsions and occasionally a condition of tetanic spasm. These various paroxysms increase in frequency and severity with the advance of the disease.'"

"Disease?" Gershon Meir frowned. "I don't understand, Nahum. What disease? What are you driving at?"

Grodin went on reading. "'The individual experiences alternate intervals of comparative quiet in which there is intense anxiety and more or less constant difficulty in respiration accompanied by a peculiar sonorous exhalation which has suggested the notion that the patient barks like a dog. In many instances—'"

"A dog!"

"'In many instances there are intermittent fits of maniacal excitement. During all this stage of the disease the patient is tormented with a viscid secretion accumulating in his mouth. From dread of swallowing this he constantly spits about himself. He may also make snapping movements of the jaws as if attempting to bite. These are actually a manifestation of the spasmodic action which affects the muscles in general. There is no great amount of fever, but the patient will be constipated, his flow of urine will be diminished and he will often feel sexual excitement.

"'After two or three days of suffering of the most terrible description the patient succumbs, with death taking place either in a paroxysm of choking or from exhaustion. The duration of the disease from the first declaration of symptoms is generally from three to five days.'"

Grodin refolded the paper, returned it to his wallet. "Rabies," he said quietly. "Hydrophobia. Its incubation period is less than a week in dogs and other lower mammals. In humans it generally takes a month to erupt. It works faster in small children, I understand. And if the bite is in the head or neck the incubation period is speeded up."

"Can't it be cured? I thought—"

"The Pasteur shots. A series of about a dozen painful injections. I believe the vaccine is introduced by a needle into the stomach. And there are other less arduous methods of vaccination if the particular strain of rabies virus can be determined. But they have to be employed immediately. Once the incubation period is complete, once the symptoms manifest themselves, then death is inevitable."

"God."

"By the time Anselmo has the slightest idea what's wrong with him—"

"It will be too late."

"Exactly," Grodin said.

"When you gave him the pentothal—"

"Yes. There was more than pentothal in the needle."

"I sensed something."

"So you said."

"But I never would have guessed—"

"No. Of course not."

Gershon Meir shuddered. "When he realizes what you did to him and how you did it—"

"Then what?" Grodin spread his hands. "Could he be more utterly our enemy than he is already? And I honestly don't think he'll guess how he was tricked. He'll most likely suppose he was exposed to rabies from an animal source. I understand you can get it from inhaling the vapors of the dung of rabid bats. Perhaps he'll hide out in a bat-infested cave and blame the bats for his illness. But it doesn't matter, Gershon. Let him know what I did to him. I almost hope he guesses, for all the good it will do him."

"God."

"I just wanted to tell you," Grodin said, his voice calmer now. "There's poetry to it, don't you think? He's walking around now like a time bomb. He could get the Pasteur shots and save himself, but he doesn't know that, and by the time he does—"

"God."

"Start the car, eh? We'd better be getting back." And the older man straightened up in his seat and rubbed the throbbing knuckles of his right hand. They ached, but all the same he was smiling.

# A BAD NIGHT
# FOR
# BURGLARS

THE BURGLAR, A slender and clean-cut chap just past thirty, was rifling a drawer in the bedside table when Archer Trebizond slipped into the bedroom. Trebizond's approach was as catfooted as if he himself were the burglar, a situation which was manifestly not the case. The burglar never did hear Trebizond, absorbed as he was in his perusal of the drawer's contents, and at length he sensed the other man's presence as a jungle beast senses the presence of a predator.

The analogy, let it be said, is scarcely accidental.

When the burglar turned his eyes on Archer Trebizond his heart fluttered and fluttered again, first at the mere fact of discovery, then at his own discovery of the gleaming revolver in Trebizond's hand. The revolver was pointed in his direction, and this the burglar found upsetting.

"Darn it all," said the burglar, approximately. "I could have sworn there was nobody home. I phoned, I rang the bell—"

"I just got here," Trebizond said.

"Just my luck. The whole week's been like that. I dented a fender on Tuesday afternoon, overturned my fish tank the night before last. An unbelievable mess all over the carpet, and I lost a mated pair of African mouthbreeders so rare they don't have a Latin name yet. I'd hate to tell you what I paid for them."

"Hard luck," Trebizond said.

"And just yesterday I was putting away a plate of fettucine and I bit the inside of my mouth. You ever done that? It's murder, and the worst part is you feel so stupid about it. And then you keep biting it over and over again because it sticks out while it's healing. At least I do." The burglar gulped a breath and ran a moist hand over a moister forehead. "And now this," he said.

"This could turn out to be worse than fenders and fish tanks," Trebizond said.

"Don't I know it. You know what I should have done? I should have spent the entire week in bed. I happen to know a safecracker who consults an astrologer before each and every job he pulls. If Jupiter's in the wrong place or Mars is squared with Uranus or something he won't go in. It sounds ridiculous, doesn't it? And yet it's eight years now since anybody put a handcuff on that man. Now who do you know who's gone eight years without getting arrested?"

"I've never been arrested," Trebizond said.

"Well, you're not a crook."

"I'm a businessman."

The burglar thought of something but let it pass. "I'm going to get the name of his astrologer," he said. "That's just what I'm going to do. Just as soon as I get out of here."

"If you get out of here," Trebizond said. "Alive," Trebizond said.

The burglar's jaw trembled just the slightest bit. Trebizond smiled, and from the burglar's point of view Trebizond's smile seemed to enlarge the black hole in the muzzle of the revolver.

"I wish you'd point that thing somewhere else," he said nervously.

"There's nothing else I want to shoot."

"You don't want to shoot me."

"Oh?"

"You don't even want to call the cops," the burglar went on. "It's really not necessary. I'm sure we can work things out between us, two civilized men coming to a civilized agreement. I've some money on me. I'm an openhanded sort and would be pleased to make a small contribution to your favorite charity, whatever it might be. We don't need policemen to intrude into the private affairs of gentlemen."

The burglar studied Trebizond carefully. This little speech had always gone over rather well in the past, especially with men of substance. It was hard to tell how it was going over now, or if it was going over at all. "In any event," he ended somewhat lamely, "you certainly don't want to shoot me."

"Why not?"

"Oh, blood on the carpet, for a starter. Messy, wouldn't you say? Your wife would be upset. Just ask her and she'll tell you shooting me would be a ghastly idea."

"She's not at home. She'll be out for the next hour or so."

"All the same, you might consider her point of view. And shooting me would be illegal, you know. Not to mention immoral."

"Not illegal," Trebizond remarked.

"I beg your pardon?"

"You're a burglar," Trebizond reminded him. "An unlawful intruder on my property. You have broken and entered. You have invaded the sanctity of my home. I can shoot you where you stand and not get so much as a parking ticket for my trouble."

"Of course you can shoot me in self-defense—"

"Are we on 'Candid Camera'?"

"No, but—"

"Is Allen Funt lurking in the shadows?"

"No, but I—"

"In your back pocket. That metal thing. What is it?"

"Just a pry bar."

"Take it out," Trebizond said. "Hand it over. Indeed. A weapon if I ever saw one. I'd state that you attacked me with it and I fired in self-defense. It would be my word against yours, and yours would remain unvoiced since you would be dead. Whom do you suppose the police would believe?"

The burglar said nothing. Trebizond smiled a satisfied smile and put the pry bar in his own pocket. It was a piece of nicely shaped steel and it had a nice heft to it. Trebizond rather liked it.

"Why would you want to kill me?"

"Perhaps I've never killed anyone. Perhaps I'd like to satisfy my curiosity. Or perhaps I got to enjoy killing in the war and have been yearning for another crack at it. There are endless possibilities."

"But—"

"The point is," said Trebizond, "you might be useful to me in that manner. As it is, you're not useful to me at all. And stop hinting about my favorite charity or other euphemisms. I don't want your money. Look about you. I've ample money of my own—that should be obvious. If I were a poor man you wouldn't have breached my threshold. How much money are you talking about, anyway? A couple of hundred dollars?"

"Five hundred," the burglar said.

"A pittance."

"I suppose. There's more at home but you'd just call that a pittance too, wouldn't you?"

"Undoubtedly." Trebizond shifted the gun to his other hand. "I told you I was a businessman," he said. "Now if there were any way in which you could be more useful to me alive than dead—"

"You're a businessman and I'm a burglar," the burglar said, brightening.

"Indeed."

"So I could steal something for you. A painting? A competitor's trade secrets? I'm really very good at what I do, as a matter of fact, although you wouldn't guess it by my performance tonight. I'm not saying I could whisk the Mona Lisa out of the Louvre, but I'm pretty good at your basic hole-and-corner job of everyday burglary. Just give me an assignment and let me show my stuff."

"Hmmmm," said Archer Trebizond.

"Name it and I'll swipe it."

"Hmmmm."

"A car, a mink coat, a diamond bracelet, a Persian carpet, a first edition, bearer bonds, incriminating evidence, eighteen-and-a-half minutes of tape—"

"What was that last?"

"Just my little joke," said the burglar. "A coin collection, a stamp collection, psychiatric records, phonograph records, police records—"

"I get the point."

"I tend to prattle when I'm nervous."

"I've noticed."

"If you could point that thing elsewhere—"

Trebizond looked down at the gun in his hand. The gun continued to point at the burglar.

"No," Trebizond said, with evident sadness. "No, I'm afraid it won't work."

"Why not?"

"In the first place, there's nothing I really need or want. Could you steal me a woman's heart? Hardly. And more to the point, how could I trust you?"

"You could trust me," the burglar said. "You have my word on that."

"My point exactly. I'd have to take your word that your word is good, and where does that lead us? Down the proverbial garden path, I'm afraid. No, once I let you out from under my roof I've lost my advantage. Even if I have a gun trained on you, once you're in the open I can't shoot you with impunity. So I'm afraid—"

"No!"

Trebizond shrugged. "Well, really," he said. "What use are you? What are you good for besides being killed? Can you do anything besides steal, sir?"

"I can make license plates."

"Hardly a valuable talent."

"I know," said the burglar sadly. "I've often wondered why the state bothered to teach me such a pointless trade. There's not even much call for counterfeit license plates, and they've got a

83

monopoly on making the legitimate ones. What else can I do? I must be able to do something. I could shine your shoes, I could polish your car—"

"What do you do when you're not stealing?"

"Hang around," said the burglar. "Go out with ladies. Feed my fish, when they're not all over my rug. Drive my car when I'm not mangling its fenders. Play a few games of chess, drink a can or two of beer, make myself a sandwich—"

"Are you any good?"

"At making sandwiches?"

"At chess."

"I'm not bad."

"I'm serious about this."

"I believe you are," the burglar said. "I'm not your average woodpusher, if that's what you want to know. I know the openings and I have a good sense of space. I don't have the patience for tournament play, but at the chess club downtown I win more games than I lose."

"You play at the club downtown?"

"Of course. I can't burgle seven nights a week, you know. Who could stand the pressure?"

"Then you *can* be of use to me," Trebizond said.

"You want to learn the game?"

"I know the game. I want you to play chess with me for an hour until my wife gets home. I'm bored, there's nothing in the house to read, I've never cared much for television and it's hard for me to find an interesting opponent at the chess table."

"So you'll spare my life in order to play chess with me."

"That's right."

"Let me get this straight," the burglar said. "There's no catch to this, is there? I don't get shot if I lose the game or anything tricky like that, I hope."

"Certainly not. Chess is a game that ought to be above gimmickry."

"I couldn't agree more," said the burglar. He sighed a long sigh. "If I didn't play chess," he said, "you wouldn't have shot me, would you?"

"It's a question that occupies the mind, isn't it?"

"It is," said the burglar.

They played in the front room. The burglar drew the white pieces in the first game, opened King's Pawn, and played what turned out to be a reasonably imaginative version of the Ruy Lopez. At the sixteenth move Trebizond forced the exchange of knight for rook, and not too long afterward the burglar resigned.

In the second game the burglar played the black pieces and offered the Sicilian Defense. He played a variation that Trebizond wasn't familiar with. The game stayed remarkably even until in the end game the burglar succeeded in developing a passed pawn. When it was clear that he would be able to queen it, Trebizond tipped over his king, resigning.

"Nice game," the burglar offered.

"You play well."

"Thank you."

"Seems a pity that—"

His voice trailed off. The burglar shot him an inquiring look. "That I'm wasting myself as a common criminal? Is that what you were going to say?"

"Let it go," Trebizond said. "It doesn't matter."

They began setting up the pieces for the third game when a key slipped into a lock. The lock turned, the door opened and Melissa Trebizond stepped into the foyer and through it to the living room.

Both men got to their feet. Mrs. Trebizond advanced, a vacant smile on her pretty face. "You found a new friend to play chess with. I'm happy for you."

Trebizond set his jaw. From his back pocket he drew the burglar's pry bar. It had an even nicer heft than he had thought. "Melissa," he said, "I've no need to waste time with a recital of your sins. No doubt you know precisely why you deserve this."

She stared at him, obviously not having understood a word he had said to her, whereupon Archer Trebizond brought the pry bar down on the top of her skull. The first blow sent her to her knees. Quickly he struck her three more times, wielding the metal bar with all his strength, then turned to look into the wide eyes of the burglar.

"You've killed her," the burglar said.

"Nonsense," said Trebizond, taking the bright revolver from his pocket once again.

"Isn't she dead?"

"I hope and pray she is," Trebizond said, "but I haven't killed her. *You've* killed her."

"I don't understand."

"The police will understand," Trebizond said, and shot the burglar in the shoulder. Then he fired again, more satisfactorily this time, and the burglar sank to the floor with a hole in his heart.

Trebizond scooped the chess pieces into their box, swept up the board and set about the business of arranging things. He suppressed an urge to whistle. He was, he decided, quite pleased with himself. Nothing was ever entirely useless, not to a man of resources. If fate sent you a lemon, you made lemonade.

# NOTHING SHORT OF HIGHWAY ROBBERY

I EASED UP on the gas pedal a few hundred yards ahead of the service station. I was putting the brakes on when my brother Newton opened his eyes and straightened up in his seat.

"We haven't got but a gallon of gas left if we got that much," I told him. "And there's nothing out ahead of us but a hundred miles of sand and a whole lot of cactus, and I already seen enough cactus to last me a spell."

He smothered a yawn with the back of his hand. "Guess I went and fell asleep," he said.

"Guess you did."

He yawned again while a fellow a few years older'n us came off of the front porch of the house and walked our way, moving slow, taking his time. He was wearing a broadbrimmed white hat against the sun and a pair of bib overalls. The house wasn't much, a one-story clapboard structure with a flat roof. The garage alongside it must have been built at the same time and designed by the same man.

He came around to my side and I told him to fill the tank. "Regular," I said.

He shook his head. "High-test is all I got," he said. "That be all right?"

I nodded and he went around the car and commenced unscrewing the gas cap. "Only carries high-test," I said, not wildly happy about it.

"It'll burn as good as the regular, Vern."

"I guess I know that. I guess I know it's another five cents a gallon or another dollar bill on a tankful of gas, and don't you just bet that's why he does it that way? Because what the hell can you do if you want regular? This bird's the only game in town."

"Well, I don't guess a dollar'll break us, Vern."

I said I guessed not and I took a look around. The pump wasn't so far to the rear that I couldn't get a look at it, and when I did I saw the price per gallon, and it wasn't just an extra nickel that old boy was taking from us. His high-test was priced a good twelve cents a gallon over everybody else's high-test.

I pointed this out to my brother and did some quick sums in my head. Twelve cents plus a nickel times, say, twenty gallons was three dollars and forty cents. I said, "Damn, Newton, you know how I hate being played for a fool."

"Well, maybe he's got his higher costs and all. Being out in the middle of nowhere and all, little town like this."

"Town? Where's the town at? Where we are ain't nothing but a wide place in the road."

And that was really all it was. Not even a crossroads, just the frame house and the garage alongside it, and on the other side of the road a cafe with a sign advertising home-cooked food and package goods. A couple cars over by the garage, two of them with their hoods up and various parts missing from them. Another car parked over by the cafe.

"Newt," I said, "you ever see a softer place'n this?"

"Don't even think about it."

"Not thinking about a thing. Just mentioning."

"We don't bother with nickels and dimes no more, Vernon. We agreed on that. By tonight we'll be in Silver City. Johnny Mack Lee's already there and first thing in the morning we'll be taking that bank off slicker'n a bald tire. You know all that."

"I know."

"So don't be exercising your mind over nickels and dimes."

"Oh, I know it," I said. "Only we could use some kind of money pretty soon. What have we got left? Hundred dollars?"

"Little better than that."

"Not much better, though."

"Well, tomorrow's payday," Newt said.

I knew he was right but it's a habit a man gets into, looking at a place and figuring how he would go about taking it off. Me and Newt, we always had a feeling for places like filling stations and liquor stores and 7–11 stores and like that. You just take 'em off nice and easy, you get in and get out and a man can make a living that way. Like the saying goes, it don't pay much but it's regular.

But then the time came that we did a onc-to-five over to the state pen and it was an education. We both of us came out of there knowing the right people and the right way to operate. One thing we swore was to swear off nickels and dimes. The man who pulls quick-dollar stickups like that, he works ten times as often and takes twenty times the risks of the man who takes his time setting up a big job and scoring it. I remember Johnny Mack Lee saying it takes no more work to knock over a bank than a bakery and the difference is dollars to doughnuts.

I looked up and saw the dude with the hat poking around under the hood. "What's he doing now, Newt? Prospecting for more gold?"

"Checking the oil, I guess."

"Hope we don't need none," I said. "'Cause you just know he's gotta be charging two dollars a quart for it."

Well, we didn't need any oil. And you had to admit he did a good job of checking under there, topping up the battery terminals and all. Then he came around and leaned against the car door.

"Oil's okay," he said. "You sure took a long drink of gas. Good you had enough to get here. And this here's the last station for a whole lot of highway."

"Well," I said. "How much do we owe you?"

He named a figure. High as it was, it came as no surprise to me since I'd already turned and read it off of the pump. Then as I was reaching in my pocket he said, "I guess you know about that fan clutch, don't you?"

"Fan clutch?"

He gave a long slow nod. "I suppose you got a few miles left in it," he said. "Thing is, it could go any minute. You want to step out of the car for a moment I can show you what I'm talking about."

Well, I got out, and Newt got out his side, and we went and joined this bird and peeked under the hood. He reached behind the radiator and took ahold of some damned thing or other and showed us how it was wobbling. "The fan clutch," he said. "You ever replace this here since you owned the car?"

Newt looked at me and I looked back at him. All either of us ever knew about a car is starting it and stopping it and the like. As a boy Newt was awful good at starting them without keys. You know how kids are.

"Now if this goes," he went on, "then there goes your water pump. Probably do a good job on your radiator at the same time. You might want to wait and have your own mechanic take care of it for you. The way it is, though, I wouldn't want to be driving too fast or too far with it. Course if you hold it down to forty miles an hour and stop from time to time so's the heat won't build up—"

His voice trailed off. Me and Newt looked at each other again. Newt asked some more about the fan clutch and the dude wobbled it again and told us more about what it did, which we pretended to pay attention to and nodded like it made sense to us.

"This fan clutch," Newt said. "What's it run to replace it?"

"Around thirty, thirty-five dollars. Depends on the model and who does the work for you, things like that."

"Take very long?"

"Maybe twenty minutes."

"Could you do it for us?"

The dude considered, cleared his throat, spat in the dirt. "Could," he allowed. "If I got the part. Let me just go and check."

90

When he walked off I said, "Brother, what's the odds that he's got that part?"

"No bet a-tall. You figure there's something wrong with our fan clutch?"

"Who knows?"

"Yeah," Newt said. "Can't figure on him being a crook and just spending his life out here in the middle of nowhere, but then you got to consider the price he gets for the gas and all. He hasn't had a customer since we pulled in, you know. Maybe he gets one car a day and tries to make a living off it."

"So tell him what to do with his fan clutch."

"Then again, Vern, maybe all he is in the world is a good mechanic trying to do us a service. Suppose we cut out of here and fifty miles down the road our fan clutch up and kicks our water pump through our radiator or whatever the hell it is. By God, Vernon, if we don't get to Silver City tonight Johnny Mack Lee's going to be vexed with us."

"That's a fact. But thirty-five dollars for a fan clutch sure eats a hole in our capital, and suppose we finally get to Silver City and find out Johnny Mack Lee got out the wrong side of bed and slipped on a banana peel or something? Meaning if we get there and there's no job and we're stuck in the middle of nowhere, then what do we do?"

"Well, I guess it's better'n being stuck in the desert."

"I guess."

Of course he had just the part he needed. You had to wonder how a little gas station like that would happen to carry a full line of fan clutches, which I never even heard of that particular part before, but when I said as much to Newt he shrugged and said maybe an out-of-the-way place like that was likely to carry a big stock because he was too far from civilization to order parts when the need for them arose.

"The thing is," he said, "all up and down the line you can read all of this either way. Either we're being taken or we're being done a favor for, and there's no way to know for sure."

While he set about doing whatever he had to do with the fan

91

clutch, we took his advice and went across the street for some coffee. "Woman who runs the place is a pretty fair cook," he said. "I take all my meals there my own self."

"Takes all his meals here," I said to Newt. "Hell, she's got him where he's got us. He don't want to eat here, he can walk sixty miles to a place more to his liking."

The car that had been parked at the cafe was gone now and we were the only customers. The woman in charge was too thin and rawboned to serve as an advertisement for her own cooking. She had her faded blonde hair tied up in a red kerchief and she was perched on a stool smoking a cigarette and studying a True Confessions magazine. We each of us ordered apple pie at a dollar a wedge and coffee at thirty-five cents a cup. While we were eating a car pulled up and a man wearing a suit and tie bought a pack of cigarettes from her. He put down a dollar bill and didn't get back but two dimes change.

"I think I know why that old boy across the street charges so much," Newt said softly. "He needs to get top dollar if he's gonna pay for his meals here."

"She does charge the earth."

"You happen to note the liquor prices? She gets seven dollars for a bottle of Ancient Age bourbon. And that's not for a quart, either. That's for a fifth."

I nodded slowly. I said, "I just wonder where they keep all that money."

"Brother, we don't even want to think on that."

"Never hurt a man to think."

"These days it's all credit cards anyways. The tourist trade is nothing but credit cards and his regular customers most likely run a monthly tab and give him a check for it."

"We'll be paying cash."

"Well, it's a bit hard to establish credit in our line of work."

"Must be other people pays him cash. And the food and liquor over here, that's gotta be all cash, or most all cash."

"And how much does it generally come to in a day? Be sensible. As little business as they're doing—"

"I already thought of that. Same time, though, look how far

they are from wherever they do their banking."

"So?"

"So they wouldn't be banking the day's receipts every night. More likely they drive in and make their deposits once a week, maybe even once every two weeks."

Newt thought about that. "Likely you're right," he allowed. "Still, we're just talking small change."

"Oh, I know."

But when we paid for our pie and coffee Newton gave the old girl a smile and told her how we sure had enjoyed the pie, which we hadn't all that much, and how her husband was doing a real good job on our car over across the street.

"Oh, he does real good work," she said.

"What he's doing for us," Newt said, "he's replacing our fan clutch. I guess you probably get a lot of people here needing new fan clutches."

"I wouldn't know about that," she said. "Thing is I don't know much about cars. He's the mechanic and I'm the cook is how we divvy things up."

"Sounds like a good system," Newt told her.


On the way across the street Newt separated two twenties from our bankroll and tucked them into his shirt pocket. Then I reminded him about the gas and he added a third twenty. He gave the rest of our stake a quick count and shook his head in annoyance. "We're getting pretty close to the bone," he said. "Johnny Mack Lee better be where's he's supposed to be."

"He's always been reliable."

"That's God's truth. And the bank, it better be the piece of cake he says it is."

"I just hope."

"Twenty thousand a man is how he has it figured. Plus he says it could run three times that. I sure wouldn't complain if it did, brother."

I said I wouldn't either. "It does make it silly to even think about nickels and dimes," I said.

"Just what I was telling you."

"I was never thinking about it, really. Not in the sense of doing it. Just mental exercise, keeps the brain in order."

He gave me a brotherly punch in the shoulder and we laughed together some. Then we went on to where the dude in the big hat was playing with our car. He gave us a big smile and held out a piece of metal for us to admire. "Your old fan clutch," he said, which I had more or less figured. "Take hold of this part. That's it, right there. Now try to turn it."

I tried to turn it and it was hard to turn. He had Newt do the same thing. "Tight," Newt said.

"Lucky you got this far with it," he said, and clucked his tongue and shook his head and heaved the old fan clutch onto a heap of old metallic junk.

I stood there wondering if a fan clutch was supposed to turn hard or easy or not at all, and if that was our original fan clutch or a piece of junk he kept around for this particular purpose, and I knew my brother Newton was wondering just the same thing. I wished they could have taught us something useful in the state pen, something that might have come in handy in later life, something like your basic auto mechanics course. But they had me melting my flesh off my bones in the prison laundry and they had Newt sewing mail sacks, which there isn't much call for in civilian life, being the state penal system has an official monopoly on the business.

Meanwhile Newt had the three twenties out of his shirt pocket and was standing there straightening them out and lining up their edges. "Let's see now," he said. "That's sixteen and change for the gas, and you said thirty to thirty-five for the fan clutch, so what's that all come to?"

It turned out that it came to just under eighty-five dollars.

The fan clutch, it seemed, had run higher than he'd thought it would. Forty-two fifty was what it came to, and that was for the part exclusive of labor. Labor tacked another twelve dollars onto our tab. And while he'd been working there under the hood, our friend had found a few things that simply needed attending to. Our fan belt, for example, was clearly on its last legs and ready to pop any minute. He showed it to us and you could see how worn it was, all frayed and just a thread or two away from popping.

So he had replaced it, and he'd replaced our radiator hoses at the same time. He fished around in his junkpile and came up with a pair of radiator hoses which he said had come off our car. The rubber was old and stiff with little cracks in the surface, and it sure smelled like something awful.

I studied the hoses and agreed they were in terrible shape. "So you just went ahead and replaced them on your own," I said.

"Well," he said, "I didn't want to bother you while you were eating."

"That was considerate," Newt said.

"I figured you fellows would want it seen to. You blow a fan belt or a hose out there, well, it's a long walk back, you know. Course I realize you didn't authorize me to do the work, so if you actually want me to take the new ones off and put the old back on—"

Of course there was no question of doing that. Newt looked at me for a minute and I looked back at him and he took out our roll, which I don't guess you could call a roll anymore from the size of it, and he peeled off another twenty and a ten and added them to the three twenties from his shirt pocket. He held the money in his hand and looked at it and then at the dude, then back at the money, then back at the dude again. You could see he was doing heavy thinking, and I had an idea where his thoughts were leading.

Finally he took in a whole lot of air and let it out in a rush and said, "Well, hell, I guess it's worth it if it leaves us with a car in good condition. Last thing either of us wants is any damn trouble with the damn car and I guess it's worth it. This fixes us up, right? Now we're in good shape with nothing to worry about, right?"

"Well," the dude said.

We looked at him.

"There is a thing I noticed."

"Oh?"

"If you'll just look right here," he said. "See how the rubber grommet's gone on the top of your shock absorber mounting, that's what called it to my attention. Now you see your car's right above the hydraulic lift, that's cause I had it up before to take a look at your shocks. Now let me just raise it up again and I can point out to you what's wrong."

Well, he pressed a switch or some such to send the car up off the ground, and then he pointed here and there underneath it to show us where the shocks were shot and something was cutting into something else and about to commence bending the frame.

"If you got the time you ought to let me take care of that for you," he said. "Because if you don't get it seen to you wind up with frame damage and your whole front end goes on you, and then where are you?"

He let us take a long look at the underside of the car. There was no question that something was pressing on something and cutting into it. What the hell it all added up to was beyond me.

"Just let me talk to my brother a minute," Newt said to him, and he took hold of my arm and we walked around the side.

"Well," he said, "what do you think? It looks like this old boy here is sticking it in pretty deep."

"It does at that. But that fan belt was shot and those hoses was the next thing to petrified."

"True."

"If they was our fan belt and hoses in the first place and not some junk he had around."

"I had that very thought, Vern."

"Now as for the shock absorbers—"

"Something sure don't look altogether perfect underneath that car. Something's sure cutting into something."

"I know it. But maybe he just went and got a file or some such thing and did some cutting himself."

"In other words, either he's a con man or he's a saint."

"Except we know he ain't a saint, not at the price he gets for gasoline, and not telling us how he eats all his meals across the road and all the time his own wife's running it."

"So what do we do? You want to go on to Silver City on those shocks? I don't even know if we got enough money to cover putting shocks on, far as that goes."

We walked around to the front and asked the price of the shocks. He worked it all out with pencil and paper and came up with a figure of forty-five dollars, including the parts and the labor and the tax and all. Newt and I went into another huddle and he counted his money and I went through my own pockets and came up with a couple of dollars, and it worked out that we could pay what we owed and get the shocks and come up with three dollars to bless ourselves with.

So I looked at Newt and he looked back at me and gave a great shrug of his shoulders. Close as we are we can say a lot without speaking.

We told the dude to go ahead and do the work.

While he installed the shocks, me and Newt went across the road and had us a couple of chicken-fried steaks. They wasn't bad at all even if the price was on the high side. We washed the steaks down with a beer apiece and then each of us had a cup of that coffee. I guess there's been times I had better coffee.

"I'd say you fellows sure were lucky you stopped here," the woman said.

"It's our lucky day, all right," Newt said. While he paid her I looked over the paperback books and magazines. Some of them looked to be old and secondhand but they weren't none of them reduced in price on account of it, and this didn't surprise me much.

What also didn't surprise us was when we got back to find the shocks installed and our friend with his big hat off and scratching his mop of hair and telling us how the rear shocks was in even worse shape than the front ones. He went and ran the car up in the air again to show us more things that didn't mean much to us.

Newton said, "Well, sir, my brother and I, we talked it over. We figure we been neglecting this here automobile and we really ought to do right by it. If those rear shocks is bad, well, let's just get 'em the hell off of there and new ones on. And while we're here I'm just about positive we're due for an oil change."

"And I'll replace the oil filter while I'm at it."

"You do that," Newt told him. "And I guess you'll find other things that can do with a bit of fixing. Now we haven't got all the time in the world or all the money in the world either, but I guess we got us a pair of hours to spare, and we consider ourselves lucky having the good fortune to run up against a mechanic who knows which end of the wrench is which. So what we'll do, we'll just find us a patch of shade to set in and you check that car over and find things to do to her. Only things that need doing, but I guess you'd be the best judge of that."

Well, I'll tell you he found things to fix. Now and then a car would roll on in and he'd have to go and sell somebody a tank of gas, but we sure got the lion's share of his time. He replaced the air filter, he cleaned the carburetor, he changed the oil and replaced the oil filter, he tuned the engine and drained and flushed the radiator and filled her with fresh coolant, he gave us new plugs and points, he did this and that and every damn thing he could think of, and I guess the only parts of that car he didn't replace were ones he didn't have replacement parts for.

Through it all Newt and I sat in a patch of shade and sipped Cokes out of the bottle. Every now and then that bird would come over and tell us what else he found that he ought to be doing, and we'd look at each other and shrug our shoulders and say for him to go ahead and do what had to be done.

"Amazing what was wrong with that car of ours," Newt said to me. "Here I thought it rode pretty good."

"Hell, I pulled in here wanting nothing in the world but a tank of gas. Maybe a quart of oil, and oil was the one thing in the world we didn't need, or it looks like."

"Should ride a whole lot better once he's done with it."

"Well I guess it should. Man's building a whole new car around the cigarette lighter."

"And the clock. Nothing wrong with that clock, outside of it loses a few minutes a day."

"Lord," Newt said, "don't you be telling him about those few minutes the clock loses. We won't never get out of here."

That dude took the two hours we gave him and about twelve minutes besides, and then he came on over into the shade and presented us with his bill. It was all neatly itemized, everything listed in the right place and all of it added up, and the figure in the bottom right-hand corner with the circle around it read $277.45.

"That there is quite a number," I said.

He put the big hat on the back of his head and ran his hand over his forehead. "Whole lot of work involved," he said. "When you take into account all of those parts and all that labor."

"Oh, that's for certain," Newt said. "And I can see they all been taken into account, all right."

"That's clear as black and white," I said. "One thing, you couldn't call this a nickel-and-dime figure."

"That you couldn't," Newton said. "Well, sir, let me just go and get some money from the car. Vern?"

We walked over to the car together. "Funny how things work out," Vern said. "I swear people get forced into things, I just swear to hell and gone they do. What did either of us want beside a tank of gas?"

"Just a tank of gas is all."

"And here we are," he said. He opened the door on the passenger side, waited for a pickup truck to pass going west to east, then popped the glove compartment. He took the .38 for himself and gave me the .32 revolver. "I'll just settle up with our good buddy here," he said, loud enough for the good buddy in question to hear him. "Meanwhile, why don't you just step across the street and pick us up something to drink later on this evening? You never know, might turn out to be a long ways between liquor stores."

I went and gave him a little punch in the upper arm. He laughed the way he does and I put the .32 in my pocket and trotted on across the road to the cafe.

# ONE THOUSAND
# DOLLARS
# A WORD

THE EDITOR'S NAME was Warren Jukes. He was a lean sharp-featured man with slender long-fingered hands and a narrow line for a mouth. His black hair was going attractively gray on top and at the temples. As usual, he wore a stylish three-piece suit. As usual, Trevathan felt logy and unkempt in comparison, like a bear having trouble shaking off the torpor of hibernation.

"Sit down, Jim," Jukes said. "Always a pleasure. Don't tell me you're bringing in another manuscript already? It never ceases to amaze me the way you keep grinding them out. Where do you get your ideas, anyway? But I guess you're tired of that question after all these years."

He was indeed, and that was not the only thing of which James Trevathan was heartily tired. But all he said was, "No, Warren. I haven't written another story."

"Oh?"

"I wanted to talk with you about the last one."

"But we talked about it yesterday," Jukes said, puzzled. "Over the telephone. I said it was fine and I was happy to have it for the magazine. What's the title, anyway? It was a play on words, but I can't remember it offhand."

"'A Stitch in Crime,'" Trevathan said.

101

"Right, that's it. Good title, good story and all of it wrapped up in your solid professional prose. What's the problem?"

"Money," Trevathan said.

"A severe case of the shorts, huh?" The editor smiled. "Well, I'll be putting a voucher through this afternoon. You'll have the check early next week. I'm afraid that's the best I can do, Jimbo. The corporate machinery can only go so fast."

"It's not the time," Trevathan said. "It's the amount. What are you paying for the story, Warren?"

"Why, the usual. How long was it? Three thousand words, wasn't it?"

"Thirty-five hundred."

"So what does that come to? Thirty-five hundred at a nickel a word is what? One seventy-five, right?"

"That's right, yes."

"So you'll have a check in that amount early next week, as soon as possible, and if you want I'll ring you when I have it in hand and you can come over and pick it up. Save waiting a couple of days for the neither-rain-nor-snow people to get it from my desk to yours."

"It's not enough."

"Beg your pardon?"

"The price," Trevathan said. He was having trouble with this conversation. He'd written a script for it in his mind on the way to Jukes's office, and he'd been infinitely more articulate then than now. "I should get more money," he managed. "A nickel a word is... Warren, that's no money at all."

"It's what we pay, Jim. It's what we've always paid."

"Exactly."

"So?"

"Do you know how long I've been writing for you people, Warren?"

"Quite a few years."

"Twenty years, Warren."

"Really?"

"I sold a story called 'Hanging by a Thread' to you twenty

102

years ago last month. It ran twenty-two hundred words and you paid me a hundred and ten bucks for it."

"Well, there you go," Jukes said.

"I've been working twenty years, Warren, and I'm getting the same money now that I got then. Everything's gone up except my income. When I wrote my first story for you I could take one of those nickels that a word of mine brought and buy a candy bar with it. Have you bought a candy bar recently, Warren?"

Jukes touched his belt buckle. "If I went and bought candy bars," he said, "my clothes wouldn't fit me."

"Candy bars are forty cents. Some of them cost thirty-five. And I still get a nickel a word. But let's forget candy bars."

"Fine with me, Jim."

"Let's talk about the magazine. When you bought 'Hanging by a Thread,' what did the magazine sell for on the stands?"

"Thirty-five cents, I guess."

"Wrong. Twenty-five. About six months later you went to thirty-five. Then you went to fifty, and after that sixty and then seventy-five. And what does the magazine sell for now?"

"A dollar a copy."

"And you still pay your authors a nickel a word. That's really wealth beyond the dreams of avarice, isn't it, Warren?"

Jukes sighed heavily, propped his elbows on his desk top, tented his fingertips. "Jim," he said, dropping his voice in pitch, "there are things you're forgetting. The magazine's no more profitable than it was twenty years ago. In fact we're working closer now than we did then. Do you know anything about the price of paper? It makes candy look pretty stable by comparison. I could talk for hours on the subject of the price of paper. Not to mention all the other printing costs, and shipping costs and more other costs than I want to mention or you want to hear about. You look at that buck-a-copy price and you think we're flying high, but it's not like that at all. We were doing better way back then. Every single cost of ours has gone through the roof."

"Except the basic one."

"How's that?"

"The price you pay for material. That's what your readers are buying from you, you know. Stories. Plots and characters. Prose and dialogue. Words. And you pay the same for them as you did twenty years ago. It's the only cost that's stayed the same."

Jukes took a pipe apart and began running a pipe cleaner through the stem. Trevathan started talking about his own costs—his rent, the price of food. When he paused for breath Warren Jukes said, "Supply and demand, Jim."

"What's that?"

"Supply and demand. Do you think it's hard for me to fill the magazine at a nickel a word? See that pile of scripts over there? That's what this morning's mail brought. Nine out of ten of those stories are from new writers who'd write for nothing if it got them into print. The other ten percent is from pros who are damned glad when they see that nickel-a-word check instead of getting their stories mailed back to them. You know, I buy just about everything you write for us, Jim. One reason is I like your work, but that's not the only reason. You've been with us for twenty years and we like to do business with our old friends. But you evidently want me to raise your word rate, and we don't pay more than five cents a word to anybody, because in the first place we haven't got any surplus in the budget and in the second place we damn well don't *have* to pay more than that. So before I raise your rate, old friend, I'll give your stories back to you. Because I don't have any choice."

Trevathan sat and digested this for a few moments. He thought of some things to say but left them unsaid. He might have asked Jukes how the editor's own salary had fluctuated over the years, but what was the point of that? He could write for a nickel a word or he could not write for them at all. That was the final word on the subject.

"Jim? Shall I put through a voucher or do you want 'A Stitch in Crime' back?"

"What would I do with it? No, I'll take the nickel a word, Warren."

"If there was a way I could make it more—"

"I understand."

"You guys should have got yourselves a union years ago. Give you a little collective muscle. Or you could try writing something else. We're in a squeeze, you know, and if we were forced to pay more for material we'd probably have to fold the magazine altogether. But there are other fields where the pay is better."

"I've been doing this for twenty years, Warren. It's all I know. My God, I've got a reputation in the field, I've got an established name—"

"Sure. That's why I'm always happy to have you in the magazine. As long as I do the editing, Jimbo, and as long as you grind out the copy, I'll be glad to buy your yarns."

"At a nickel a word."

"Well—"

"Nothing personal, Warren. I'm just a little bitter. That's all."

"Hey, think nothing of it." Jukes got to his feet, came around from behind his desk. "So you got something off your chest, and we cleared the air a little. Now you know where you stand. Now you can go on home and knock off something sensational and get it to me, and if it's up to your usual professional standard you'll have another check coming your way. That's the way to double the old income, you know. Just double the old production."

"Good idea," Trevathan said.

"Of course it is. And maybe you can try something for another market while you're at it. It's not too late to branch out, Jim. God knows I don't want to lose you, but if you're having trouble getting by on what we can pay you, well—"

"It's a thought," Trevathan said.

*Five cents a word.*

Trevathan sat at his battered Underwood and stared at a blank sheet of paper. The paper had gone up a dollar a ream in the past year, and he could swear they'd cheapened the quality in the process. Everything cost more, he thought, except his own well-chosen words. They were still trading steadily at a nickel apiece.

Not too late to branch out, Jukes had told him. But that was a sight easier to say than to do. He'd tried writing for other kinds of markets, but detective stories were the only kind he'd ever had any luck with. His mind didn't seem to produce viable fictional ideas in other areas. When he'd tried writing longer works, novels, he'd always gotten hopelessly bogged down. He was a short-story writer, recognized and frequently anthologized, and he was prolific enough to keep himself alive that way, but—

But he was sick of living marginally, sick of grinding out story after story. And heartily sick of going through life on a nickel a word.

What would a decent word rate be?

Well, if they paid him twenty-five cents a word, then he'd at least be keeping pace with the price of a candy bar. Of course after twenty years you wanted to do a little better than stay even. Say they paid him a dollar a word. There were writers who earned that much. Hell, there were writers who earned a good deal more than that, writers whose books wound up on best-seller lists, writers who got six-figure prices for screenplays, writers who wrote themselves rich.

*One thousand dollars a word.*

The phrase popped into his mind, stunning in its simplicity, and before he was aware of it his fingers had typed the words on the page before him. He sat and looked at it, then worked the carriage return lever and typed the phrase again.

*One thousand dollars a word.*

He studied what he had typed, his mind racing on ahead, playing with ideas, shaking itself loose from its usual stereotyped thought patterns. Well, why not? Why shouldn't he earn a thousand dollars a word? Why not branch out into a new field?

Why not?

He took the sheet from the typewriter, crumpled it into a ball, pegged it in the general direction of the wastebasket. He rolled a new sheet in its place and sat looking at its blankness, waiting, thinking. Finally, word by halting word, he began to type.

Trevathan rarely rewrote his short stories. At a nickel a word he could not afford to. Furthermore, he had acquired a facility over the years which enabled him to turn out acceptable copy in first draft. Now, however, he was trying something altogether new and different, and so he felt the need to take his time getting it precisely right. Time and again he yanked false starts from the typewriter, crumpled them, hurled them at the wastebasket.

Until finally he had something he liked.

He read it through for the fourth or fifth time, then took it from the typewriter and read it again. It did the job, he decided. It was concise and clear and very much to the point.

He reached for the phone. When he'd gotten through to Jukes he said, "Warren? I've decided to take your advice."

"Wrote another story for us? Glad to hear it."

"No," he said, "another piece of advice you gave me. I'm branching out in a new direction."

"Well, I think that's terrific," Jukes said. "I really mean it. Getting to work on something big? A novel?"

"No, a short piece."

"But in a more remunerative area?"

"Definitely. I'm expecting to net a thousand dollars a word for what I'm doing this afternoon."

"A thousand—" Warren Jukes let out a laugh, making a sound similar to the yelp of a startled terrier. "Well, I don't know what you're up to, Jim, but let me wish you the best of luck with it. I'll tell you one thing. I'm damned glad you haven't lost your sense of humor."

Trevathan looked again at what he'd written. "*I've got a gun. Please fill this paper sack with thirty thousand dollars in used tens and twenties and fifties or I'll be forced to blow your stupid head off.*"

"Oh, I've still got my sense of humor," he said. "Know what I'm going to do, Warren? I'm going to laugh all the way to the bank."

# THE GENTLE WAY

I WAS AT the animal shelter over an hour that morning before I found the lamb. She was right out in plain sight in the middle of the barnyard, but the routine called for me to run through the inside chores before taking care of the outside animals. I arrived at the shelter around seven, so I had two hours to get things in shape before Will Haggerty arrived at nine to open up for business.

First on the list that morning was the oven. Will and I had had to put down a dog the night before, a rangy Doberman with an unbreakable vicious streak. The dog had come to us two months ago, less than a month after I started working there. He'd been a beloved family pet for a year and a half before almost taking an arm off a seven-year-old neighbor boy. Two hours after that the Dobe was in a cage at the far end of the shelter. "Please try and find a good home for Rex," the owners begged us. "Maybe a farm, someplace where he has room to run."

Will had said all the right things and they left, smiling bravely. When they were gone Will sighed and went back to look at the dog and talk to him. He turned to me. "We could put a fifty-dollar adoption tag on him and move him out of here in a week, Eddie, but I won't do it. A farm—now this is just what your average farmer needs, isn't it? Good old Rex is a killer. He'd rip up cats and chickens. Give him room to run and he'd go after sheep and calves. No Dobe is worth a damn unless he's trained by an expert and the best experts won't get a hundred percent success. Train one right and he's still no family pet. He'll be a good guard dog, a good attack dog, but who wants to live with one of those? I know people who swear by them, but I never yet met a Dobe I could trust."

"So what happens now?"

"We tag the cage 'Not For Adoption' and give the poor beast food and water. Maybe I'll turn up a trainer who wants to take a chance on him, but frankly I doubt it. Rex here is just too old and too mean. It's not teaching him new tricks but making him forget the ones he already knows, and that's a whole lot easier said than done."

Rex was the first animal we had to put away since I went to work for Will. There must have been a dozen people who walked past the cage and asked to adopt him. Some of them wanted to give him a try even after they heard why he wasn't available. We wouldn't let him go. Will worked with him a few times and only confirmed what he already knew. The dog was vicious, and his first taste of blood had finished him; but we kept him around for weeks even after we knew what we had to do.

We were standing in front of the Doberman's cage when Will dropped a big hand on my shoulder and shook his head sadly. "No sense putting it off anymore," he said. "That cage is no place for him and there's no other place he can go. Might as well get it over."

"You want me to help?"

"He's a big old boy and it'd be easier with two of us, but I'm not going to tell you to. God knows I got no stomach for it myself."

I said I'd stick around.

He got a pistol and loaded it with tranquilizer darts, then filled a hypodermic syringe with morphine. We walked back to Rex's cage and Will kept the pistol out of sight at his side until Rex was facing the other way. He raised the gun and fired quickly, planting two darts an inch apart in the big dog's shoulder. Rex dropped like a stone.

Will crawled into the cage and hunkered down next to him. He had the needle poised but hesitated. The tranquilizer darts would keep the dog unconscious for fifteen or twenty minutes. The morphine would kill. There were tears flowing down Will Haggerty's weathered face. I tried to look away but couldn't, and I watched him find a vein and fill the comatose dog with a lethal dose of morphine.

We put him in the wheelbarrow and took him inside. The other animals seemed restless, but that may have been my imagination. I had opened the lid of the incinerator while Will was preparing the morphine. The two of us got the dead dog out of the wheelbarrow and into the big metal box. I closed the lid and Will threw the switch without hesitation. Then we turned away and walked into another room.

We had used the oven before. We would pick up dogs on the street, dogs run down in traffic. Or dogs would die at home and people would bring us their bodies for disposal. Twice in the time I'd been there we'd had auto victims who were alive when we found them but could not possibly be saved. Those had received morphine shots and gone into the incinerator, but that had been very different. Rex was a beautiful animal in splendid health and it went against the grain to kill him.

"I hate it," Will had told me. "There's nothing worse. I'll keep an animal forever if there's any chance of placing him. There are those in this business who burn half the dogs they get and sell the others to research labs. I never yet let one go for research and never will. And I never yet burned one that I had the slightest hope for."

I opened the oven and swept out a little pile of powdery white ash, unable to believe that nothing more remained of the Doberman. I was glad when the job was done and the oven closed. It was a relief to get busy with the routine work of feeding and watering the dogs and cats, cleaning cages, sweeping up.

Then I went out to the barnyard and found the dead lamb.

The shelter is in the middle of the city, a drab, gray, hopeless part of a generally hopeless town. The barnyard covers about a quarter of an acre girdled by eight feet of cyclone fencing. We keep farm animals there; chickens, ducks and geese, ponies and pigs and sheep. Some had been pets that outgrew their welcome. Others were injured animals we had patched up. Some of them came through cruelty cases we prosecuted, on the rare occasions when Will managed to get a court order divesting the owner of his charges. Supermarkets brought us their distressed produce as feed, and a farmer who owed Will a favor had sent over a load of hay a couple of weeks ago. The barnyard was open to the public during normal business hours, and kids from all over the city would come in and play with the animals.

In theory, the barnyard exists to generate goodwill for the shelter operation. The stray-dog contract with the city is a virtual guarantee of Will's operating expenses. I hadn't worked for him a week, however, before I knew that was just an excuse. He loved to walk among his animals, loved to slip a sugar cube to a pony, scratch a pig's back with a long stick, or just stand chewing a dead cigar and watching the ducks and geese.

The lamb had been born at the shelter shortly after I started working there. Ewes often need assistance at lambing time, and Will had delivered her while I stood around feeling nervous. We named the lamb Fluff, which was accurate if unimaginative, and she was predictably the hit of the barnyard. Everybody loved her—except for the person who killed her.

He had used a knife, and he had used it over and over again. The ground was littered with bloody patches of wool. I took one look and was violently ill, something that hadn't happened since the days of college beer parties. I stood there for what must have been a long time. Then I went inside and called Will.

"You'd better come down here," I said. "Somebody killed Fluff."

When he got here we put her in the oven and he threw the switch. We made coffee and sat in the office letting it get cold on the desk in front of us. It was past nine and time to open the front doors, but neither of us was in a hurry.

After a while he said, "Well, we haven't had one of these for six months. I suppose we were overdue."

"This has happened before?"

He looked at me. "I keep forgetting how young you are."

"What's that supposed to mean?"

"It may have sounded nastier than I meant it. I guess I'm feeling nasty, that's all. Yes, it's happened before, and it will happen again. Kids. They come over the fence and kill something."

"Why?"

"Because they want to. Because they'd like to kill a person but they're not ready for that yet, so they practice on an animal that never knew there was evil on earth. One time, two years ago, a batch of them killed fifteen chickens, the whole flock. Chopped their heads off. Left everything else alone, just killed the chickens. The police asked them why and they said it was fun watching them run around headless. *It was fun.*"

I didn't say anything.

"It's always kids, Eddie. Rotten kids from rotten homes. The police pick them up, but they're children, so they run them through juvenile court and it shakes up the kids and terrifies the parents. The kids are released in their parents' custody and maybe the parents pay a fine and the kids learn a lesson. They learn not to break into this particular barnyard and not to kill these particular animals." He took the cellophane from a cigar and rolled it between his palms. "Some of the time I don't call the police. There's a gentler way to go about it and it works better in the long run. I'd rather do it that way this time, but I'd need your help."

"How do you mean?"

"Catch him ourselves." He took his time lighting the cigar. "They always try it again. We can stake out the place as easily as the cops can, and when we take him we can operate more flexibly than they can. There's a method I've worked out. It lets them understand our operation, gives them a better perspective."

"I think I understand."

"But it means staying up all night for the next night or two, so it's a question of whether you want to give up the time."

"Sure."

"Won't be more than two nights, I would say. He'll be back."

"How do you know there's just one of them?"

"Because there was only one dead animal, son. If you got two there's going to be a minimum of two dead animals. Everybody has to have a turn. It always seems to work that way, anyhow."

We staked out the place that night and the night after. We took turns sleeping during daylight hours, and we were both planted behind cover in the barnyard all through the dark hours. The killer stayed away two nights running. We decided to give it three more tries, but one was all we needed.

Around one in the morning of the third night we heard someone at the fence. I could just make out a shape in the darkness. He would climb halfway up the fence, then hesitate and drop back to the ground. He seemed to be trying to get up the courage to climb all the way over.

I had a tranquilizer dart pistol and I was dying to try dropping him then and there while he was outlined against the fence. I was afraid he would sense our presence and be warned off, but I forced myself to wait. Finally he climbed all the way up, poised there on the balls of his tennis shoes, and jumped toward us.

We had our flashlights on him before he hit the ground, big five-cell jobs that threw a blinding beam.

"Hold it right there," Will boomed out, striding toward him. He had a dart pistol in his right hand and was holding it out in front of the flashlight so that the boy could see it. All it could shoot were the trank darts, but you couldn't tell that by looking at it.

Either the kid panicked or he figured nobody would shoot him for climbing a barnyard fence. He was quick as a snake. He got three-quarters of the way up the fence when Will put a dart into his shoulder, and he hit the ground the way Rex had hit the floor of his cage.

Will hoisted him easily onto his shoulder and toted him into the office. We turned on a desk lamp and propped the kid in a chair. He was about thirteen or fourteen, skinny, with a mop of lifeless black hair. In the pockets of his jeans we found three clasp knives and a switchblade, and on his belt he had a hunting knife in a sheath. There were stains in the hunting knife's blood groove, and in one of the clasp knives we found bits of bloody wool.

"Just follow my play, Eddie," Will told me. "There's a technique I worked out and you'll see how it goes."

We keep milk in a little fridge, mostly for the cats and puppies. Will poured out a glass of it and put it on the desk. The kid opened his eyes after about twelve minutes. His face was deadly pale and his blue eyes burned in the white face.

Will said, "How you feeling? Never run, son, when someone holds a gun on you. There's milk in front of you. You look a little peaked and it'll do you good."

"I don't want any milk."

"Well, it's there if you change your mind. I guess you wanted to have a look at our animals. Just your hard luck you picked tonight." He reached over and rumpled the boy's hair affectionately. "See, there was a gang of troublemakers here a few nights ago. We know who they are, we had trouble with them before. They hang out in Sayreville over to the north. They broke in the other night and killed a poor little lamb."

I was watching the kid's face. His mind wasn't all that quick and it dawned on him rather slowly that we didn't know he was Fluff's killer.

"But it's one thing to know who they are and another thing to prove it," Will went on. "So we thought we'd try catching them in the act. You just happened to drop in at the wrong time. I thought you were too young to be one of them, but when you started to bolt I couldn't take chances. That was a tranquilizer dart, by the way. We use it on animals that are impossible to control."

*Like the kid himself*, I thought, but Will was talking to him now in the gentle voice he uses on high-strung dogs and spooked ponies, showing him the pistol and the darts and explaining how they work.

"I guess those punks won't be here tonight after all," Will said.

"You wouldn't believe what they did to a poor innocent creature. Well, they'll be back sooner or later, and when they do return we'll get them."

"What will happen to them then?" the kid asked.

"A whole lot more than they counted on, son. First off the cops will take them in the back room and pound hell out of them—kill a cop or an animal in this town and the police tend to throw the book away—but those kids won't have a mark on them. Then they'll sit in jail until their case comes up, and then they'll be in a reformatory for a minimum of three years. And I wouldn't want to tell you what happens to them in reform school. Let's just say it won't be a Sunday school picnic and let it go at that."

"Well, I guess they deserve it," the kid said.

"You bet they do."

"Anybody who'd do a thing like that," the kid added.

Will heaved a sigh. "Well, now that you're here, son, maybe we can make it up to you for scaring you like that. How about a guided tour of the place? Give you some kind of an idea of the operation we're running here."

I don't know whether the kid was enthusiastic about the idea or whether he just had the sense to give that impression. Either way, he tagged along as we led him all through the place, inside and out. We showed him around the barnyard, pointed out Fluff's mother, talked about how Fluff had been born. We showed him the dog and cat cages and the small animal section with mice and hamsters and gerbils. He was full of questions and Will gave him detailed answers.

It wasn't hard to see what Will was doing. First, we were making it obvious that we knew a decent kid like him couldn't possibly be an animal killer. We let him know that we suspected somebody else for the act and that he was home free. We reinforced things by telling him his act would have earned him precisely the sort of treatment it *should* have earned him—a good beating and a stiff sentence. Then, while all that soaked in, we made him feel a part of the animal shelter instead of an enemy.

116

It looked good, but I had my doubts. The kid was having too much fun making the most of the situation. He was going to go home convinced we were a couple of damn fools who couldn't recognize a villain when he almost literally fell into our laps. Still, I didn't see how we could get worse results than the police got by following the book—and Will had done this before, so I wasn't going to give him an argument.

"And this here is the incinerator," Will said finally.

"For garbage?"

"Used to be. But there's an ordinance against burning garbage within city limits, on account of the air pollution. What we use it for is disposal of dead animals." He hung his head. "Poor little Fluff went in here. All that was left of her was enough ashes to fill an envelope—a small one at that."

The kid was impressed. "How long does it take?"

"No time at all. She heats up to something like three thousand degrees Fahrenheit and nothing lasts long at that temperature." Will unhooked the cover, raised it up. "You're just about tall enough to see in there. Enough room for two or three big dogs at a time."

"I'll say."

"You could pretty near fit a pony in there."

"You sure could," the kid said. He thought for a moment, still staring down into the oven. "What would happen if you put an animal in there while it was still alive?"

"Now there's an interesting question," Will allowed. "Of course I would never do that to an animal."

"Of course not."

"Because it would be cruel."

"Sure, but I was just wondering."

"But a dirty little lamb-killing brat like you," he said, talking and moving at the same time, gripping the boy by the scruff of the neck and the seat of the pants and heaving him in one motion into the incinerator, "a brat like you is another story entirely."

The lid was closing before the kid even thought to scream. When it slammed shut and Will hooked the catch, you could barely hear the boy's voice. You could tell that he was yelling in terror, and there were also sounds of him kicking at the walls. Of course the big metal box didn't budge an inch.

"If that isn't brilliant," I said.

"I was wondering if you knew what I was leading up to."

"I didn't. I followed the psychology but didn't think it would really work. But this is just perfect."

"I'm glad you think so."

"Just perfect. Why, after the scare he's getting right now, he'll never want to look at another animal."

"The scare?" Will's face had a look on it I had never seen before. "You think all this is to *scare* him?"

He reached over and threw the switch.

# THE EHRENGRAF OBLIGATION

WILLIAM TELLIFORD GAVE his head a tentative scratch, in part because it itched, in part out of puzzlement. It itched because he had been unable to wash his lank brown hair during the four days he'd thus far spent in jail. He was puzzled because this dapper man before him was proposing to get him out of jail.

"I don't understand," he said. "The court appointed an attorney for me. A younger man, I think he said his name was Trabner. You're not associated with him or anything, are you?"

"Certainly not."

"Your name is—"

"Martin Ehrengraf."

"Well, I appreciate your coming to see me, Mr. Ehrengraf, but I've already got a lawyer, this Mr. Trabner, and—"

"Are you satisfied with Mr. Trabner?"

Telliford lowered his eyes, focusing his gaze upon the little lawyer's shoes, a pair of highly polished black wing tips. "I suppose he's all right," he said slowly.

"But?"

"But he doesn't believe I'm innocent. I mean he seems to take it for granted I'm guilty and the best thing I can do is plead guilty to manslaughter or something. He's talking in terms of making some kind of deal with the district attorney, like it's a foregone conclusion that I have to go to prison and the only question is how long."

"Then you've answered my question," Ehrengraf said, a smile flickering on his thin lips. "You're unsatisfied with your lawyer. The court has appointed him. It remains for you to disappoint him, as it were, and to engage me in his stead. You have the right to do this, you know."

"But I don't have the money. Trabner was going to defend me for free, which is about as much as I can afford. I don't know what kind of fees you charge for something like this but I'll bet they're substantial. That suit of yours didn't come from the Salvation Army."

Ehrengraf beamed. His suit, charcoal gray flannel with a nipped-in waist, had been made for him by a most exclusive tailor. His shirt was pink, with a button-down collar. His vest was a tattersall check, red and black on a cream background, and his tie showed half-inch stripes of red and charcoal gray. "My fees are on the high side," he allowed. "To undertake your defense I would ordinarily set a fee of eighty thousand dollars."

"Eighty dollars would strain my budget," William Telliford said. "Eighty thousand, well, it might take me ten years to earn that much."

"But I propose to defend you free of charge, sir."

William Telliford stared, not least because he could not recall the last time anyone had thought to call him *sir*. He was, it must be said, a rather unprepossessing young man, tending to slouch and sprawl. His jeans needed patching at the knees. His plaid flannel shirt needed washing and ironing. His chukka boots needed soles and heels, and his socks needed replacement altogether.

"But—"

"But why?"

Telliford nodded.

"Because you are a poet," said Martin Ehrengraf.

"Poets," said Ehrengraf, "are the unacknowledged legislators of the universe."

"That's beautiful," Robin Littlefield said. She didn't know just what to make of this little man but he was certainly impressive. "Could you say that again? I want to remember it."

"Poets are the unacknowledged legislators of the universe. But don't credit me with the observation. Shelley said it first."

"Is she your wife?"

The lawyer's deeply set dark eyes narrowed perceptibly. "Percy Bysshe Shelley," he said gently. "Born 1792, died 1822. The poet."

"Oh."

"So your young man is one of the world's unacknowledged legislators. Or you might prefer the lines Arthur O'Shaughnessy wrote. 'We are the music makers,/And we are the dreamers of dreams.' You know the poem?"

"I don't think so."

"I like the second stanza," said Ehrengraf, and tilted his head to one side and quoted it:

> With wonderful deathless ditties
> We build up the world's greatest
>   cities,
> And out of a fabulous story
> We fashion an empire's glory:
> One man with a dream, at
>   pleasure,
> Shall go forth and conquer a crown;
> And three with a new song's
>   measure
> Can trample an empire down.

"You have a wonderful way of speaking. But I, uh, I don't really know much about poetry."

"You reserve your enthusiasm for Mr. Telliford's poems, no doubt."

"Well, I like it when Bill reads them to me. I like the way they sound, but I'll have to admit I don't always know what he's getting at."

Ehrengraf beamed, spread his hands. "But they sound good, don't they? Miss Littlefield, dare we require more of a poem than it please our ears? I don't read much modern poetry, Miss Littlefield. I prefer the bards of an earlier and more innocent age. Their verses are often simpler, but I don't pretend to understand any number of my favorite poems. Half the time I don't know just what Blake's getting at, Miss Littlefield, but that doesn't keep me from enjoying his work. That sonnet of your young man's, that poem about riding a train across Kansas and looking at the moon. I'm sure you remember it."

"Sort of."

"He writes of the moon 'stroking desperate tides in the liquid land.' That's a lovely line, Miss Littlefield, and who cares whether the poem itself is fully comprehensible? Who'd raise such a niggling point? William Telliford is a poet and I'm under an obligation to defend him. I'm certain he couldn't have murdered that woman."

Robin gnawed a thumbnail. "The police are pretty sure he did it," she said. "The fire axe was missing from the hallway of our building and the glass case where it was kept was smashed open. And Janice Penrose, he used to live with her before he met me, well, they say he was still going around her place sometimes when I was working at the diner. And they never found the fire axe, but Bill came home with his jeans and shirt covered with blood and couldn't remember what happened. And he was seen in her neighborhood, and he'd been drinking, plus he smoked a lot of dope that afternoon and he was always taking pills. Ups and downs, like, plus some green capsules he stole from somebody's medicine chest and we were never quite sure what they were, but they do weird things to your head."

"The artist is so often the subject of his own experiment," Ehrengraf said sympathetically. "Think of De Quincey. Consider Coleridge, waking from an opium dream with all of 'Kubla Khan' fixed in his mind, just waiting for him to write it down. Of course he was interrupted by that dashed man from Porlock, but the lines he did manage to save are so wonderful. You know the poem, Miss Littlefield?"

"I think we had to read it in school."

"Perhaps."

"Or didn't he write something about an albatross? Some guy shot an albatross, something like that."

"Something like that."

"The thing is," William Telliford said, "the more I think about it, the more I come to the conclusion that I must have killed Jan. I mean, who else would kill her?"

"You're innocent," Ehrengraf told him.

"You really think so? I can't remember what happened that day. I was doing some drugs and hitting the wine pretty good, and then I found this bottle of bourbon that I didn't think we still had, and I started drinking that, and that's about the last thing I remember. I must have gone right into blackout and the next thing I knew I was walking around covered with blood. And I've got a way of being violent when I'm drunk. When I lived with Jan I beat her up a few times, and I did the same with Robin. That's one of the reasons her father hates me."

"Her father hates you?"

"Despises me. Oh, I can't really blame him. He's this self-made man with more money than God and I'm squeezing by on food stamps. There's not much of a living in poetry."

"It's an outrage."

"Right. When Robin and I moved in together, well, her old man had a fit. Up to then he was laying a pretty heavy check on her the first of every month, but as soon as she moved in with me that was the end of that song. No more money for her. Here's her little brother going to this fancy private school and her mother dripping in sables and emeralds and diamonds and mink, and here's Robin slinging hash in a greasy spoon because her father doesn't care for the company she's keeping."

"Interesting."

"The man really hates me. Some people take to me and some people don't, but he just couldn't stomach me. Thought I was the lowest of the low. It really grinds a person down, you know. All the pressure he was putting on Robin, and both of us being as broke as we were, I'll tell you, it reached the point where I couldn't get any writing done."

"That's terrible," Ehrengraf said, his face clouded with concern. "The poetry left you?"

"That's what happened. It just wouldn't come to me. I'd sit there all day staring at a blank sheet of paper, and finally I'd say the hell with it and fire up a joint or get into the wine, and there's another day down the old chute. And then finally I found that bottle of bourbon and the next thing I knew—" the poet managed a brave smile "—well, according to you, I'm innocent."

"Of course you are innocent, sir."

"I wish I was convinced of that, Mr. Ehrengraf. I don't even see how *you* can be convinced."

"Because you are a poet," the diminutive attorney said. "Because, further, you are a client of Martin H. Ehrengraf. My clients are always innocent. That is the Ehrengraf presumption. Indeed, my income depends upon the innocence of my clients."

"I don't follow you."

"It's simple enough. My fees, as we've said, are quite high. But I collect them only if my efforts are successful. If a client of mine goes to prison, Mr. Telliford, he pays me nothing. I'm not even reimbursed for my expenses."

"That's incredible," Telliford said. "I never heard of anything like that. Do many lawyers work that way?"

"I believe I'm the only one. It's a pity more don't take up the custom. Other professionals as well, for that matter. Consider how much higher the percentage of successful operations might be if surgeons were paid on the basis of their results."

"Isn't that the truth. Hey, you know what's ironic?"

"What?"

"Mr. Littlefield. Robin's father. He could pay you that eighty thousand out of petty cash and never miss it. That's the kind of money he's got. But the way he feels about me, he'd pay to *send* me to prison, not to keep me out of it. In other words, if you worked for him you'd only get paid if you lost your case. Don't you think that's ironic?"

"Yes," said Ehrengraf. "I do indeed."

When William Telliford stepped into Ehrengraf's office, the lawyer scarcely recognized him. The poet's beard was gone and his hair had received the attention of a fashionable barber. His jacket was black velvet, his trousers a cream-colored flannel. He was wearing a raw silk shirt and a bold paisley ascot.

He smiled broadly at Ehrengraf's reaction. "I guess I look different," he said.

"Different," Ehrengraf agreed.

"Well, I don't have to live like a slob now." The young man sat down in one of Ehrengraf's chairs, shot his cuff and checked the time on an oversized gold watch. "Robin'll be coming by for me in half an hour," he said, "but I wanted to take the time to let you know how much I appreciated what you tried to do for me. You believed in my innocence when I didn't even have that much faith in myself. And I'm sure you would have been terrific in the courtroom if it had come to that."

"Fortunately it didn't."

"Right, but whoever would have guessed how it would turn out? Imagine old Jasper Littlefield killing Jan to frame me and get me out of his daughter's life. That's really a tough one to swallow. But he came over looking for Robin, and he found me drunk, and then it was evidently just a matter of taking the fire axe out of the case and taking me along with him to Jan's place and killing her and smearing her blood all over me. I must have been in worse than a blackout when it happened. I must have been passed out cold for him to be sure I wouldn't remember any of it."

"So it would seem."

"The police never did find the fire axe, and I wondered about that at the time. What I'd done with it, I mean, because deep down inside I really figured I must have been guilty. But what happened was Mr. Littlefield took the axe along with him, and then when he went crazy it was there for him to use."

"And use it he did."

"He sure did," Telliford said. "According to some psychologist they interviewed for one of the papers, he must have been repressing his basic instincts all his life. When he killed Jan for the purpose of framing me, it set something off inside him, some undercurrent of violence he'd been smothering for years and years. And then finally he up and dug out the fire axe, and he did a job on his wife and his son, chopped them both to hell and gone, and then he made a phone call to the police and confessed what he'd done and told about murdering Jan at the same time."

"Considerate of him," said Ehrengraf, "to make that phone call."

"I'll have to give him that," the poet said. "And then, before the cops could get there and pick him up, he took the fire axe and chopped through the veins in his wrists and bled to death."

"And you're a free man."

"And glad of it," Telliford said. "I'll tell you, it looks to me as though I'm sitting on top of the world. Robin's crazy about me and I'm all she's got 'in the world—me and the couple of million bucks her father left her. With the rest of the family dead, she inherits every penny. No more slinging hash. No more starving in a garret. No more dressing like a slob. You like my new wardrobe?"

"It's quite a change," Ehrengraf said diplomatically.

"Well, I realize now that I was getting sick of the way I looked, the life I was leading. Now I can live the way I want. I've got the freedom to do as I please with my life."

"That's wonderful."

"And you're the man who believed in me when nobody else did, myself included." Telliford smiled with genuine warmth. "I can't tell you how grateful I am. I was talking with Robin, and I had the idea that we ought to pay you your fee. You didn't actually get me off, of course, but your system is that you get paid no matter how your client gets off, just so he doesn't wind up in jail. That's how you explained it, isn't it?"

"That's right."

"That's what I said to Robin. But she said we didn't have any agreement to pay you eighty thousand dollars, as a matter of fact we didn't have any agreement to pay you anything, because you volunteered your services. In fact I would have gotten off the same way with my court-appointed attorney. I said that wasn't the point, but Robin said after all it's her money and she didn't see the point of giving you an eighty-thousand-dollar handout, that you were obviously well off and didn't need charity."

"Her father's daughter, I'd say."

"Huh? Anyway, it's her money and her decision to make, but I got her to agree that we'd pay for any expenses you had. So if you can come up with a figure—"

Ehrengraf shook his head. "You don't owe me a cent," he insisted. "I took your case out of a sense of obligation. And your lady friend is quite correct—I am not a charity case. Furthermore, my expenses on your behalf were extremely low, and in any case I should be more than happy to stand the cost myself."

"Well, if you're absolutely certain—"

"Quite certain, thank you." Ehrengraf smiled. "I'm most satisfied with the outcome of the case. Of course I regret the loss of Miss Littlefield's mother and brother, but at least there's a happy ending to it all. You're out of prison, you have no worries about money, your future is assured and you can return to the serious business of writing poetry."

"Yeah," Telliford said.

"Is something wrong?"

"Not really. Just what you said about poetry."

"Oh?"

"I suppose I'll get back to it sooner or later."

"Don't tell me your muse has deserted you?"

"Oh, I don't know," the young man said nervously. "It's just that, oh, I don't really seem to care much about poetry now, you know what I mean?"

"I'm not sure that I do."

"Well, I've got everything I want, you know? I've got the money to go all over the world and try all the things I've always wanted to try, and, oh, poetry just doesn't seem very important anymore." He laughed. "I remember what a kick I used to get when I'd check the mailbox and some little magazine would send me a check for one of my poems. Now what I usually got was fifty cents a line for poems, and that's from the magazines that paid anything, and most of them just gave you copies of the issue with the poem in it and that was that. That sonnet you liked, 'On A Train Through Kansas,' the magazine that took it paid me twenty-five cents a line. So I made three dollars and fifty cents for that poem, and by the time I submitted it here and there and everywhere, hell, my postage came to pretty nearly as much as I got for it."

"It's a scandal."

"But the thing is, when I didn't have any money, even a little check helped. Now, though, it's hard to take the whole thing seriously. But besides that, I just don't get poetic ideas anymore. And I just don't feel it." He forced a smile. "It's funny. Getting away from poetry hasn't been bothering me, but now that I'm talking with you about it I find myself feeling bad. As though by giving up poetry I'm letting you down or something."

"You're not letting *me* down," Ehrengraf said. "But to dismiss the talent you have, to let it languish—"

"Well, I just don't know if I've got it anymore," Telliford said. "That's the whole thing. I sit down and try to write a poem and it's just not *there*, you know what I mean? And Robin says why waste my time, that nobody really cares about poetry nowadays anyway, and I figure maybe she's right."

"Her father's daughter."

"Huh? Well, I'll tell you something that's ironic, anyway. I was having trouble writing poetry before I went to jail, what with the hassles from Robin's old man and all our problems and getting into the wine and the grass too much. And I'm having more troubles now, now that we've got plenty of money and Robin's father's out of our hair. But you know when I was really having no trouble at all?"

"When?"

"During the time I was in jail. There I was, stuck in that rotten cell with a lifetime in the penitentiary staring me in the face, and I swear I was averaging a poem every day. My mind was just clicking along. And I was writing good stuff, too." The young man drew an alligator billfold from the breast pocket of the velvet jacket, removed and unfolded a sheet of paper. "You liked the Kansas poem," he said, "so why don't you see what you think of this one?"

Ehrengraf read the poem. It seemed to be about birds, and included the line *"Puppets dance from bloody strings."* Ehrengraf wasn't sure what the poem meant but he knew he liked the sound of that line.

"It's very good," he said.

"Yeah, I thought you'd like it. And I wrote it in the jug, just wrote the words down like they were flowing out of a faucet, and now all I can write is checks. It's ironic, isn't it?"

"It certainly is."

It was a little over two weeks later when Ehrengraf met yet again with William Telliford. Once again, the meeting took place in the jail cell where the two had first made one another's acquaintance.

"Mr. Ehrengraf," the young man said. "Gee, I didn't know if you would show up. I figured you'd wash your hands of me."

"Why should I do that, sir?"

"Because they say I killed Robin. But I swear I didn't do it!"

"Of course you didn't."

"I could have killed Jan, for all I knew. Because I was unconscious at the time, or in a blackout, or whatever it was. So I didn't know what happened. But I was away from the apartment when Robin was killed and I was awake. I hadn't even been drinking much."

"We'll simply prove where you were."

Telliford shook his head. "What we can't prove is that Robin was alive when I left the apartment. I know she was, but how are we going to prove it?"

"We'll find a way," Ehrengraf said soothingly. "We know you're innocent, don't we?"

"Right."

"Then there is nothing to worry about. Someone else must have gone to your house, taking that fire axe along for the express purpose of framing you for murder. Someone jealous of your success, perhaps. Someone who begrudged you your happiness."

"But who?"

"Leave that to me, sir. It's my job."

"Your job," Telliford said. "Well, this time you'll get well paid for your job, Mr. Ehrengraf. And your system is perfect for my case, let me tell you."

"How do you mean?"

"If I'm found innocent, I'll inherit all the money Robin inherited from her father. She made me her beneficiary. So I'll be able to pay you whatever you ask, eighty thousand dollars or even more."

"Eighty thousand will be satisfactory."

"And I'll pay it with pleasure. But if I'm found guilty, well, I won't get a dime."

"Because one cannot legally profit from a crime."

"Right. So if you'll take the case on your usual terms—"

"I work on no other terms," Ehrengraf said. "And I would trust no one else with your case." He took a deep breath and held it in his lungs for a moment before continuing. "Mr. Telliford," he said, "your case is going to be a difficult one. You must appreciate that."

"I do."

"Of course I'll do everything in my power on your behalf, acting always in your best interest. But you must recognize that the possibility exists that you will be convicted."

"And for a crime I didn't commit."

"Such miscarriages of justice do occasionally come to pass. It's tragic, I agree, but don't despair. Even if you're convicted, the appeal process is an exhaustive one. We can appeal your case again and again. You may have to serve some time in prison, Mr. Telliford, but there's always hope. And you know what Lovelace had to say on the subject."

"Lovelace?"

"Richard Lovelace. Born 1618, died 1657. 'To Althea, from Prison,' Mr. Telliford.

130

*Stone walls do not a prison make,*
*Nor iron bars a cage;*
*Minds innocent and quiet take*
*That for an hermitage.*
*If I have freedom in my love,*
*And in my soul am free,*
*Angels alone, that soar above,*
*Enjoy such liberty.*

Telliford shuddered. "'Stone walls and iron bars,'" he said.
"Have faith, sir."

"I'll try."

"At least you have your poetry. Are you sufficiently supplied
with paper and pencil? I'll make sure your needs are seen to."

"Maybe it would help me to write some poetry. Maybe it would
take my mind off things."

"Perhaps it would. And I'll devote myself wholeheartedly to
your defense, sir, whether I ever see a penny for my troubles or
not." He drew himself up to his full height. "After all," he said,
"it's my obligation. *'I could not love thee, dear, so much, / Loved
I not Honour more.'* That's also Lovelace, Mr. Telliford. *'To
Lucasta, Going to the Wars.'* Good day, Mr. Telliford. You have
nothing to worry about."

# WHEN THIS MAN DIES

THE NIGHT BEFORE the first letter came, he had Speckled Band in the feature at Saratoga. The horse went off at nine-to-two from the number one pole and Edgar Kraft had two hundred dollars on him, half to win and half to place. Speckled Band went to the front and stayed there. The odds-on favorite, a four-year-old named Sheila's Kid, challenged around the clubhouse turn and got hung up on the outside. Kraft was counting his money. In the stretch, Speckled Band broke stride, galloped home madly, was summarily disqualified and placed fourth. Kraft tore up his tickets and went home.

So he was in no mood for jokes that morning. He opened five of the six letters that came in the morning mail, and all five were bills, none of which he had any prospect of paying in the immediate future. He put them in a drawer in his desk. There were already several bills in that drawer. He opened the final letter and was at first relieved to discover that it was not a bill, not a notice of payment due, not a threat to repossess car or furniture. It was, instead, a very simple message typed in the center of a large sheet of plain typing paper.

First a name:

## SOMETIMES THEY BITE

### Mr. Joseph H. Neimann

And below that:

### When this man dies
### You will receive
### Five hundred dollars.

He was in no mood for jokes. Trotters that lead all the way and then break in the stretch do not contribute to a man's sense of humor. He looked at the sheet of paper, turned it over to see if there was anything further on its reverse, turned it over again to read the message once more, picked up the envelope, saw nothing on it but his own name and a local postmark, said something unprintable about some idiots and their idea of a joke and tore everything up and threw it away, message and envelope and all.

In the course of the next week he thought about the letter once, maybe twice. No more than that. He had problems of his own. He had never heard of anyone named Joseph H. Neimann and entertained no hopes of receiving five hundred dollars in the event of the man's death. He did not mention the cryptic message to his wife. When the man from Superior Finance called to ask him if he had any hopes of meeting his note on time, he did not say anything about the legacy that Mr. Neimann meant to leave him.

He went on doing his work from one day to the next, working with the quiet desperation of a man who knows his income, while better than nothing, will never quite get around to equaling his expenditures. He went to the track twice, won thirty dollars one night, lost twenty-three the next. He came quite close to forgetting entirely about Mr. Joseph H. Neimann and the mysterious correspondent.

Then the second letter came. He opened it mechanically, unfolded a large sheet of plain white paper. Ten fresh fifty-dollar bills fluttered down upon the top of his desk. In the center of the sheet of paper someone had typed:

### Thank You

Edgar Kraft did not make the connection immediately. He tried to think what he might have done that would merit anyone's thanks, not to mention anyone's five hundred dollars. It took him a moment, and then he recalled that other letter and rushed out of his office and down the street to a drugstore. He bought a morning paper, turned to the obituaries.

Joseph Henry Neimann, 67, of 413 Park Place, had died the previous afternoon in County Hospital after an illness of several months' duration. He left a widow, three children and four grandchildren. Funeral services would be private, flowers were please to be omitted.

He put three hundred dollars in his checking account and two hundred dollars in his wallet. He made his payment on the car, paid his rent, cleared up a handful of small bills. The mess in his desk drawer was substantially less baleful, although by no means completely cleared up. He still owed money, but he owed less now than before the timely death of Joseph Henry Neimann. The man from Superior Finance had been appeased by a partial payment; he would stop making a nuisance of himself, at least for the time being.

That night, Kraft took his wife to the track. He even let her make a couple of impossible hunch bets. He lost forty dollars and it hardly bothered him at all.

When the next letter came he did not tear it up. He recognized the typing on the envelope, and he turned it over in his hands for a few moments before opening it, like a child with a wrapped present. He was somewhat more apprehensive than child with present, however; he couldn't help feeling that the mysterious benefactor would want something in return for his five hundred dollars.

He opened the letter. No demands, however. Just the usual sheet of plain paper, with another name typed in its center:

MR. RAYMOND ANDERSEN

And below that:

## SOMETIMES THEY BITE

WHEN THIS MAN DIES
YOU WILL RECEIVE
SEVEN HUNDRED FIFTY DOLLARS.

For the next few days he kept telling himself that he did not wish anything unpleasant for Mr. Raymond Andersen. He didn't know the man, he had never heard of him, and he was not the sort to wish death upon some total stranger. And yet—

Each morning he bought a paper and turned at once to the death notices, searching almost against his will for the name of Mr. Raymond Andersen. *I don't wish him harm,* he would think each time. But seven hundred fifty dollars was a happy sum. If something were going to happen to Mr. Raymond Andersen, he might as well profit by it. It wasn't as though he was doing anything to cause Andersen's death. He was even unwilling to wish for it. But if something happened...

Something happened. Five days after the letter came, he found Andersen's obituary in the morning paper. Andersen was an old man, a very old man, and he had died in his bed at a home for the aged after a long illness. His heart jumped when he read the notice with a combination of excitement and guilt. But what was there to feel guilty about? He hadn't done anything. And death, for a sick old man like Raymond Andersen, was more a cause for relief than grief, more a blessing than a tragedy.

But why would anyone want to pay him seven hundred fifty dollars?

Nevertheless, someone did. The letter came the following morning, after a wretched night during which Kraft tossed and turned and batted two possibilities back and forth—that the letter would come and that it would not. It did come, and it brought the promised seven hundred fifty dollars in fifties and hundreds. And the same message:

THANK YOU

For what? He had not the slightest idea. But he looked at the two-word message again before putting it carefully away.

*You're welcome,* he thought. *You're entirely welcome.*

For two weeks no letter came. He kept waiting for the mail, kept hoping for another windfall like the two that had come so far. There were times when he would sit at his desk for twenty or thirty minutes at a time, staring off into space and thinking about the letters and the money. He would have done better keeping his mind on his work, but this was not easy. His job brought him five thousand dollars a year, and for that sum he had to work forty to fifty hours a week. His anonymous pen pal had thus far brought him a quarter as much as he earned in a year, and he had done nothing at all for the money.

The seven-fifty had helped, but he was still in hot water. On a sudden female whim his wife had had the living room recarpeted. The rent was due. There was another payment due on the car. He had one very good night at the track, but a few other visits took back his winnings and more.

And then the letter came, along with a circular inviting him to buy a dehumidifier for his basement and an appeal for funds from some dubious charity. He swept circular and appeal into his wastebasket and tore open the plain white envelope. The message was the usual sort:

MR. CLAUDE PIERCE

And below the name:

WHEN THIS MAN DIES
YOU WILL RECEIVE
ONE THOUSAND DOLLARS.

Kraft's hands were shaking slightly as he put the envelope and letter away in his desk. One thousand dollars—the price had gone up again, this time to a fairly staggering figure. Mr. Claude Pierce. Did he know anyone named Claude Pierce? He did not. Was Claude Pierce sick? Was he a lonely old man, dying somewhere of a terminal illness?

Kraft hoped so. He hated himself for the wish, but he could not smother it. He hoped Claude Pierce was dying.

This time he did a little research. He thumbed through the

137

phone book until he found a listing for a Claude Pierce on Honeydale Drive. He closed the book then and tried to put the whole business out of his mind, an enterprise foredoomed to failure. Finally he gave up, looked up the listing once more, looked at the man's name and thought that this man was going to die. It was inevitable, wasn't it? They sent him some man's name in the mail, and then the man died, and then Edgar Kraft was paid. Obviously, Claude Pierce was a doomed man.

He called Pierce's number. A woman answered, and Kraft asked if Mr. Pierce was in.

"Mr. Pierce is in the hospital," the woman said. "Who's calling, please?"

"Thank you," Kraft said.

Of course, he thought. They, whoever they were, simply found people in hospitals who were about to die, and they paid money to Edgar Kraft when the inevitable occurred, and that was all. The why of it was impenetrable. But so few things made sense in Kraft's life that he did not want to question the whole affair too closely. Perhaps his unknown correspondent was like that lunatic on television who gave away a million dollars every week. If someone wanted to give Kraft money, Kraft wouldn't argue with him.

That afternoon he called the hospital. Claude Pierce had been admitted two days ago for major surgery, a nurse told Kraft. His condition was listed as *good*.

Well, he would have a relapse, Kraft thought. He was doomed—the letterwriter had ordained his death. He felt momentarily sorry for Claude Pierce, and then he turned his attention to the entries at Saratoga. There was a horse named Orange Pips which Kraft had been watching for some time. The horse had a good post now, and if he was ever going to win, this was the time.

Kraft went to the track. Orange Pips ran out of the money. In the morning Kraft failed to find Pierce's obituary. When he called the hospital, the nurse told him that Pierce was recovering very nicely.

Impossible, Kraft thought.

For three weeks Claude Pierce lay in his hospital bed, and for three weeks Edgar Kraft followed his condition with more interest than Pierce's doctor could have displayed. Once Pierce took a turn for the worse and slipped into a coma. The nurse's voice was grave over the phone, and Kraft bowed his head, resigned to the inevitable. A day later Pierce had rallied remarkably. The nurse sounded positively cheerful, and Kraft fought off a sudden wave of rage that threatened to overwhelm him.

From that point on, Pierce improved steadily. He was released, finally, a whole man again, and Kraft could not understand quite what had happened. Something had gone wrong. When Pierce died, he was to receive a thousand dollars. Pierce had been sick, Pierce had been close to death, and then, inexplicably, Pierce had been snatched from the very jaws of death, with a thousand dollars simultaneously snatched from Edgar Kraft.

He waited for another letter. No letter came.

With the rent two weeks overdue, with a payment on the car past due, with the man from Superior Finance calling him far too often, Kraft's mind began to work against him. *When this man dies*, the letter had said. There had been no strings attached, no time limit on Pierce's death. After all, Pierce could not live forever. No one did. And whenever Pierce did happen to draw his last breath, he would get that thousand dollars.

Suppose something happened to Pierce—

He thought it over against his own will. It would not be hard, he kept telling himself. No one knew that he had any interest whatsoever in Claude Pierce. If he picked his time well, if he did the dirty business and got it done with and hurried off into the night, no one would know. The police would never think of him in the same breath with Claude Pierce, if police were in the habit of thinking in breaths. He did not know Pierce, he had no obvious motive for killing Pierce, and—

He couldn't do it, he told himself. He simply could not do it. He was no killer. And something as senseless as this, something so thoroughly absurd, was unthinkable.

139

He would manage without the thousand dollars. Somehow, he would live without the money. True, he had already spent it a dozen times over in his mind. True, he had been counting and recounting it when Pierce lay in a coma. But he would get along without it. What else could he do?

The next morning headlines shrieked Pierce's name at Edgar Kraft. The previous night someone had broken into the Pierce home on Honeydale Drive and had knifed Claude Pierce in his bed. The murderer had escaped unseen. No possible motive for the slaying of Pierce could be established. The police were baffled.

Kraft got slightly sick to his stomach as he read the story. His first reaction was a pure and simple onrush of unbearable guilt, as though he had been the man with the knife, as though he himself had broken in during the night to stab silently and flee promptly, mission accomplished. He could not shake this guilt away. He knew well enough that he had done nothing, that he had killed no one. But he had conceived of the act, he had willed that it be done, and he could not escape the feeling that he was a murderer, at heart if not in fact.

His blood money came on schedule. One thousand dollars, ten fresh hundreds this time. And the message. *Thank you.*

Don't thank me, he thought, holding the bills in his hand, holding them tenderly. Don't thank me!

MR. LEON DENNISON

WHEN THIS MAN DIES
YOU WILL RECEIVE
FIFTEEN HUNDRED DOLLARS.

Kraft did not keep the letter. He was breathing heavily when he read it, his heart pounding. He read it twice through, and then he took it and the envelope it had come in, and all the other letters and envelopes that he had so carefully saved, and he tore them all into little bits and flushed them down the toilet.

He had a headache. He took aspirin, but it did not help his headache at all. He sat at his desk and did no work until lunchtime. He went to the luncheonette around the corner and ate lunch without tasting his food. During the afternoon he found that, for the first time, he could not make heads or tails out of the list of entries at Saratoga. He couldn't concentrate on a thing, and he left the office early and took a long walk.

*Mr. Leon Dennison.*

Dennison lived in an apartment on Cadbury Avenue. No one answered his phone. Dennison was an attorney, and he had an office listing. When Kraft called it a secretary answered and told him that Mr. Dennison was in conference. Would he care to leave his name?

*When this man dies.*

But Dennison would not die, he thought. Not in a hospital bed, at any rate. Dennison was perfectly all right, he was at work and the person who had written all those letters knew very well that Dennison was all right, that he was not sick.

*Fifteen hundred dollars.*

But how, he wondered. He did not own a gun and had not the slightest idea how to get one. A knife? Someone had used a knife on Claude Pierce, he remembered. And a knife would probably not be hard to get his hands on. But a knife seemed somehow unnatural to him.

How, then? By automobile? He could do it that way, he could lie in wait for Dennison and run him down in his car. It would not be difficult, and it would probably be certain enough. Still, the police were supposed to be able to find hit-and-run drivers fairly easily. There was something about paint scrapings, or blood on your own bumper or something. He didn't know the details, but they always did seem to catch hit-and-run drivers.

Forget it, he told himself. You are not a killer.

He didn't forget it. For two days he tried to think of other things and failed miserably. He thought about Dennison, and he thought about fifteen hundred dollars and he thought about murder.

*When this man dies—*

One time he got up early in the morning and drove to Cadbury Avenue. He watched Leon Dennison's apartment, and he saw

Dennison emerge, and when Dennison crossed the street toward his parked car Kraft settled his own foot on the accelerator and ached to put the pedal on the floor and send the car hurtling toward Leon Dennison. But he didn't do it. He waited.

So clever. Suppose he were caught in the act? Nothing linked him with the person who wrote him the letters. He hadn't even kept the letters, but even if he had, they were untraceable.

*Fifteen hundred dollars—*

On a Thursday afternoon he called his wife and told her he was going directly to Saratoga. She complained mechanically before bowing to the inevitable. He drove to Cadbury Avenue and parked his car. When the doorman slipped down to the corner for a cup of coffee, Kraft ducked into the building and found Leon Dennison's apartment. The door was locked, but he managed to spring the lock with the blade of a penknife. He was sweating freely as he worked on the lock, expecting every moment someone to come up behind him and lay a hand on his shoulder. The lock gave, and he went inside and closed it after him.

But something happened the moment he entered the apartment. All the fear, all the anxiety, all of this suddenly left Edgar Kraft. He was mysteriously calm now. Everything was prearranged, he told himself. Joseph H. Neimann had been doomed, and Raymond Andersen had been doomed, and Claude Pierce had been doomed and each of them had died. Now Leon Dennison was similarly doomed, and he too would die.

It seemed very simple. And Edgar Kraft himself was nothing but a part of this grand design, nothing but a cog in a gigantic machine. He would do his part without worrying about it. Everything could only go according to plan.

Everything did. He waited three hours for Leon Dennison to come home, waited in calm silence. When a key turned in the lock, he stepped swiftly and noiselessly to the side of the door, a fireplace andiron held high overhead. The door opened and Leon Dennison entered, quite alone.

The andiron descended.

Leon Dennison fell without a murmur. He collapsed, lay still. The andiron rose and fell twice more, just for insurance, and

Leon Dennison never moved and never uttered a sound. Kraft had only to wipe off the andiron and a few other surfaces to eliminate any fingerprints he might have left behind. He left the building by the service entrance. No one saw him.

He waited all that night for the rush of guilt. He was surprised when it failed to come. But he had already been a murderer—by wishing for Andersen's death, by planning Pierce's murder. The simple translation of his impulses from thought to deed was no impetus for further guilt.

There was no letter the next day. The following morning the usual envelope was waiting for him. It was quite bulky; it was filled with fifteen hundred-dollar bills.

The note was different. It said *Thank You*, of course. But beneath that there was another line:

HOW DO YOU LIKE YOUR NEW JOB?

# COLLECTING
# ACKERMANS

ON AN OTHERWISE unremarkable October afternoon, Florence Ackerman's doorbell sounded. Miss Ackerman, who had been watching a game show on television and clucking at the mental lethargy of the panelists, walked over to the intercom control and demanded to know who was there.

"Western Union," a male voice announced.

Miss Ackerman repeated the clucking sound she had most recently aimed at Charles Nelson Reilly. She clucked this time at people who lost their keys and rang other tenants' bells in order to gain admittance to the building. She clucked at would-be muggers and rapists who might pass themselves off as messengers or deliverymen for an opportunity to lurk in the hallways and stairwell. In years past this building had had a doorman, but the new landlord had curtailed services, aiming to reduce his overhead and antagonize longstanding tenants at the same time.

"Telegram for Miz Ackerman," the voice added.

And was it indeed a telegram? It was possible, Miss Ackerman acknowledged. People were forever dying and other people were apt to communicate such data by means of a telegram. It was easier to buzz whoever it was inside than to brood about it. The door to her own apartment would remain locked, needless to say, and the other tenants could look out for themselves. Florence

Ackerman had been looking out for her own self for her whole life and the rest of the planet could go and do the same.

She pressed the buzzer, then went to the door and put her eye to the peephole. She was a small birdlike woman and she had to come up onto her toes to see through the peephole, but she stayed on her toes until her caller came into view. He was a youngish man and he wore a large pair of mirrored sunglasses. Besides obscuring much of his face, the sunglasses kept Miss Ackerman from noticing much about the rest of his appearance. Her attention was inescapably drawn to the twin images of her own peephole reflected in the lenses.

The young man, unaware that he was being watched, rapped on the door with his knuckles. "Telegram," he said.

"Slide it under the door."

"You have to sign for it."

"That's ridiculous," Miss Ackerman said. "One never has to sign for a telegram. As a matter of fact they're generally phoned in nowadays."

"This one you got to sign for."

Miss Ackerman's face, by no means dull to begin with, sharpened. She who had been the scourge of several generations of fourth-grade pupils was not to be intimidated by a pair of mirrored sunglasses. "Slide it under the door," she demanded. "Then I'll open the door and sign your book." If there was indeed anything to be slid beneath the door, she thought, and she rather doubted that there was.

"I can't."

"Oh?"

"It's a singin' telegram. Singin' telegram for Miz Ackerman, what it says here."

"And you're to sing it to me?"

"Yeah."

"Then sing it."

"Lady, are you kiddin'? I'm gonna sing a telegram through a closed door? Like forget it."

Miss Ackerman made the clucking noise again. "I don't believe you have a telegram for me," she said. "Western Union suspended

146

their singing telegram service some time ago. I remember reading an article to that effect in the *Times*." She did not bother to add that the likelihood of anyone's ever sending a singing telegram to her was several degrees short of infinitesimal.

"All I know is I'm supposed to sing this, but if you don't want to open the door—"

"I wouldn't dream of opening my door."

"—then the hell with you, Miz Ackerman. No disrespect intended, but I'll just tell 'em I sang it to you and who cares what you say."

"You're not even a good liar, young man. I'm calling the police now. I advise you to be well out of the neighborhood by the time they arrive."

"You know what you can do," the young man said, but in apparent contradiction to his words he went on to tell Miss Ackerman what she could do. While we needn't concern ourselves with his suggestion, let it be noted that Miss Ackerman could not possibly have followed it, nor, given her character and temperament, would she have been likely at all to make the attempt.

Neither did she call the police. People who say "I am calling the police now" hardly ever do. Miss Ackerman did think of calling her local precinct but decided it would be a waste of time. In all likelihood the young man, whatever his game, was already on his way, never to return. And Miss Ackerman recalled a time two years previously, just a few months after her retirement, when she returned from an afternoon chamber music concert to find her apartment burglarized and several hundred dollars worth of articles missing. She had called the police, naively assuming there was a point to such a course of action, and she'd only managed to spend several hours of her time making out reports and listing serial numbers, and a sympathetic detective had as much as told her nothing would come of the effort.

Actually, calling the police wouldn't really have done her any good this time, either.

Miss Ackerman returned to her chair and, without too much difficulty, picked up the threads of the game show. She did not for a moment wonder who might have sent her a singing telegram, knowing with cool certainty that no one had done so, that there had been no telegram, that the young man had intended rape or robbery or some other unpleasantness that would have made her life substantially worse than it already was. That robbers and rapists and such abounded was no news to Miss Ackerman. She had lived all her life in New York and took in her stride the possibility of such mistreatment, even as residents of California take in their stride the possibility of an earthquake, even as farmers on the Vesuvian slopes acknowledge that it is in the nature of volcanoes periodically to erupt. Miss Ackerman sat in her chair, leaving it to make a cup of tea, returning to it teacup in hand, and concentrated on her television program.

The following afternoon, as she wheeled her little cart of groceries around the corner, a pair of wiry hands seized her without ceremony and yanked her into the narrow passageway between a pair of brick buildings. A gloved hand covered her mouth, the fingers digging into her cheek.

She heard a voice at her ear: "Happy birthday to you, you old hairbag, happy birthday to you." Then she felt a sharp pain in her chest, and then she felt nothing, ever.

"Retired schoolteacher," Freitag said. "On her way home with her groceries. Hell of a thing, huh? Knifed for what she had in her purse, and what could she have, anyway? Livin' on Social Security and a pension and the way inflation eats you up nowadays she wouldn't of had much on her. Why stick a knife in a little old lady like her, huh? He didn't have to kill her."

"Maybe she screamed," Ken Poolings suggested. "And he got panicky."

"Nobody heard a scream. Not that it proves anything either way." They were back at the stationhouse and Jack Freitag was drinking lukewarm coffee out of a styrofoam container. But for the styrofoam the beverage would have been utterly tasteless. "Ackerman, Ackerman, Ackerman. It's hell the way these parasites prey on old folks. It's the judges who have to answer for it. They put the creeps back on the street. What they ought to do is kill the little bastards, but that's not humane. Sticking a knife in a little old lady, *that's* humane. Ackerman, Ackerman. Why does that name do something to me?"

"She was a teacher. Maybe you were in one of her classes."

Freitag shook his head. "I grew up in Chelsea. West Twenty-fourth Street. Miss Ackerman taught all her life here in Washington Heights just three blocks from the place where she lived. And she didn't even have to leave the neighborhood to get herself killed. Ackerman. Oh, I know what it was. Remember three or maybe it was four days ago, this faggot in the West Village? Brought some other faggot home with him and got hisself killed for his troubles? They found him all tied up with things carved in him. It was all over page three of the *Daily News*. Ritual murder, sadist cult, sex perversion, blah blah blah. His name was Ackerman."

"Which one?"

"The dead one. They didn't pick up the guy who did it yet. I don't know if they got a make or not."

"Does it make any difference?"

"Not to me it don't." Freitag finished his coffee, threw his empty container at the green metal wastebasket, then watched as it circled the rim and fell on the floor. "The Knicks stink this year," he said. "But you don't care about basketball, do you?"

"Hockey's my game."

"Hockey," Freitag said. "Well, the Rangers stink, too. Only they stink on ice." He leaned back in his chair and laughed at his own wit and stopped thinking of two murder victims who both happened to be named Ackerman.

Mildred Ackerman lay on her back. Her skin was slick with perspiration, her limbs heavy with spent passion. The man who was lying beside her stirred, placed a hand upon her flesh and began to stroke her. "Oh, Bill," she said. "That feels so nice. I love the way you touch me."

The man went on stroking her.

"You have the nicest touch. Firm but gentle. I sensed that about you when I saw you." She opened her eyes, turned to face him. "Do you believe in intuition, Bill? I do. I think it's possible to know a great deal about someone just on the basis of your intuitive feelings."

"And what did you sense about me?"

"That you would be strong but gentle. That we'd be very good together. It was good for you, wasn't it?"

"Couldn't you tell?"

Millie giggled.

"So you're divorced," he said.

"Uh-huh. You? I'll bet you're married, aren't you? It doesn't bother me if you are."

"I'm not. How long ago were you divorced?"

"It's almost five years now. It'll be exactly five years in January. That's since we split, but then it was another six months before the divorce went through. Why?"

"And Ackerman was your husband's name?"

"Yeah. Wallace Ackerman."

"No kids?"

"No, I wanted to but he didn't."

"A lot of women take their maiden names back after a divorce."

She laughed aloud. "They don't have a maiden name like I did. You wouldn't believe the name I was born with."

"Try me."

"Plonk. Millie Plonk. I think I married Wally just to get rid of it. I mean Mildred's bad enough, but Plonk? Like forget it. I don't think you even told me *your* last name."

"Didn't I?" The hand moved distractingly over Millie's abdomen. "So you decided to go on being an Ackerman, huh?"

"Sure. Why not?"

"Why not indeed."

"It's not a bad name."

"Mmmm," the man said. "This is a nice place you got here, incidentally. Been living here long?"

"Ever since the divorce. It's a little small. Just a studio."

"But it's a good-sized studio, and you must have a terrific view. Your window looks out on the river, doesn't it?"

"Oh, sure. And you know, eighteen flights up, it's gotta be a pretty decent view."

"It bothers some people to live that high up in the air."

"Never bothered me."

"Eighteen floors," the man said. "If a person went out that window there wouldn't be much left of her, would there?"

"Jeez, don't even talk like that."

"You couldn't have an autopsy, could you? Couldn't determine whether she was alive or dead when she went out the window."

"Come on, Bill. That's creepy."

"Your ex-husband living in New York?"

"Wally? I think I heard something about him moving out to the West Coast, but to be honest I don't know if he's alive or dead."

"Hmmm."

"And who cares? You ask the damnedest questions, Bill."

"Do I?"

"Uh-huh. But you got the nicest hands in the world, I swear to God. You touch me so nice. And your eyes, you've got beautiful eyes. I guess you've heard that before?"

"Not really."

"Well, how could anybody tell? Those crazy glasses you wear, a person tries to look into your eyes and she's looking into a couple of mirrors. It's a sin having such beautiful eyes and hiding them."

"Eighteen floors, that's quite a drop."

"Huh?"

"Nothing," he said, and smiled. "Just thinking out loud."

Freitag looked up when his partner entered the room. "You look a little green in the face," he said. "Something the matter?"

"Oh, I was just looking at the *Post* and there's this story that's enough to make you sick. This guy out in Sheepshead Bay, and he's a policeman, too."

"What are you talking about?"

Poolings shrugged. "It's nothing that doesn't happen every couple of months. This policeman, he was depressed or he had a fight with his wife or something, I don't know what. So he shot her dead, and then he had two kids, a boy and a girl, and he shot them to death in their sleep and then he went and ate his gun. Blew his brains out."

"Jesus."

"You just wonder what goes through a guy's mind that he does something like that. Does he just go completely crazy or what? I can't understand a person who does something like that."

"I can't understand people, period. Was this somebody you knew?"

"No, he lives in Sheepshead Bay. *Lived* in Sheepshead Bay. Anyway, he wasn't with the department. He was a Transit Authority cop."

"Anybody spends all his time in the subways, it's got to take its toll. Has to drive you crazy sooner or later."

"I guess."

Freitag plucked a cigarette from the pack in his shirt pocket, tapped it on the top of his desk, held it between his thumb and forefinger, frowned at it and returned it to the pack. He was trying to cut back to a pack a day and was not having much success. "Maybe he was trying to quit smoking," he suggested. "Maybe it was making him nervous and he just couldn't stand it any more."

"That seems a little farfetched, doesn't it?"

"Does it? Does it really?" Freitag got the cigarette out again, put it in his mouth, lit it. "It don't sound all that farfetched to me. What was this guy's name, anyway?"

"The TA cop? Hell, I don't know. Why?"

"I might know him. I know a lot of transit cops."

"It's in the *Post*. Bluestein's reading it."

"I don't suppose it matters, anyway. There's a ton of transit cops and I don't know that many of them. Anyway, the ones I know aren't crazy."

"I didn't even notice his name," Poolings said. "Let me just go take a look. Maybe I know him, as far as that goes."

Poolings went out, returning moments later with a troubled look on his face. Freitag looked questioningly at him.

"Rudy Ackerman," he said.

"Nobody I know. Hey."

"Yeah, right. Another Ackerman."

"That's three Ackermans, Ken."

"It's six Ackermans if you count the wife and kids."

"Yeah, but three incidents. I mean it's no coincidence that this TA cop and his wife and kids all had the same last name, but when you add in the schoolteacher and the faggot, then you got a coincidence."

"It's a common name."

"Is it? How common, Ken?" Freitag leaned forward, stubbed out his cigarette, picked up a Manhattan telephone directory and flipped it open. "Ackerman, Ackerman," he said, turning pages. "Here we are. Yeah, it's common. There's close to two columns of Ackermans in Manhattan alone. And then there's some that spell it with two *n*'s. I wonder."

"You wonder what?"

"If there's a connection."

Poolings sat on the edge of Freitag's desk. "How could there be a connection?"

"Damned if I know."

"There couldn't, Jack."

"An old schoolteacher gets stabbed by a mugger in Washington Heights. A faggot picks up the wrong kind of rough trade and gets tied up and tortured to death. And a TA cop goes berserk and kills his wife and kids and himself. No connection."

"Except for them all having the same last name."

"Yeah. And the two of us just happened to notice that because we investigated the one killing and read about the other two."

"Right."

"So maybe nobody else even knows that there were three homicides involving Ackermans. Maybe you and me are the only people in the city who happened to notice this little coincidence."

"So?"

"So maybe there's something we didn't notice," Freitag said. He got to his feet. "Maybe there have been more than three. Maybe if we pull a printout of deaths over the past few weeks we're going to find Ackermans scattered all over it."

"Are you serious, Jack?"

"Sounds crazy, don't it?"

"Yeah, that's how it sounds, all right."

"If there's just the three it don't prove a thing, right? I mean, it's a common name and you got lots of people dying violently in New York City. When you have eight million people in a city it's no big surprise that you average three or four murders a day. The rate's not even so high compared to other cities. With three or four homicides a day, well, when you got three Ackermans over a couple of weeks, that's not too crazy all by itself to be pure coincidence, right?"

"Right."

"Suppose it turns out there's more than the three."

"You've got a hunch, Jack. Haven't you?"

Freitag nodded. "That's what I got, all right. A hunch. Let's just see if I'm nuts or not. Let's find out."

"A fifth of Courvoisier, V.S.O.P." Mel Ackerman used a step-ladder to reach the bottle. "Here we are, sir. Now will there be anything else?"

"All the money in the register," the man said.

Ackerman's heart turned over. He saw the gun in the man's hand and his own hands trembled so violently that he almost dropped the bottle of cognac. "Jesus," he said. "Could you point that somewhere else? I get very nervous."

"The money," the man said.

"Yeah, right. I wish you guys would pick on somebody else once in a while. This makes the fourth time I been held up in the past two years. You'd think I'd be used to it by now, wouldn't you? Listen, I'm insured, I don't care about the money, just be careful with the gun, huh? There's not much money in the register but you're welcome to every penny I got." He punched the No Sale key and scooped up bills, emptying all of the compartments. Beneath the removable tray he had several hundred dollars in large bills, but he didn't intend to call them to the robber's attention. Sometimes a gunman made you take out the tray and hand over everything. Other times the man would take what you gave him and be anxious to get the hell out. Mel

Ackerman didn't much care either way. Just so he got out of this alive, just so the maniac would take the money and leave without firing his gun.

"Four times in two years," Ackerman said, talking as he emptied the register, taking note of the holdup man's physical appearance as he did so. Tall but not too tall, young, probably still in his twenties. White. Good build. No beard, no moustache. Big mirrored sunglasses that hid a lot of his face.

"Here we go," Ackerman said, handing over the bills. "No muss, no fuss. You want me to lie down behind the counter while you go on your way?"

"What for?"

"Beats me. The last guy that held me up, he told me so I did it. Maybe he got the idea from a television program or something. Don't forget the brandy."

"I don't drink."

"You just come to liquor stores to rob 'em, huh?" Mel was beginning to relax now. "This is the only way we get your business, is that right?"

"I've never held up a liquor store before."

"So you had to start with me? To what do I owe the honor?"

"Your name."

"My name?"

"You're Melvin Ackerman, aren't you?"

"So?"

"So this is what you get," the man said, and shot Mel Ackerman three times in the chest.

"It's crazy," Freitag said. "What it is is crazy. Twenty-two people named Ackerman died in the past month. Listen to this. Arnold Ackerman, fifty-six years of age, lived in Flushing. Jumped or fell in front of the E train."

"Or was pushed."

"Or was pushed," Freitag agreed. "Wilma Ackerman, sixty-two years old, lived in Flatbush. Heart attack. Mildred Ackerman, thirty-six, East Eighty-seventh Street, fell from an eighteenth-story window. Rudolph Ackerman, that's the Transit Authority

155

cop, killed his wife and kids and shot himself. Florence Ackerman was stabbed, Samuel Ackerman fell down a flight of stairs, Lucy Ackerman took an overdose of sleeping pills, Walter P. Ackerman was electrocuted when a radio fell in the bathtub with him, Melvin Ackerman's the one who just got shot in a holdup—" Freitag spread his hands. "It's unbelievable. And it's completely crazy."

"Some of the deaths must be natural," Poolings said. "Here's one. Sarah Ackerman, seventy-eight years old, spent two months as a terminal cancer patient at St. Vincent's and finally died last week. Now that has to be coincidental."

"Uh-huh. Unless somebody slipped onto the ward and held a pillow over her face because he didn't happen to like her last name."

"That seems pretty farfetched, Jack."

"Farfetched? Is it any more farfetched than the rest of it? Is it any crazier than the way all these other Ackermans got it? Some nut case is running around killing people who have nothing in common but their last names. There's no way they're related, you know. Some of these Ackermans are Jewish and some are gentiles. It's one of those names that can be either. Hell, this guy Wilson Ackerman was black. So it's not somebody with a grudge against a particular family. It's somebody who has a thing about the name, but why?"

"Maybe somebody's collecting Ambroses," Poolings suggested.

"Huh? Where'd you get Ambrose?"

"Oh, it's something I read once," Poolings said. "This writer Charles Fort used to write about freaky things that happen, and one thing he wrote was that a guy named Ambrose had walked around the corner and disappeared, and the writer Ambrose Bierce had disappeared in Mexico, and he said maybe somebody was collecting Ambroses."

"That's ridiculous."

"Yeah. But what I meant—"

"Maybe somebody's collecting Ackermans."

"Right."

"Killing them. Killing everybody with that last name and doing

156

it differently each time. Every mass murderer I ever heard of had a murder method he was nuts about and used it over and over, but this guy never does it the same way twice. We got—what is it, twenty-two deaths here? Even if some of them just happened, there's no question that at least fifteen out of twenty-two have to be the work of this nut, whoever he is. He's going to a lot of trouble to keep this operation of his from looking like what it is. Most of these killings look like suicide or accidental death, and the others were set up to look like isolated homicides in the course of a robbery or whatever. That's how he managed to knock off this many Ackermans before anybody suspected anything. Ken, what gets me is the question of why. Why is he doing this?"

"He must be crazy."

"Of course he's crazy, but being crazy don't mean you don't have reasons for what you do. It's just that they're crazy reasons. What kind of reasons could he have?"

"Revenge."

"Against all the Ackermans in the world?"

Poolings shrugged. "What else? Maybe somebody named Ackerman did him dirty once upon a time and he wants to get even with all the Ackermans in the world. I don't see what difference it makes as far as catching him is concerned, and once we catch him the easiest way to find out the reason is to ask him."

"*If* we catch him."

"Sooner or later we'll catch him, Jack."

"Either that or the city'll run out of Ackermans. Maybe *his* name is Ackerman."

"How do you figure that?"

"Getting even with his father, hating himself, *I* don't know. You want to start looking somewhere, it's gotta be easier to start with people named Ackerman than with people not named Ackerman."

"Even so there's a hell of a lot of Ackermans. It's going to be some job checking them all out. There's got to be a few hundred in the five boroughs, plus God knows how many who don't have telephones. And if the guy we're looking for is a drifter living in a dump of a hotel somewhere, there's no way to find him, and

157

that's if he's even using his name in the first place, which he probably isn't, considering the way he feels about the name."

Freitag lit a cigarette. "Maybe he *likes* the name," he said. "Maybe he wants to be the only one left with it."

"You really think we should check all the Ackermans?"

"Well, the job gets easier every day, Ken. 'Cause every day there's fewer Ackermans to check on."

"God."

"Yeah."

"Do we just do this ourselves, Jack?"

"I don't see how we can. We better take it upstairs and let the brass figure out what to do with it. You know what's gonna happen."

"What?"

"It's gonna get in the papers."

"Oh, God."

"Yeah." Freitag drew on his cigarette, coughed, cursed and took another drag anyway. "The newspapers. At which point all the Ackermans left in the city start panicking, and so does everybody else, and don't ask me what our crazy does because I don't have any idea. Well, it'll be somebody else's worry." He got to his feet. "And that's what we need—for it to be somebody else's worry. Let's take this to the lieutenant right now and let him figure out what to do with it."

The pink rubber ball came bouncing crazily down the driveway toward the street. The street was a quiet suburban cul-de-sac in a recently developed neighborhood on Staten Island. The house was a three-bedroom expandable colonial ranchette. The driveway was concrete, with the footprints of a largish dog evident in two of its squares. The small boy who came bouncing crazily after the rubber ball was towheaded and azure-eyed and, when a rangy young man emerged from behind the barberry hedge and speared the ball one-handed, seemed suitably amazed.

"Gotcha," the man said, and flipped the ball underhand to the small boy, who missed it, but picked it up on the second bounce.

158

"Hi," the boy said.

"Hi yourself."

"Thanks," the boy said, and looked at the pink rubber ball in his hand. "It was gonna go in the street."

"Sure looked that way."

"I'm not supposed to go in the street. On account of the cars."

"Makes sense."

"But sometimes the dumb ball goes in the street anyhow, and then what am I supposed to do?"

"It's a problem," the man agreed, reaching over to rumple the boy's straw-colored hair. "How old are you, my good young man?"

"Five and a half."

"That's a good age."

"Goin' on six."

"A logical assumption."

"Those are funny glasses you got on."

"These?" The man took them off, looked at them for a moment, then put them on. "Mirrors," he said.

"Yeah, I know. They're funny."

"They are indeed. What's your name?"

"Mark."

"I bet I know your last name."

"Oh, yeah?"

"I bet it's Ackerman."

"How'd you know?" The boy wrinkled up his face in a frown. "Aw, I bet you know my daddy."

"We're old friends. Is he home?"

"You silly. He's workin'."

"I should have guessed as much. What else would Hale Ackerman be doing on such a beautiful sunshiny day, hmmmm? How about your mommy? She home?"

"Yeah. She's watchin' the teevee."

"And you're playing in the driveway."

"Yeah."

The man rumpled the boy's hair again. Pitching his voice theatrically low, he said, "It's a tough business, son, but that doesn't mean it's a *heartless* business. Keep that in mind."

"Huh?"

"Nothing. A pleasure meeting you, Mark, me lad. Tell your parents they're lucky to have you. Luckier than they'll ever have to know."

"Whatcha mean?"

"Nothing," the man said agreeably. "Now I have to walk all the way back to the ferry slip and take the dumb old boat all the way back to Manhattan and then I have to go to. . ." he consulted a slip of paper from his pocket ". . .to Seaman Avenue way the hell up in Washington Heights. Pardon me. Way the *heck* up in Washington Heights. Let's just hope *they* don't turn out to have a charming kid."

"You're funny."

"You bet," the man said.

"Police protection," the lieutenant was saying. He was a beefy man with an abundance of jaw. He had not been born looking particularly happy, and years of police work had drawn deep lines of disappointment around his eyes and mouth. "That's the first step, but how do you even go about offering it? There's a couple of hundred people named Ackerman in the five boroughs and one's as likely to be a target as the next one. And we don't know who the hell we're protecting 'em *from*. We don't know if this is one maniac or a platoon of them. Meaning we have to take every dead Ackerman on this list and backtrack, looking for some common element, which since we haven't been looking for it all along we're about as likely to find it as a virgin on Eighth Avenue. Twenty-two years ago I coulda gone with the police or the fire department and I couldn't make up my mind. You know what I did? I tossed a goddamn coin. It hadda come up heads."

"As far as protecting these people—"

"As far as protecting 'em, how do you do that without you let out the story? And when the story gets out it's all over the papers, and suppose you're a guy named Ackerman and you find out some moron just declared war on your last name?"

"I suppose you get out of town."

"Maybe you get out of town, and maybe you have a heart attack, and maybe you call the mayor's office and yell a lot, and maybe you sit in your apartment with a loaded gun and shoot the mailman when he does something you figure is suspicious. And maybe if you're some *other* lunatic you read the story and it's like tellin' a kid don't put beans up your nose, so you go out and join in the Ackerman hunt yourself. Or if you're another kind of lunatic which we're all of us familiar with you call up the police and confess. Just to give the nice cops something to do."

A cop groaned.

"Yeah," the lieutenant said. "That about sums it up. So the one thing you don't want is for this to get in the papers, but—"

"But it's too late for that," said a voice from the doorway. And a uniformed patrolman entered the office holding a fresh copy of the New York *Post*. "Either somebody told them or they went and put two and two together."

"I coulda been a fireman," the lieutenant said. "I woulda got to slide down the pole and wear one of those hats and everything, but instead the goddamn coin had to come up heads."

The young man paid the cashier and carried his tray of food across the lunchroom to a long table at the rear. A half dozen people were already sitting there. The young man joined them, ate his macaroni and cheese, sipped his coffee and listened as they discussed the Ackerman murders.

"I think it's a cult thing," one girl was saying. "They have this sort of thing all the time out in California, like surfing and est and all those West Coast trips. In order to be a member you have to kill somebody named Ackerman."

"That's a theory," a bearded young man said. "Personally, I'd guess the whole business is more logically motivated than that. It looks to me like a chain murder."

Someone wanted to know what that was.

"A chain murder," the bearded man said. "Our murderer has a strong motive to kill a certain individual whose name happens to be Ackerman. Only problem is his motive is so strong that

161

he'd be suspected immediately. So instead he kills a whole slew of Ackermans and the one particular victim he has a reason to kill is no more than one face in a crowd. So his motive gets lost in the shuffle." The speaker smiled. "Happens all the time in mystery stories. Now it's happening in real life. Not the first time life imitates art."

"Too logical," a young woman objected. "Besides, all these murders had different methods and a lot of them were disguised so as not to look like murders at all. A chain murderer wouldn't want to operate that way, would he?"

"He might. If he was very, very clever—"

"But he'd be too clever for his own good, don't you think? No, I think he had a grudge against one Ackerman and decided to exterminate the whole tribe. Like Hitler and the Jews."

The conversation went on in this fashion, with the young man who was eating macaroni and cheese contributing nothing at all to it. Gradually the talk trailed off and so indeed did the people at the table, until only the young man and the girl next to whom he'd seated himself remained. She took a sip of coffee, drew on her cigarette and smiled at him. "You didn't say anything," she said. "About the Ackerman murders."

"No," he agreed. "People certainly had some interesting ideas."

"And what did you think?"

"I think I'm happy my name isn't Ackerman."

"What is it?"

"Bill. Bill Trenholme."

"I'm Emily Kuystendahl."

"Emily," he said. "Pretty name."

"Thank you. What do you think? Really?"

"Really?"

"Uh-huh."

"Well," he said, "I don't think much of the theories everybody was coming up with. Chain murders and cult homicide and all the rest of it. I have a theory of my own, but of course that's all it is. Just a theory."

"I'd really like to hear it."

"You would?"

"Definitely."

Their eyes met and wordless messages were exchanged. He smiled and she smiled in reply. "Well," he said, after a moment. "First of all, I think it was just one guy. Not a group of killers. From the way it was timed. And because he keeps changing the murder method I think he wanted to keep what he was doing undiscovered as long as possible."

"That makes sense. But why?"

"I think it was a source of fun for him."

"A source of fun?"

The man nodded. "This is just hypothesis," he said, "but let's suppose he just killed a person once for the sheer hell of it. To find out what it felt like, say. To enlarge his area of personal experience."

"God."

"Can you accept that hypothetically?"

"I guess so. Sure."

"Okay. Now we can suppose further that he liked it, got some kind of a kick out of it. Otherwise he wouldn't have wanted to continue. There's certainly precedent for it. Not all the homicidal maniacs down through history have been driven men. Some of them have just gotten a kick out of it so they kept right on doing it."

"That gives me the shivers."

"It's a frightening concept," he agreed. "But let's suppose that the first person this clown killed was named Ackerman, and that he wanted to go on killing people and he wanted to make a game out of it. So he—"

"A game!"

"Sure, why not? He could just keep on with it, having his weird jollies and seeing how long it would take for the police and the press to figure out what was going on. There are a lot of Ackermans. It's a common name, but not so common that a pattern wouldn't begin to emerge sooner or later. Think how many Smiths there are in the city, for instance. I don't suppose police in the different boroughs coordinate their activities so closely, and I guess the Bureau of Vital Statistics doesn't bother to note if a lot of fatalities have the same last name, so it's a question of how long it takes for the pattern to emerge in and of itself. Well, it's done so now, and what does the score stand at now? Twenty-seven?"

"That's what the paper said, I think."

"It's quite a total when you stop and think of it. And there may have been a few Ackermans not accounted for. A body or two in the river, for instance."

"You make it sound—"

"Yes?"

"I don't know. It gives me the willies to think about it. Will he just keep on now? Until they catch him?"

"You think they'll catch him?"

"Well, sooner or later, won't they? The Ackermans know to be careful now and the police will have stakeouts. Is that what they call it? Stakeouts?"

"That's what they call it on television."

"Don't you think they'll catch him?"

The young man thought it over. "I'm sure they'll catch him," he said, "*if* he keeps it up."

"You mean he might stop?"

"I would. If I were him."

"If you were him. What a thought!"

"Just projecting a little. But to continue with it, if I were this creep, I'd leave the rest of the world's Ackermans alone from here on in."

"Because it would be too dangerous?"

"Because it wouldn't be any fun for me."

"Fun!"

"Oh, come on," he said, smiling. "Once you get past the evilness of it, which I grant you is overwhelming, can't you see how it would be fun for a demented mind? But try not to think of him as fundamentally cruel. Think of him as someone responding to a challenge. Well, now the police and the newspapers and the Ackermans themselves know what's going on, so at this point it's not a game anymore. The game's over and if he were to go on with it he'd just be conducting a personal war of extermination. And if he doesn't really have any genuine grudge against Ackermans, well, I say he'd let them alone."

She looked at him and her eyes were thoughtful. "Then he might just stop altogether."

"Sure."

"And get away with it?"

"I suppose. Unless they pick him up for killing somebody else." Her eyes widened and he grinned. "Oh, really, Emily, you can't expect him to stop this new hobby of his entirely, can you? Not if he's been having so much fun at it? I don't think killers like that ever stop, not once it gets in their blood. They don't stop until the long arm of the law catches up with them."

"The way you said that."

"Pardon me?"

"'The long arm of the law.' As if it's sort of a joke."

"Well, when you see how this character operated, he does make the law look like something of a joke, doesn't he?"

"I guess he does."

He smiled, got to his feet. "Getting close in here. Which way are you headed? I'll walk you home."

"Well, I have to go uptown—"

"Then that's the way I'm headed."

"And if I had to go downtown?"

"Then I'd have urgent business in that direction, Emily."

On the street she said, "But what do you suppose he'll do? Assuming you're right that he'll stop killing Ackermans but he'll go on killing. Will he just pick out innocent victims at random?"

"Not if he's a compulsive type, and he certainly looks like one to me. No, I guess he'd just pick out another whole category of people."

"Another last name? Just sifting through the telephone directory and seeing what strikes his fancy? God, that's a terrifying idea. I'll tell you something, I'm glad my name's not such a common one. There aren't enough Kuystendahls in the world to make it very interesting for him."

"Or Trenholmes. But there are plenty of Emilys, aren't there?"

"Huh?"

"Well, he doesn't have to pick his next victims by last name. In fact, he'd probably avoid that because the police would pick up on something, like that in a minute after this business with the Ackermans. He could establish some other kind of category. Men with beards, say. Oldsmobile owners."

"Oh, my God."

"People wearing brown shoes. Bourbon drinkers. Or, uh, girls named Emily."

"That's not funny, Bill."

"Well, no reason why it would have to be Emily. *Any* first name—that's the whole point, the random nature of it. He could pick guys named Bill, as far as that goes. Either way it would probably take the police a while to tip to it, don't you think?"

"I don't know."

"You upset, Emily?"

"Not upset, exactly."

"You certainly don't have anything to worry about," he said, and slipped an arm protectively around her waist. "I'll take good care of you, baby."

"Oh, will you?"

"Count on it."

They walked together in silence for awhile and after a few moments she relaxed in his embrace. As they waited for a light to change he said, "Collecting Emilys."

"Pardon?"

"Just talking to myself," he said. "Nothing important."

# THE DETTWEILER SOLUTION

SOMETIMES YOU JUST can't win for losing. Business was so bad over at Dettweiler Bros. Fine Fashions for Men that Seth Dettweiler went on back to the store one Thursday night and poured out a five-gallon can of lead-free gasoline where he figured as it would do the most good. He lit a fresh Philip Morris King Size and balanced it on the edge of the counter so as it would burn for a couple of minutes and then get unbalanced enough to drop into the pool of gasoline. Then he got into an Oldsmobile that was about five days clear of a repossession notice and drove on home.

You couldn't have had a better fire dropping napalm on a paper mill. Time it was done you could sift those ashes and not find so much as a collar button. It was far and away the most spectacularly total fire Schuyler County had ever seen, so much so that Maybrook Fidelity Insurance would have been a little tentative about settling a claim under ordinary circumstances. But the way things stood there wasn't the slightest suspicion of arson, because what kind of a dimwitted hulk goes and burns down his business establishment a full week after his fire insurance has lapsed?

No fooling.

167

See, it was Seth's brother Porter who took care of paying bills and such, and a little over a month ago the fire-insurance payment had been due, and Porter looked at the bill and at the bank balance and back and 'forth for awhile and then he put the bill in a drawer. Two weeks later there was a reminder notice, and two weeks after that there was a notice that the grace period had expired and the insurance was no longer in force, and then a week after that there was one pluperfect hell of a bonfire.

Seth and Porter had always got on pretty good. (They took after each other quite a bit, folks said. Especially Porter.) Seth was forty-two years of age, and he had that long Dettweiler face topping a jutting Van Dine jaw. (Their mother was a Van Dine hailing from just the other side of Oak Falls.) Porter was thirty-nine, equipped with the same style face and jaw. They both had black hair that lay flat on their heads like shoe polish put on in slapdash fashion. Seth had more hair left than Porter, in spite of being the older brother by three years. I could describe them in greater detail, right down to scars and warts and sundry distinguishing marks, but it's my guess that you'd enjoy reading all that about as much as I'd enjoy writing it, which is to say less than somewhat. So let's get on with it.

I was saying they got on pretty good, rarely raising their voices one to the other, rarely disagreeing seriously about anything much. Now the fire didn't entirely change the habits of a lifetime but you couldn't honestly say that it did anything to improve their relationship. You'd have to allow that it caused a definite strain.

"What I can't understand," Seth said, "is how anybody who is fool enough to let fire insurance lapse can be an even greater fool by not telling his brother about it. That in a nutshell is what I can't understand."

"What beats *me*," Porter said, "is how the same person who has the nerve to fire a place of business for the insurance also does so without consulting his partner, especially when his partner just happens to be his brother."

"Allus I was trying to do," said Seth, "was save you from the criminal culpability of being an accessory before, to and after the fact, plus figuring you might be too chickenhearted to go along with it."

"Allus I was trying to do," said Porter, "was save you from worrying about financial matters you would be powerless to contend with, plus figuring it would just be an occasion for me to hear further from you on the subject of those bow ties."

"Well, you did buy one powerful lot of bow ties."

"I knew it."

"Something like a Pullman car full of bow ties, and it's not like every man and boy in Schuyler County's been getting this mad passion for bow ties of late."

"I just knew it."

"I wasn't the one brought up the subject, but since you went and mentioned those bow ties—"

"Maybe I should of mentioned the spats," Porter said.

"Oh, I don't want to hear about spats."

"No more than I wanted to hear about bow ties. Did we sell one single damn pair of spats?"

"We did."

"We did?"

"Feller bought one about fifteen months back. Had Maryland plates on his car, as I recall. Said he always wanted spats and didn't know they still made 'em."

"Well, selling one pair out of a gross isn't too bad."

"Now you leave off," Seth said.

"And you leave off of bow ties?"

"I guess."

"Anyway, the bow ties and the spats all burned up in the same damn fire," Porter said.

"You know what they say about ill winds," Seth said. "I guess there's a particle of truth in it, what they say."

While it didn't do the Dettweiler brothers much good to discuss spats and bow ties, it didn't solve their problems to leave off mentioning spats and bow ties. By the time they finished their conversation all they were back to was square one, and the view from that spot wasn't the world's best.

The only solution was bankruptcy, and it didn't look to be all that much of a solution.

"I don't mind going bankrupt," one of the brothers said. (I think it was Seth. Makes no nevermind, actually. Seth, Porter, it's all the same who said it.) "I don't mind going bankrupt, but I sure do hate the thought of being broke."

"Me too," said the other brother. (Porter, probably.)

"I've thought about bankruptcy from time to time."

"Me too."

"But there's a time and a place for bankruptcy."

"Well, the place is all right. No better place for bankruptcy than Schuyler County."

"That's true enough," said Seth. (Unless it was Porter.) "But this is surely not the time. Time to go bankrupt is in good times when you got a lot of money on hand. Only the damnedest kind of fool goes bankrupt when he's stony broke busted and there's a depression going on."

What they were both thinking on during this conversation was a fellow name of Joe Bob Rathburton who was in the construction business over to the other end of Schuyler County. I myself don't know of a man in this part of the state with enough intelligence to bail out a leaky rowboat who doesn't respect Joe Bob Rathburton to hell and back as a man with good business sense. It was about two years ago that Joe Bob went bankrupt and he did it the right way. First of all he did it coming off the best year's worth of business he'd ever done in his life. Then what he did was he paid off the car and the house and the boat and put them all in his wife's name. (His wife was Mabel Washburn, but no relation to the Washburns who have the Schuyler County First National Bank. That's another family entirely.)

Once that was done, Joe Bob took out every loan and raised every dollar he possibly could, and he turned all that capital into green folding cash and sealed it in quart Mason jars which he buried out back of an old pear tree that's sixty-plus years old and still bears fruit like crazy. And then he declared bankruptcy and sat back in his Mission rocker with a beer and a cigar and a real big-tooth smile.

"If I could think of anything worth doing," Porter Dettweiler said one night, "why, I guess I'd just go ahead and do it."

"Can't argue with that," Seth said.

"But I can't," Porter said.

"Nor I either."

"You might pass that old jug over here for a moment."

"Soon as I pour a tad for myself, if you've no objection."

"None whatsoever," said Porter.

They were over at Porter's place on the evening when this particular conversation occurred. They had taken to spending most of their evenings at Porter's on account of Seth had a wife at home, plus a daughter named Rachel who'd been working at the Ben Franklin store ever since dropping out of the junior college over at Monroe Center. Seth didn't have but the one daughter. Porter had two sons and a daughter, but they were all living with Porter's ex-wife, who had divorced him two years back and moved clear to Georgia. They were living in Valdosta now, as far as Porter knew. Least that was where he sent the check every month.

"Alimony jail," said Porter.

"How's that?"

"What I said was alimony jail. Where you go when you quit paying on your alimony."

"They got a special jug set aside for men don't pay their alimony?"

"Just an expression. I guess they put you into whatever jug's the handiest. All I got to do is quit sendin' Gert her checks and let her have them cart me away. Get my three meals a day and a roof over my head and the whole world could quit nagging me night and day for money I haven't got."

"You could never stand it. Bein' in a jail day in and day out, night in and night out."

171

"I know it," Porter said unhappily. "There anything left in that there jug, on the subject of jugs?"

"Some. Anyway, you haven't paid Gert a penny in how long? Three months?"

"Call it five."

"And she ain't throwed you in jail yet. Least you haven't got her close to hand so's she can talk money to you."

"Linda Mae givin' you trouble?"

"She did. Keeps a civil tongue since I beat up on her the last time."

"Lord knew what he was doin'," Porter said, "makin' men stronger than women. You ever give any thought to what life would be like if wives could beat up on their husbands instead of the other way around?"

"Now I don't even want to think about that," Seth said.

You'll notice nobody was mentioning spats or bow ties. Even with the jug of corn getting discernibly lighter every time it passed from one set of hands to the other, these two subjects did not come up. Neither did anyone speak of the shortsightedness of failing to keep up fire insurance or the myopia of incinerating a building without ascertaining that such insurance was in force. Tempers had cooled with the ashes of Dettweiler Bros. Fine Fashions for Men, and once again Seth and Porter were on the best of terms.

Which just makes what happened thereafter all the more tragic.

"What I think I got," Porter said, "is no way to turn."

(This wasn't the same evening, but if you put the two evenings side by side under a microscope you'd be hard pressed to tell them apart each from the other. They were at Porter's little house over alongside the tracks of the old spur off the Wyandotte & Southern, which I couldn't tell you the last time there was a train on that spur, and they had their feet up and their shoes off, and there was a jug of corn in the picture. Most of their evenings had come to take on this particular shade.)

"Couldn't get work if I wanted to," Porter said, "which I don't, and if I did I couldn't make enough to matter, and my debts is up to my ears and rising steady."

"It doesn't look to be gettin' better," Seth said. "On the other hand, how can it get worse?"

"I keep thinking the same."

"And?"

"And it keeps getting worse."

"I guess you know what you're talkin' about," Seth said. He scratched his bulldog chin, which hadn't been in the same room with a razor in more than a day or two. "What I been thinkin' about," he said, "is killin' myself."

"You been thinking of that?"

"Sure have."

"I think on it from time to time myself," Porter admitted. "Mostly nights when I can't sleep. It can be a powerful comfort around about three in the morning. You think of all the different ways and the next thing you know you're asleep. Beats the stuffing out of counting sheep jumping fences. You seen one sheep you seen 'em all is always been my thoughts on the subject, whereas there's any number of ways of doing away with your yourself."

"I'd take a certain satisfaction in it," Seth said, more or less warming to the subject. "What I'd leave is this note tellin' Linda Mae how her and Rachel'll be taken care of with the insurance, just to get the bitch's hopes up, and then she can find out for her own self that I cashed in that insurance back in January to make the payment on the Oldsmobile. You know it's pure uncut hell gettin' along without an automobile now."

"You don't have to tell me."

"Just put a rope around my neck," said Seth, smothering a hiccup, "and my damn troubles'll be over."

"And mine in the bargain," Porter said.

"By you doin' your own self in?"

"Be no need," Porter said, "if you did *yourself* in."

"How you figure that?"

"What I figure is a hundred thousand dollars," Porter said.

"Lord love a duck, if I had a hundred thousand dollars I could declare bankruptcy and live like a king!"

Seth looked at him, got up, walked over to him and took the jug away from him. He took a swig and socked the cork in place, but kept hold of the jug.

"Brother," he said, "I just guess you've had enough of this here."

"What makes you say that, brother?"

"Me killin' myself and you gettin' rich, you don't make sense. What you think you're talkin' about, anyhow?"

"Insurance," Porter said. "Insurance, that's what I think I'm talking about. Insurance."

Porter explained the whole thing. It seems there was this life insurance policy their father had taken out on them when they weren't but boys. Face amount of a hundred thousand dollars, double indemnity for accidental death. It was payable to him while they were alive, but upon his death the beneficiary changed. If Porter was to die the money went to Seth. And vice versa.

"And you knew about this all along?"

"Sure did," Porter said.

"And never cashed it in? Not the policy on me and not the policy on you?"

"Couldn't cash 'em in," Porter said. "I guess I woulda if I coulda, but I couldn't so I didn't."

"And you didn't let these here policies lapse?" Seth said. "On account of occasionally a person can be just the least bit absentminded and forget about keeping a policy in force. That's been known to happen," Seth said, looking off to one side, "in matters relating to fire insurance, for example, and I just thought to mention it."

(I have the feeling he wasn't the only one to worry on that score. You may have had similar thoughts yourself, figuring you know how the story's going to end, what with the insurance not valid and all. Set your mind at rest. If that was the way it had happened I'd never be taking the trouble to write it up for you. I got to select stories with some satisfaction in them if I'm going

174

to stand a chance of selling them to the magazine, and I hope you don't figure I'm sitting here poking away at this typewriter for the sheer physical pleasure of it. If I just want to exercise my fingers I'll send them walking through the Yellow Pages if it's all the same to you.)

"Couldn't let 'em lapse," Porter said. "They're all paid up. What you call twenty-payment life, meaning you pay it in for twenty years and then you got it free and clear. And the way pa did it, you can't borrow on it or nothing. All you can do is wait and see who dies."

"Well, I'll be."

"Except we don't have to wait to see who dies."

"Why, I guess not. I just guess a man can take matters into his own hands if he's of a mind to."

"He surely can," Porter said.

"Man wants to kill himself, that's what he can go and do."

"No law against it," Porter said.

Now you know and I know that that last is not strictly true. There's a definite no-question law against suicide in our state, and most likely in yours as well. It's harder to make it stand up than a calf with four broken legs, however, and I don't recall that anyone hereabouts was ever prosecuted for it, or likely will be. It does make you wonder some what they had in mind writing that particular law into the books.

"I'll just have another taste of that there corn," Porter said, "and why don't you have a pull on the jug your own self? You have any idea just when you might go and do it?"

"I'm studying on it," Seth said.

"There's a lot to be said for doing something soon as a man's mind's made up on the subject. Not to be hurrying you or anything of the sort, but they say that he who hesitates is last." Porter scratched his chin. "Or some such," he said.

"I just might do it tonight."

"By God," Porter said.

"Get the damn thing over with. Glory Hallelujah and my troubles is over."

"And so is mine," said Porter.

"You'll be in the money then," said Seth, "and I'll be in the boneyard, and both of us is free and clear. You can just buy me a decent funeral and then go bankrupt in style."

"Give you Johnny Millbourne's number-one funeral," Porter promised. "Brassbound casket and all. I mean, price is no object if I'm going bankrupt anyway. Let old Johnny swing for the money."

"You a damn good man, brother."

"You the best man in the world, brother."

The jug passed back and forth a couple more times. At one point Seth announced that he was ready, and he was halfway out the door before he recollected that his car had been repossessed, which interfered with his plans to drive it off a cliff. He came back in and sat down again and had another drink on the strength of it all, and then suddenly he sat forward and stared hard at Porter.

"This policy thing," he said.

"What about it?"

"It's on both of us, is what you said."

"If I said it then must be it's the truth."

"Well then," Seth said, and sat back, arms folded on his chest.

"Well then what?"

"Well then if *you* was to kill yourself, then *I'd* get the money and *you'd* get the funeral."

"I don't see what you're getting at," Porter said slowly.

"Seems to me either one of us can go and do it," Seth said. "And here's the two of us just takin' it for granted that I'm to be the one to go and do it, and I think we should think on that a little more thoroughly."

"Why, being as you're older, Seth."

"What's that to do with anything?"

"Why, you got less years to give up."

"Still be givin' up all that's left. Older or younger don't cut no ice."

Porter thought about it. "After all," he said, "it was your idea."

"That don't cut ice neither. I could mention I got a wife and child."

"I could mention I got a wife and three children."

"Ex-wife."

"All the same."

"Let's face it," Seth said. "Gert and your three don't add up to anything and neither do Linda Mae and Rachel."

"Got to agree," Porter said.

"So."

"One thing. You being the one who put us in this mess, what with firing the store, it just seems you might be the one to get us out of it."

"You bein' the one let the insurance lapse through your own stupidity, you could get us out of this mess through insurance, thus evenin' things up again."

"Now talkin' about stupidity—"

"Yes, talkin' about stupidity—"

"Spats!"

"Bow ties, damn you! *Bow ties!*"

You might have known it would come to that.


Now I've told you Seth and Porter generally got along pretty well and here's further evidence of it. Confronted by such a stalemate, a good many people would have wrote off the whole affair and decided not to take the suicide route at all. But not even spats and bow ties could deflect Seth and Porter from the road they'd figured out as the most logical to pursue.

So what they did, one of them tossed a coin, and the other one called it while it was in the air, and they let it hit the floor and roll, and I don't recollect whether it was heads or tails, or who tossed and who called—what's significant is that Seth won.

"Well now," Seth said. "I feel I been reprieved. Just let me have that coin. I want to keep it for a luck charm."

"Two out of three."

"We already said once is as good as a million," Seth said, "so you just forget that two-out-of-three business. You got a week like we agreed but if I was you I'd get it over soon as I could."

"I got a week," Porter said.

"You'll get the brassbound casket and everything, and you can

177

have Minnie Lucy Boxwood sing at your funeral if you want. Expense don't matter at all. What's your favorite song?"

"I suppose 'Your Cheatin' Heart.'"

"Minnie Lucy does that real pretty."

"I guess she does."

"Now you be sure and make it accidental," Seth said. "Two hundred thousand dollars goes just about twice as far as one hundred thousand dollars. Won't cost you a thing to make it accidental, just like we talked about it. What I would do is borrow Fritz Chenoweth's half-ton pickup and go up on the old Harburton Road where it takes that curve. Have yourself a belly full of corn and just keep goin' straight when the road doesn't. Lord knows I almost did that myself enough times without tryin'. Had two wheels over the edge less'n a month ago."

"That close?"

"That close."

"I'll be doggone," Porter said.

Thing is, Seth went on home after he failed to convince Porter to do it right away, and that was when things began to fall into the muck. Because Porter started thinking things over. I have a hunch it would have worked about the same way if Porter had won the flip, with Seth thinking things over. They were a whole lot alike, those two. Like two peas in a pod.

What occurred to Porter was would Seth have gone through with it if he lost, and what Porter decided was that he wouldn't. Not that there was any way for him to prove it one way or the other, but when you can't prove something you generally tend to decide on believing in what you want to believe, and Porter Dettweiler was no exception. Seth, he decided, would not have killed himself and didn't never have no intention of killing himself, which meant that for Porter to go through with killing his own self amounted to nothing more than damned foolishness.

Now it's hard to say just when he figured out what to do, but it was in the next two days, because on the third day he went over and borrowed that pickup off Fritz Chenoweth. "I got the back all loaded down with a couple sacks of concrete mix and a

178

keg of nails and I don't know what all," Fritz said. "You want to unload it back of my smaller barn if you need the room."

"Oh, that's all right," Porter told him. "I guess I'll just leave it loaded and be grateful for the traction."

"Well, you keep it overnight if you have a mind," Fritz said.

"I just might do that," Porter said, and he went over to Seth's house. "Let's you and me go for a ride," he told Seth. "Something we was talking about the other night, and I went and got me a new slant on it which the two of us ought to discuss before things go wrong altogether."

"Be right with you," Seth said, "soon as I finish this sandwich."

"Oh, just bring it along."

"I guess," said Seth.

No sooner was the pickup truck backed down and out of the driveway than Porter said, "Now will you just have a look over there, brother."

"How's that?" said Seth, and turned his head obligingly to the right, whereupon Porter gave him a good lick upside the head with a monkey wrench he'd brought along expressly for that purpose. He got him right where you have a soft spot if you're a little baby. (You also have a soft spot there if someone gets you just right with a monkey wrench.) Seth made a little sound which amounted to no more than letting his breath out, and then he went out like an icebox light when you have closed the door on it.

Now as to whether or not Seth was dead at this point I could not honestly tell you, unless I were to make up an answer knowing how slim is the likelihood of anyone presuming to contradict me. But the plain fact is that he might have been dead and he might not and even Seth could not have told you, being at the very least stone-unconscious at the time.

What Porter did was drive up the old Harburton Road, I guess figuring that he might as well stick to as much of the original plan as possible. There's a particular place where the road does a reasonably convincing imitation of a fishhook, and that spot's been described as Schuyler County's best natural brake on the population explosion since they stamped out the typhoid. A whole lot of folks fail to make that curve every year, most of them young ones with plenty of breeding years left in them. Now and then there's a movement to put up a guard rail, but the ecology people are against it so it never gets anywheres.

If you miss that curve, the next land you touch is a good five hundred feet closer to sea level.

So Porter pulls over to the side of the road and then he gets out of the car and maneuvers Seth (or Seth's body, whichever the case may have been) so as he's behind the wheel. Then he stands alongside the car working the gas pedal with one hand and the steering wheel with the other and putting the fool truck in gear and doing this and that and the other thing so he can run the truck up to the edge and over, and thinking hard every minute about those two hundred thousand pretty green dollars that are destined to make his bankruptcy considerably easier to contend with.

Well, I told you right off that sometimes you can't win for losing, which was the case for Porter and Seth both, and another way of putting it is to say that when everything goes wrong there's nothing goes right. Here's what happened. Porter slipped on a piece of loose gravel while he was pushing, and the truck had to go on its own, and where it went was halfway and no further, with its back wheel hung up on a hunk of tree limb or some such and its two front wheels hanging out over nothing and its motor stalled out deader'n a smoked fish.

Porter said himself a whole mess of bad words. Then he wasted considerable time shoving the back of that truck, forgetting it was in gear and not about to budge. Then he remembered and said a few more bad words and put the thing in neutral, which involved a long reach across Seth to get to the floor shift and a lot of coordination to manipulate it and the clutch pedal at the same time. Then Porter got out of the truck and gave the door a slam, and just about then a beat-up old Chevy with Indiana plates pulls up and this fellow leaps out screaming that he's got a tow rope and he'll pull the truck to safety.

You can't hardly blame Porter for the rest of it. He wasn't the type to be great at contingency planning anyhow, and who could allow for something like this? What he did, he gave this great sob and just plain hurled himself at the back of that truck, it being in neutral now, and the truck went sailing like a kite in a tornado, and Porter, well, what he did was follow right along after it. It wasn't part of his plan but he just had himself too much momentum to manage any last-minute change of direction.

According to the fellow from Indiana, who it turned out was a veterinarian from Bloomington, Porter fell far enough to get off a couple of genuinely rank words on the way down. Last words or not, you sure wouldn't go and engrave them on any tombstone.

Speaking of which, he has the last word in tombstones, Vermont granite and all, and his brother Seth has one just like it. They had a double-barreled funeral, the best Johnny Millbourne had to offer, and they each of them reposed in a brass-bound casket, the top-of-the-line model. Minnie Lucy Boxwood sang "Your Cheatin' Heart," which was Porter's favorite song, plus she sang Seth's favorite, which was "Old Buttermilk Sky," plus she also sang free gratis "My Buddy" as a testament to brotherly love.

And Linda Mae and Rachel got themselves two hundred thousand dollars from the insurance company, which is what Gert and her kids in Valdosta, Georgia, also got. And Seth and Porter have an end to their miseries, which was all they really wanted before they got their heads turned around at the idea of all that money.

The only thing funnier than how things don't work out is how they do.

# FUNNY
# YOU
# SHOULD ASK

ON WHAT A less original writer might deign to describe as a fateful day, young Robert Tillinghast approached the proprietor of a shop called Earth Forms. "Actually," he said, "I don't think I can buy anything today, but there's a question I'd like to ask you. It's been on my mind for the longest time. I was looking at those recycled jeans over by the far wall."

"I'll be getting a hundred pair in Monday afternoon," the proprietor said.

"Is that right?"

"It certainly is."

"A hundred pair," Robert marveled. "That's certainly quite a lot."

"It's the minimum order."

"Is that a fact? And they'll all be the same quality and condition as the ones you have on display over on the far wall?"

"Absolutely. Of course, I won't know what sizes I'll be getting."

"I guess that's just a matter of chance."

"It is. But they'll all be first-quality name brands, and they'll all be in good condition, broken in but not broken to bits. That's a sort of an expression I made up to describe them."

"I like it," said Robert, not too sincerely. "You know, there's a question that's been nagging at my mind for the longest time.

Now you get six dollars a pair for the recycled jeans, is that right?" It was. "And it probably wouldn't be out of line to guess that they cost you about half that amount?" The proprietor, after a moment's reflection, agreed that it wouldn't be far out of line to make that estimate.

"Well, that's the whole thing," Robert said. "You notice the jeans I'm wearing?"

The proprietor glanced at them. They were nothing remarkable, a pair of oft-washed Lee Riders that were just beginning to go thin at the knees. "Very nice," the man said. "I'd get six dollars for them without a whole lot of trouble."

"But I wouldn't want to sell them."

"And of course not. Why should you? They're just getting to the comfortable stage."

"Exactly!" Robert grew intense, and his eyes bulged slightly. This was apt to happen when he grew intense, although he didn't know it, never having seen himself at such times. "Exactly," he repeated. "The recycled jeans you see in the shops, this shop and other shops, are just at the point where they're breaking in right. They're never really worn out. Unless you only put the better pairs on display?"

"No, they're all like that."

"That's what everybody says." Robert had had much the same conversation before in the course of his travels. "All top quality, all in excellent condition, and all in the same stage of wear."

"So?"

"So," Robert said in triumph, "who throws them out?"

"Oh."

"The company that sells them. Where do they get them from?"

"You know," the proprietor said, "it's funny you should ask. The same question's occurred to me. People buy these jeans because this is the way they want 'em. But who in the world sells them?"

"That's what I'd like to know. Not that it would do me any good to have the answer, but the question preys on my mind."

"Who sells them? I could understand about young children's jeans that kids would outgrow them, but what about the adult sizes? Unless kids grow up and don't want to wear jeans any more."

"I'll be wearing jeans as long as I live," Robert said recklessly. "I'll never get too old for jeans."

The proprietor seemed not to have heard. "Now maybe it's different out in the farm country," he said. "I buy these jeans from a firm in Rockford, Illinois—"

"I've heard of the firm," Robert said. "They seem to be the only people supplying recycled jeans."

"Only one I know of. Now maybe things are different in their area and people like brand-new jeans and once they break in somewhat they think of them as worn out. That's possible, don't you suppose?"

"I guess it's possible."

"Because it's the only explanation I can think of. After all, what could they afford to pay for the jeans? A dollar a pair? A dollar and a half at the outside? Who would sell 'em good-condition jeans for that amount of money?" The man shook his head. "Funny you should ask a question that I've asked myself so many times and never put into words."

"That Rockford firm," Robert said. "That's another thing I don't understand. Why would they develop a sideline business like recycled jeans?"

"Well, you never know about that," the man said. "Diversification is the keynote of American business these days. Take me, for example. I started out selling flowerpots, and now I sell flowerpots and guitar strings and recapped tires and recycled jeans. Now there are people who would call that an unusual combination."

"I suppose there are," said Robert.

An obsession of the sort that gripped Robert is a curious thing. After a certain amount of time it is either metamorphosized into neurosis or it is tamed, surfacing periodically as a vehicle for casual conversation. Young Robert Tillinghast, neurotic enough in other respects, suppressed his curiosity on the subject of recycled jeans and only raised the question at times when it seemed particularly apropos.

And it did seem apropos often enough. Robert was touring the country, depending for his locomotion upon the kindness of passing motorists. As charitable as his hosts were, they were apt to insist upon a quid pro quo of conversation, and Robert had learned to converse extemporaneously upon a variety of subjects. One of these was that of recycled blue jeans, a subject close at once to his heart and his skin, and Robert's own jeans often served as the lead-in to this line of conversation, being either funky and mellow or altogether disreputable, depending upon one's point of view, which in turn largely depended (it must be said) upon one's age.

One day in West Virginia, on that stretch of Interstate 79 leading from Morgantown down to Charleston, Robert thumbed a ride with a man who, though not many years older than himself, drove a late-model Cadillac. Robert, his backpack in the back seat and his body in the front, could not have been more pleased. He had come to feel that hitching a ride in an expensive car endowed one with all the privileges of ownership without the nuisance of making the payments.

Then, as the car cruised southward, Robert noticed that the driver was glancing repeatedly at his, which is to say Robert's, legs. Covert glances at that, sidelong and meaningful. Robert sighed inwardly. This, too, was part of the game, and had ceased to shock him. But he had so been looking forward to riding in this car and now he would have to get out.

The driver said, "Just admiring your jeans."

"I guess they're just beginning to break in," Robert said, relaxing now. "I've certainly had them a while."

"Well, they look just right now. Got a lot of wear left in them."

"I guess they'll last for years," Robert said. "With the proper treatment. You know, that brings up something I've been wondering about for a long time." And he went into his routine, which had become rather a little set piece by this time, ending with the question that had plagued him from the start. "So where on earth does that Rockford company get all these jeans? Who provides them?"

"Funny you should ask," the young man said. "I don't suppose you noticed my license plates before you got in?" Robert admitted he hadn't. "Few people do," the young man said. "Land of Lincoln is the slogan on them, and they're from Illinois. And I'm from Rockford. As a matter of fact, I'm with that very company."

"But that's incredible! For the longest time I've wanted to know the answers to my questions, and now at long last—" He broke off. "Why are we leaving the Interstate?"

"Bypass some traffic approaching Charleston. There's construction ahead and it can be a real bottleneck. Yes, I'm with the company."

"In sales, I suppose? Servicing accounts? You certainly have enough accounts. Why, it seems every store in the country buys recycled jeans from you people."

"Our distribution is rather good," the young man said, "and our sales force does a good job. But I'm in Acquisitions, myself. I go out and round up the jeans. Then in Rockford they're washed to clean and sterilize them, patched if they need it and—"

"You're actually in Acquisitions?"

"That's a fact."

"Well, this *is* my lucky day," Robert exclaimed. "You're just the man to give me all the answers. Where do you get the jeans? Who sells them to you? What do you pay for them? What sort of person sells perfectly good jeans?"

"That's a whole lot of questions at once."

Robert laughed, happy with himself, his host, and the world. "I just don't know where to start and it's got me rattled. Say, this bypass is a small road, isn't it? I guess not many people know about it and that's why there's no other traffic on it. Poor saps'll all get tangled in traffic going into Charleston."

"We'll miss all that."

"That's good luck. Let's see, where can I begin? All right, here's the big question and I've always been puzzled by this one. What's a company like yours doing in the recycled jeans business?"

"Well," said the young man, "diversification is the keynote of American business these days."

"But a company like yours," Robert said. "Rockford Dog Food,

187

Inc. How did you ever think to get into the business in the first place?"

"Funny you should ask," said the young man, braking the car smoothly to a stop.

# LIKE A THIEF
# IN
# THE NIGHT

AT 11:30 THE television anchorman counseled her to stay tuned for the late show, a vintage Hitchcock film starring Cary Grant. For a moment she was tempted. Then she crossed the room and switched off the set.

There was a last cup of coffee in the pot. She poured it and stood at the window with it, a tall and slender woman, attractive, dressed in the suit and silk blouse she'd worn that day at the office. A woman who could look at once efficient and elegant, and who stood now sipping black coffee from a bone-china cup and gazing south and west.

Her apartment was on the twenty-second floor of a building located at the corner of Lexington Avenue and Seventy-sixth Street, and her vista was quite spectacular. A midtown skyscraper blocked her view of the building where Tavistock Corp. did its business, but she fancied she could see right through it with x-ray vision.

The cleaning crew would be finishing up now, she knew, returning their mops and buckets to the cupboards and changing into street clothes, preparing to go off-shift at midnight. They would leave a couple of lights on in Tavistock's seventeenth floor suite as well as elsewhere throughout the building. And the halls would remain lighted, and here and there in the building some-one would be working all night, and—

She liked Hitchcock movies, especially the early ones, and she was in love with Cary Grant. But she also liked good clothes and bone-china cups and the view from her apartment and the com-fortable, well-appointed apartment itself. And so she rinsed the cup in the sink and put on a coat and took the elevator to the lobby, where the florid-faced doorman made a great show of hailing her a cab.

There would be other nights, and other movies.

The taxi dropped her in front of an office building in the West Thirties. She pushed through the revolving door and her footsteps on the marble floor sounded impossibly loud to her. The security guard, seated at a small table by the bank of elevators, looked up from his magazine at her approach. She said, "Hello, Eddie," and gave him a quick smile.

"Hey, how ya doin'," he said, and she bent to sign herself in as his attention returned to his magazine. In the appropriate spaces she scribbled *Elaine Halder, Tavistock, 1704,* and, after a glance at her watch, *12:15.*

She got into a waiting elevator and the doors closed without a sound. She'd be alone up there, she thought. She'd glanced at the record sheet while signing it, and no one had signed in for Tavistock or any other office on seventeen.

Well, she wouldn't be long.

When the elevator doors opened she stepped out and stood for a moment in the corridor, getting her bearings. She took a key from her purse and stared at it for a moment as if it were an artifact from some unfamiliar civilization. Then she turned and began walking the length of the freshly mopped corridor, hearing nothing but the echo of her boisterous footsteps.

1704. An oak door, a square of frosted glass, unmarked but for the suite number and the name of the company. She took another thoughtful glance at the key before fitting it carefully into the lock.

It turned easily. She pushed the door inward and stepped inside, letting the door swing shut behind her.

And gasped.

There was a man not a dozen yards from her.

"Hello," he said.

He was standing beside a rosewood-topped desk, the center drawer of which was open, and there was a spark in his eyes and a tentative smile on his lips. He was wearing a gray suit patterned in a windowpane check. His shirt collar was buttoned down, his narrow tie neatly knotted. He was two or three years older than she, she supposed, and perhaps that many inches taller.

Her hand was pressed to her breast, as if to still a pounding heart. But her heart wasn't really pounding. She managed a smile. "You startled me," she said. "I didn't know anyone would be here."

"We're even."

"I beg your pardon?"

"I wasn't expecting company."

He had nice white even teeth, she noticed. She was apt to notice teeth. And he had an open and friendly face, which was also something she was inclined to notice, and why was she suddenly thinking of Cary Grant? The movie she hadn't seen, of course, that plus this Hollywood meet-cute opening, with the two of them encountering each other unexpectedly in this silent tomb of an office, and—

And he was wearing rubber gloves.

Her face must have registered something because he frowned, puzzled. Then he raised his hands and flexed his fingers. "Oh, these," he said. "Would it help if I spoke of an eczema brought on by exposure to the night air?"

"There's a lot of that going around."

"I knew you'd understand."

"You're a prowler."

"The word has the nastiest connotations," he objected. "One imagines a lot of lurking in shrubbery. There's no shrubbery here beyond the odd rubber plant and I wouldn't lurk in it if there were."

"A thief, then."

"A thief, yes. More specifically, a burglar. I might have stripped the gloves off when you stuck your key in the lock but I'd been so busy listening to your footsteps and hoping they'd lead to another office that I quite forgot I was wearing these things. Not that it would have made much difference. Another minute and you'd have realized that you've never set eyes on me before, and at that point you'd have wondered what I was doing here."

"What *are* you doing here?"

"My kid brother needs an operation."

"I thought that might be it. Surgery for his eczema."

He nodded. "Without it he'll never play the trumpet again. May I be permitted an observation?"

"I don't see why not."

"I observe that you're afraid of me."

"And here I thought I was doing such a super job of hiding it."

"You were, but I'm an incredibly perceptive human being. You're afraid I'll do something violent, that he who is capable of theft is equally capable of mayhem."

"Are you?"

"Not even in fantasy. I'm your basic pacifist. When I was a kid my favorite book was *Ferdinand the Bull.*"

"I remember him. He didn't want to fight. He just wanted to smell the flowers."

"Can you blame him?" He smiled again, and the adverb that came to her was *disarmingly.* More like Alan Alda than Cary Grant, she decided. Well, that was all right. There was nothing wrong with Alan Alda.

"*You're* afraid of *me,*" she said suddenly.

"How'd you figure that? A slight quiver in the old upper lip?"

"No. It just came to me. But why? What could I do to you?"

"You could call the, uh, cops."

"I wouldn't do that."

"And I wouldn't hurt you."

"I know you wouldn't."

"Well," he said, and sighed theatrically. "Aren't you glad we got all that out of the way?"

She was, rather. It was good to know that neither of them had anything to fear from the other. As if in recognition of this change in their relationship she took off her coat and hung it on the pipe rack, where a checked topcoat was already hanging. His, she assumed. How readily he made himself at home!

She turned to find he was making himself further at home, rummaging deliberately in the drawers of the desk. What cheek, she thought, and felt herself beginning to smile.

She asked him what he was doing.

"Foraging," he said, then drew himself up sharply. "This isn't your desk, is it?"

"No."

"Thank heaven for that."

"What were you looking for, anyway?"

He thought for a moment, then shook his head. "Nope," he said. "You'd think I could come up with a decent story but I can't. I'm looking for something to steal."

"Nothing specific?"

"I like to keep an open mind. I didn't come here to cart off the IBM Selectrics. But you'd be surprised how many people leave cash in their desks."

"And you just take what you find?"

He hung his head. "I know," he said. "It's a moral failing. You don't have to tell me."

"Do people really leave cash in an unlocked desk drawer?"

"Sometimes. And sometimes they lock the drawers, but that doesn't make them all that much harder to open."

"You can pick locks?"

"A limited and eccentric talent," he allowed, "but it's all I know."

"How did you get in here? I suppose you picked the office lock."

"Hardly a great challenge."

"But how did you get past Eddie?"

"Eddie? Oh, you must be talking about the chap in the lobby. He's not quite as formidable as the Berlin Wall, you know. I got here around eight. They tend to be less suspicious at an earlier hour. I scrawled a name on the sheet and walked on by. Then I found an empty office that they'd already finished cleaning and curled up on the couch for a nap."

"You're kidding."

"Have I ever lied to you in the past? The cleaning crew leaves at midnight. At about that time I let myself out of Mr. Higginbotham's office—that's where I've taken to napping, he's a patent attorney with the most comfortable old leather couch. And then I make my rounds."

She looked at him. "You've come to this building before."

"I stop by every little once in a while."

"You make it sound like a vending machine route."

"There are similarities, aren't there? I never looked at it that way."

"And then you make your rounds. You break into offices—"

"I never break anything. Let's say I let myself into offices."

"And you steal money from desks—"

"Also jewelry, when I run across it. Anything valuable and portable. Sometimes there's a safe. That saves a lot of looking around. You know right away that's where they keep the good stuff."

"And you can open safes?"

"Not every safe," he said modestly, "and not every single time, but—" he switched to a Cockney accent "—I has the touch, mum."

"And then what do you do? Wait until morning to leave?"

"What for? I'm well-dressed. I look respectable. Besides, security guards are posted to keep unauthorized persons out of a building, not to prevent them from leaving. It might be different if I tried rolling a Xerox machine through the lobby, but I don't steal anything that won't fit in my pockets or my attaché case. And I don't wear my rubber gloves when I saunter past the guard. That wouldn't do."

"I don't suppose it would. What do I call you?"

"'That damned burglar,' I suppose. That's what everybody calls me. But you—" he extended a rubber-covered forefinger "—you may call me Bernie."

"Bernie the Burglar."

"And what shall I call you?"

"Elaine'll do."

"Elaine," he said. "Elaine, Elaine. Not Elaine Halder, by any chance?"

"How did you—?"

"Elaine Halder," he said. "And that explains what brings you to these offices in the middle of the night. You look startled. I can't imagine why. 'You know my methods, Watson.' What's the matter?"

"Nothing."

"Don't be frightened, for God's sake. Knowing your name doesn't give me mystical powers over your destiny. I just have a good memory and your name stuck in it." He crooked a thumb at a closed door on the far side of the room. "I've already been in the boss's office. I saw your note on his desk. I'm afraid I'll have to admit I read it. I'm a snoop. It's a serious character defect, I know."

"Like larceny."

"Something along those lines. Let's see now. Elaine Halder leaves the office, having placed on her boss's desk a letter of resignation. Elaine Halder returns in the small hours of the morning. A subtle pattern begins to emerge, my dear."

"Oh?"

"Of course. You've had second thoughts and you want to retrieve the letter before himself gets a chance to read it. Not a bad idea, given some of the choice things you had to say about him. Just let me open up for you, all right? I'm the tidy type and I locked up after I was through in there."

"Did you find anything to steal?"

"Eighty-five bucks and a pair of gold cuff links." He bent over the lock, probing its innards with a splinter of spring steel. "Nothing to write home about, but every little bit helps. I'm sure you have a key that fits this door—you had to in order to leave the resignation in the first place, didn't you? But how many chances do I get to show off? Not that a lock like this one presents much of a challenge, not to the nimble digits of Bernie the Burglar, and—ah, *there* we are!"

"Extraordinary."

"It's so seldom I have an audience."

He stood aside, held the door for her. On the threshold she was struck by the notion that there would be a dead body in the private office. George Tavistock himself, slumped over his desk with the figured hilt of a letter opener protruding from his back.

But of course there was no such thing. The office was devoid of clutter, let alone corpses, nor was there any sign that it had been lately burglarized.

A single sheet of paper lay on top of the desk blotter. She walked over, picked it up. Her eyes scanned its half dozen sentences as if she were reading them for the first time, then dropped to the elaborately styled signature, a far cry from the loose scrawl with which she'd signed the register in the lobby.

She read the note through again, then put it back where it had been.

"Not changing your mind again?"

She shook her head. "I never changed it in the first place. That's not why I came back here tonight."

"You couldn't have dropped in just for the pleasure of my company."

"I might have, if I'd known you were going to be here. No, I came back because—" She paused, drew a deliberate breath. "You might say I wanted to clean out my desk."

"Didn't you already do that? Isn't your desk right across there? The one with your name plate on it? Forward of me, I know, but I already had a peek, and the drawers bore a striking resemblance to the cupboard of one Ms. Hubbard."

"You went through my desk."

He spread his hands apologetically. "I meant nothing personal," he said. "At the time, I didn't even know you."

"That's a point."

196

"And searching an empty desk isn't that great a violation of privacy, is it? Nothing to be seen beyond paper clips and rubber bands and the odd felt tipped pen. So if you've come to clean out that lot—"

"I meant it metaphorically," she explained. "There are things in this office that belong to me. Projects I worked on that I ought to have copies of to show to prospective employers."

"And won't Mr. Tavistock see to it that you get copies?"

She laughed sharply. "You don't know the man," she said.

"And thank God for that. I couldn't rob someone I knew."

"He would think I intended to divulge corporate secrets to the competition. The minute he reads my letter of resignation I'll be persona non grata in this office. I probably won't even be able to get into the building. I didn't even realize any of this until I'd gotten home tonight, and I didn't really know what to do, and then—"

"Then you decided to try a little burglary."

"Hardly that."

"Oh?"

"I have a key."

"And I have a cunning little piece of spring steel, and they both perform the signal function of admitting us where we have no right to be."

"But I work here!"

"Worked."

"My resignation hasn't been accepted yet. I'm still an employee."

"Technically. Still, you've come like a thief in the night. You may have signed in downstairs and let yourself in with a key, and you're not wearing gloves or padding around in crepe-soled shoes, but we're not all that different, you and I, are we?"

She set her jaw. "I have a right to the fruits of my labor," she said.

"And so have I, and heaven help the person whose property rights get in our way."

She walked around him to the three-drawer filing cabinet to the right of Tavistock's desk. It was locked.

She turned, but Bernie was already at her elbow. "Allow me," he said, and in no time at all he had tickled the locking mechanism and was drawing the top drawer open.

"Thank you," she said.

"Oh, don't thank me," he said. "Professional courtesy. No thanks required."

She was busy for the next thirty minutes, selecting documents from the filing cabinet and from Tavistock's desk, as well as a few items from the unlocked cabinets in the outer office. She ran everything through the Xerox copier and replaced the originals where she'd found them. While she was doing all this, her burglar friend worked his way through the office's remaining desks. He was in no evident hurry, and it struck her that he was deliberately dawdling so as not to finish before her.

Now and then she would look up from what she was doing to observe him at his work. Once she caught him looking at her, and when their eyes met he winked and smiled, and she felt her cheeks burning.

He was attractive, certainly. And unquestionably likable, and in no way intimidating. Nor did he come across like a criminal. His speech was that of an educated person, he had an eye for clothes, his manners were impeccable—

What on earth was she thinking of?

By the time she had finished she had an inch-thick sheaf of paper in a manila file folder. She slipped her coat on, tucked the folder under her arm.

"You're certainly neat," he said. "A place for everything and everything right back in its place. I like that."

"Well, you're that way yourself, aren't you? You even take the trouble to lock up after yourself."

"It's not that much trouble. And there's a point to it. If one doesn't leave a mess, sometimes it takes them weeks to realize they've been robbed. The longer it takes, the less chance anybody'll figure out whodunit."

"And here I thought you were just naturally neat."

"As it happens I am, but it's a professional asset. Of course your neatness has much the same purpose, doesn't it? They'll never know you've been here tonight, especially since you haven't actually taken anything away with you. Just copies."

"That's right."

"Speaking of which, would you care to put them in my attaché case? So that you aren't noticed leaving the building with them in hand? I'll grant you the chap downstairs wouldn't notice an earthquake if it registered less than seven-point-four on the Richter scale, but it's that seemingly pointless attention to detail that enables me to persist in my chosen occupation instead of making license plates and sewing mail sacks as a guest of the governor. Are you ready, Elaine? Or would you like to take one last look around for auld lang syne?"

"I've had my last look around. And I'm not much on auld lang syne."

He held the door for her, switched off the overhead lights, drew the door shut. While she locked it with her key he stripped off his rubber gloves and put them in the attaché case where her papers reposed. Then, side by side, they walked the length of the corridor to the elevator. Her footsteps echoed. His, cushioned by his crepe soles, were quite soundless.

Hers stopped, too, when they reached the elevator, and they waited in silence. They had met, she thought, as thieves in the night, and now they were going to pass like ships in the night.

The elevator came, floated them down to the lobby. The lobby guard looked up at them, neither recognition nor interest showing in his eyes. She said, "Hi, Eddie. Everything going all right?"

"Hey, how ya doin'," he said.

There were only three entries below hers on the register sheet, three persons who'd arrived after her. She signed herself out, listing the time after a glance at her watch: 1:56. She'd been upstairs for better than an hour and a half.

Outside, the wind had an edge to it. She turned to him, glanced at his attaché case, suddenly remembered the first schoolboy who'd carried her books. She could surely have carried her own books, just as she could have safely carried the folder of papers past Eagle-eye Eddie.

Still, it was not unpleasant to have one's books carried.

"Well," she began, "I'd better take my papers, and—"

"Where are you headed?"

"Seventy-sixth Street."

"East or west?"

"East. But—"

"We'll share a cab," he said. "Compliments of petty cash." And he was at the curb, a hand raised, and a cab appeared as if conjured up and then he was holding the door for her.

She got in.

"Seventy-sixth," he told the driver. "And what?"

"Lexington," she said.

"Lexington," he said.

Her mind raced during the taxi ride. It was all over the place and she couldn't keep up with it. She felt in turn like a schoolgirl, like a damsel in peril, like Grace Kelly in a Hitchcock film. When the cab reached her corner she indicated her building, and he leaned forward to relay the information to the driver.

"Would you like to come up for coffee?"

The line had run through her mind like a mantra in the course of the ride. Yet she couldn't believe she was actually speaking the words.

"Yes," he said. "I'd like that."

She steeled herself as they approached her doorman, but the man was discretion personified. He didn't even greet her by name, merely holding the door for her and her escort and wishing them a good night. Upstairs, she thought of demanding that Bernie open her door without the keys, but decided she didn't want any demonstrations just then of her essential vulnerability. She unlocked the several locks herself.

"I'll make coffee," she said. "Or would you just as soon have a drink?"

"Sounds good."

200

"Scotch? Or cognac?"

"Cognac."

While she was pouring the drinks he walked around her living room, looking at the pictures on the walls and the books on the shelves. Guests did this sort of thing all the time, but this particular guest was a criminal, after all, and so she imagined him taking a burglar's inventory of her possessions. That Chagall aquatint he was studying—she'd paid five hundred for it at auction and it was probably worth close to three times that by now.

Surely he'd have better luck foraging in her apartment than in a suite of deserted offices.

Surely he'd realize as much himself.

She handed him his brandy. "To criminal enterprise," he said, and she raised her glass in response.

"I'll give you those papers. Before I forget."

"All right."

He opened the attaché case, handed them over. She placed the folder on the LaVerne coffee table and carried her brandy across to the window. The deep carpet muffled her footsteps as effectively as if she'd been wearing crepe-soled shoes.

*You have nothing to be afraid of*, she told herself. *And you're not afraid, and—*

"An impressive view," he said, close behind her.

"Yes."

"You could see your office from here. If that building weren't in the way."

"I was thinking that earlier."

"Beautiful," he said, softly, and then his arms were encircling her from behind and his lips were on the nape of her neck.

"'Elaine the fair, Elaine the lovable,'" he quoted. "'Elaine, the lily maid of Astolat.'" His lips nuzzled her ear. "But you must hear that all the time."

She smiled. "Oh, not so often," she said. "Less often than you'd think."

The sky was just growing light when he left. She lay alone for a few minutes, then went to lock up after him.

And laughed aloud when she found that he'd locked up after himself, without a key.

It was late but she didn't think she'd ever been less tired. She put up a fresh pot of coffee, poured a cup when it was ready and sat at the kitchen table reading through the papers she'd taken from the office. She wouldn't have had half of them without Bernie's assistance, she realized. She could never have opened the file cabinet in Tavistock's office.

"*Elaine the fair, Elaine the lovable. Elaine, the lily maid of Astolat.*"

She smiled.

A few minutes after nine, when she was sure Jennings Colliard would be at his desk, she dialed his private number.

"It's Andrea," she told him. "I succeeded beyond our wildest dreams. I've got copies of Tavistock's complete marketing plan for fall and winter, along with a couple of dozen test and survey reports and a lot of other documents you'll want a chance to analyze. And I put all the originals back where they came from, so nobody at Tavistock'll ever know what happened."

"Remarkable."

"I thought you'd approve. Having a key to their office helped, and knowing the doorman's name didn't hurt any. Oh, and I also have some news that's worth knowing. I don't know if George Tavistock is in his office yet, but if so he's reading a letter of resignation even as we speak. The Lily Maid of Astolat has had it."

"What are you talking about, Andrea?"

"Elaine Halder. She cleaned out her desk and left him a note saying bye-bye. I thought you'd like to be the first kid on your block to know that."

"And of course you're right."

"I'd come in now but I'm exhausted. Do you want to send a messenger over?"

"Right away. And you get some sleep."

"I intend to."

"You've done spectacularly well, Andrea. There will be something extra in your stocking."

"I thought there might be," she said.

She hung up the phone and stood once again at the window, looking out at the city, reviewing the night's events. It had been quite perfect, she decided, and if there was the slightest flaw it was that she'd missed the Cary Grant movie.

But it would be on again soon. They ran it frequently. People evidently liked that sort of thing.

# GOING
# THROUGH
# THE MOTIONS

ON THE WAY home I had picked up a sack of burgers and fries at the fast-food place near the Interstate off-ramp. I popped a beer, but before I got it poured or the meal eaten I checked my phone answering machine. There was a message from Anson Pollard asking me to call him right away. His voice didn't sound right, and there was something familiar in what was wrong with it.

I ate a hamburger and drank half a beer, then made the call. He said, "Thank God, Lou. Can you come over here?"

"What's the matter?"

"Come over and I'll tell you."

I went back to the kitchen table, unwrapped a second hamburger, then wrapped it up again. I bagged the food and put it in the fridge, poured the beer down the sink.

The streetlights came on while I was driving across town to his place. No question, the days were getting longer. Not much left of spring. I switched on my headlights and thought how fast the years were starting to go, and how Anson's voice hadn't sounded right.

I parked at the head of his big circular driveway. My engine went on coughing for ten or twenty seconds after I cut the ignition. It'll do that, and the kid at the garage can't seem to figure out what to do about it. I'd had to buy my own car after the last election, and this had been as good as I could afford. Of course it didn't settle into that coughing routine until I'd owned it a month, and now it wouldn't quit.

Anson had the door open before I got to it. "Lou," he said, and gripped me by the shoulders.

He was only a year older than me, which made him forty-two, but he was showing all those years and more. He was balding and carried too much weight, but that wasn't what did it. His whole face was drawn and desperate, and I put that together with his tone of voice and knew what I'd been reminded of over the phone. He'd sounded the same way three years ago when Paula died.

"What's the matter, Anse?"

He shook his head. "Come inside," he said. I followed him to the room where he kept the liquor. Without asking he poured us each a full measure of straight bourbon. I didn't much want a drink but I took it and held onto it while he drank his all the way down. He shuddered, then took a deep breath and let it out slowly.

"Beth's been kidnapped," he said.

"When?"

"This afternoon. She left school at the usual time. She never got home. This was in the mailbox when I got home. It hadn't gone through the mails. They just stuck it in the box."

I removed a sheet of paper from the envelope he handed me, unfolded it. Words cut from a newspaper, fastened in place with rubber cement. I brought the paper close to my face and sniffed at it.

He asked me what I was doing. "Sometimes you can tell by the smell when the thing was prepared. The solvent evaporates, so if you can still smell it it's recent."

"Does it matter when they prepared the note?"

"Probably not. Force of habit, I guess." I'd been sheriff for three terms before Wallace Hines rode into office on the governor's coattails. Old habits die hard.

"I just can't understand it," he was saying. "She knew not to

206

get in a stranger's car. I don't know how many times I told her "

"I used to talk about that at school assemblies, Anse. 'Don't go with strangers. Don't accept food or candy from people you don't know. Cross at corners. Don't ever play in an old icebox.' Lord, all the things you have to tell them."

"I can't understand it."

"How old is Bethie?" I'd almost said *was*, caught myself in time. That would have crushed him. The idea that she might already be dead was one neither of us would voice. It hung in the room like a silent third party to the conversation.

"She's nine. Ten in August. Lou, she's all I've got in the world, all that's left to me of Paula. Lou, I've got to get her back."

I looked at the note again. "Says a quarter of a million dollars," I said.

"I know."

"Have you got it?"

"I can raise it. I'll go talk to Jim McVeigh at the bank tomorrow. He doesn't have to know what I need it for. I've borrowed large sums in cash before on a signature loan, for a real estate deal or something like that. He won't ask too many questions."

"Says old bills, out of sequence. Nothing larger than a twenty. He'll fill an order like that and think it's for real estate?"

He poured himself another drink. I still hadn't touched mine. "Maybe he'll figure it out," he allowed. "He still won't ask questions. And he won't carry tales, either."

"Well, you're a good customer down there. And a major stockholder, aren't you?"

"I have some shares, yes."

I looked at the note, then at him. "Says no police and no FBI," I said. "What do you think about that?"

"That's what I was going to ask you."

"Well, you might want to call Wally Hines. They tell me he's the sheriff."

"You don't think much of Hines."

"Not a whole lot," I admitted, "but I'm prejudiced on the subject. He doesn't run the department the way I did. Well, I didn't do things the way my predecessor did, either. Old Bill

Hurley. He probably didn't think much of me, old Hurley."

"Should I call Hines?"

"I wouldn't. It says here they'll kill her if you do. I don't know that they're watching the house, but it wouldn't be hard for them to know if the sheriff's office came in on the operation." I shrugged. "I don't know what Hines could do, to tell you the truth. You want to pay the ransom?"

"Of course I do."

"Hines could maybe set up a stakeout, catch the kidnapper when he picks up the ransom. But they generally don't release the victim until after they get away clean with the ransom." If ever, I thought. "Now as far as the FBI is concerned, they know their job. They can look at the note and figure out what newspaper the words came from, where the paper was purchased, the envelope, all of that. They'll dust for fingerprints and find mine and yours, but I don't guess the kidnapper's were on here in the first place. What you might want to do, you might want to call the Bureau as soon as you get Bethie back. They've got the machinery and the know-how to nail those boys afterward."

"But you wouldn't call them until then?"

"I wouldn't," I said. "Not that I'm going to tell you what to do or not to do, but I wouldn't do it myself. Not if it were my little girl."

We talked about some things. He poured another drink and I finally got around to sipping at the one he'd poured me when I first walked in. We'd been in that same room three years ago, drinking the same brand of whiskey. He'd managed to hold himself together through Paula's funeral, and after everybody else cleared out and Bethie was asleep he and I settled in with a couple of bottles. Tonight I would take it easy on the booze, but that night three years ago I'd matched him drink for drink.

Out of the blue he said, "She could have been, you know." I missed the connection. "Could have been your little girl," he explained. "Bethie could have. If you'd have married Paula."

"If your grandmother had wheels she'd be a tea cart."

"'But she'd still be your grandmother.' Isn't that what we used to say? You could have married Paula."

208

"She had too much sense for that." Though the cards might have played that way, if Anson Polland hadn't come along. Now Paula was three years dead, dead of anaphylactic shock from a bee sting, if you can believe it. And the woman I'd married, and a far cry from Paula she was, had left me and gone to California. I heard someone say that the Lord took the United States by the state of Maine and lifted, so that everything loose wound up in Southern California. Well, she was and she did, and now Anse and I were a couple of solitary birds going long in the tooth. Take away thirty pounds and a few million dollars and a nine-year-old girl with freckles and you'd be hard pressed to tell us apart.

Take away a nine-year-old girl with freckles. Somebody'd done just that.

"You'll see me through this," he said. "Won't you, Lou?"

"If it's what you want."

"I wish to hell you were still sheriff. The voters of this county never had any sense."

"Maybe it's better that I'm not. This way I'm just a private citizen, nobody for the kidnappers to get excited about."

"I want you to work for me after this is over."

"Well, now."

"We can work out the details later. By God, I should have hired you the minute the election results came in. I figured we knew each other too well, we'd been through too much together. But you can do better working for me than you're doing now, and I can use you, I know I can. We'll talk about it later."

"We'll see."

"Lou, we'll get her back, won't we?"

"Sure we will, Anse. Of course we will."


Well, you have to go through the motions. There was no phone call that night. If the victim's alive they generally make a call and let you hear their voice. On tape, maybe, but reading that day's newspaper so you can place the recording in time. Any proof they can give you that the person's alive makes it that much more certain you'll pay the ransom.

Of course nothing's hard and fast. Kidnapping's an amateur crime and every fool who tries it has to make up his own rules. So it didn't necessarily prove anything that there was no call.

I hung around, waiting it out with him. He hit the bourbon pretty hard but he was always a man who could take on a heavy load without showing it much. Somewhere along the way I went into the kitchen and made a pot of coffee.

A little past midnight I said, "I don't guess there's going to be a call tonight, Anse. I'm gonna head for home."

He wanted me to stay over. He had reasons—in case there was a call in the middle of the night, in case something called for action. I told him he had my number and he could call me at any hour. What we both knew is his real reason was he didn't want to be alone there, and I thought about staying with him and decided I didn't want to. The hours were just taking too long to go by, and I didn't figure I'd get a good night's sleep under his roof.

I drove right on home. I kept it under the speed limit because I didn't want one of Wally Hines's eager beavers coming up behind me with the siren wailing. They'll do that now. We hardly ever gave out tickets to local people when I was running the show, just a warning and a soft one at that. We saved the tickets for the leadfoot tourists. Well, another man's apt to have his own way of doing things.

In my own house I popped a beer and ate my leftover hamburger. It was cold with the grease congealed on it but I was hungry enough to get it down. I could have had something out of Anse's refrigerator but I hadn't been hungry while I was there.

I sat in a chair and put on Johnny Carson but didn't even try to pay attention. I thought how little Bethie was dead and buried somewhere that nobody would likely ever find her. Because that was the way it read, even if it wasn't what Anse and I dared to say to each other. I sat there and thought how Paula was dead of a bee sting and my wife was on the other side of the continent and now Bethie. Thoughts swirled around in my head like water going down a bathtub drain.

I was up a long while. The television was still on when they were playing the "Star-Spangled Banner," and I might as well have been watching programs in Japanese for all the sense they made to me.

Somewhere down the line I went to bed.

I was eating a sweet roll and drinking a cup of coffee when he called. There'd been a phone call just moments earlier from the kidnapper, he told me, his voice hoarse with the strain of it all.

"He whispered. I was half asleep, I could barely make out what he was saying. I was afraid to ask him to repeat anything. I was just afraid, Lou."

"You get everything?"

"I think so. I have to buy a special suitcase, I have to pack it a certain way and chuck it into a culvert at a certain time." He mentioned some of the specifics. I was only half listening. Then he said, "I asked them to let me talk to Bethie."

"And?"

"It was as if he didn't even hear me. He just went on telling me things, and I asked him again and he hung up."

She was dead and in the ground, I thought.

I said, "He probably made the call from a pay phone. Most likely they're keeping her at a farmhouse somewhere and he wouldn't want to chance a trace on the call. He wouldn't have her along to let her talk, he wouldn't want to take the chance. And he'd speed up the conversation to keep it from being traced at all."

"I thought of that, Lou. I just wished I could have heard her voice."

He'd never hear her voice again, I thought. My mind filled with an image of a child's broken body on a patch of ground, and a big man a few yards from her, holding a shovel, digging. I blinked my eyes, trying to chase the image, but it just went and hovered there on the edge of thought.

"You'll hear it soon enough," I said. "You'll have her back soon."

"Can you come over, Lou?"

"Hell, I'm on my way."

I poured what was left of my coffee down the sink. I took the sweet roll with me, ate it on the way to the car. The sun was up but there was no warmth in it yet.

In the picture I'd had, with the child's corpse and the man digging, a light rain had been falling. But there'd been no rain yesterday and it didn't look likely today. A man's mind'll do tricky things, fill in details on its own. A scene like that, gloomy and all, it seems like there ought to be rain. So the mind just sketches it in.

On the way to the bank he said, "Lou, I want to hire you."

"Well, I don't know," I said. "I guess we can talk about it after Bethie's back and all this is over, but I'm not even sure I want to stay around town, Anse. I've been talking with some people down in Florida and there might be something for me down there."

"I can do better for you than some crackers down in Florida," he said gruffly. "But I'm not talking about that, I'm talking about now. I want to hire you to help me get Bethie back."

I shook my head. "You can't pay me for that, Anson."

"Why the hell not?"

"Because I won't take the money. Did you even think I would?"

"No. I guess I just wish you would. I'm going to have to lean on you some, Lou. It seems a lot to ask as a favor."

"It's not such a much," I said. "All I'll be doing is standing alongside you and backing you up." Going through the motions with you, I thought.

I waited in the car while he went into the bank. I might have played the radio but he'd taken the keys with him. Force of habit, I guess. I just sat and waited.

He didn't have the money when he came out. "Jim has to make a call or two to get that much cash together," he explained. "It'll be ready by two this afternoon."

"Did he want to know what it was for?"

"I told him I had a chance to purchase an Impressionist paint-

GOING THROUGH THE MOTIONS

ing from a collector who'd had financial reverses. The painting's provenance was clear but the sale had to be a secret and the payment had to be in cash for tax purposes."

"That's a better story than a real estate deal."

He managed a smile. "It seemed more imaginative. He didn't question it. We'd better buy that suitcase."

We parked in front of a luggage and leather goods store on Grandview Avenue. I remembered they'd had a holdup there while I was sheriff. The proprietor had been shot in the shoulder but had recovered well enough. I went in with him and Anson bought a plaid canvas suitcase. The whisperer had described the bag very precisely.

"He's a fussy son of a bitch," I said. "Maybe he's got an outfit he wants it to match."

Anse paid cash for the bag. On the drive back to his house I said, "What you were saying yesterday, Anse, that Bethie could have been mine. She's spit and image of you. You'd hardly guess she was Paula's child."

"She has her mother's softness, though."

A child's crumpled body, a man turning shovelfuls of earth, a light rain falling. I kept putting the rain into that picture. A mind's a damn stubborn thing.

"Maybe she does," I said. "But one look at her and you know she's her father's daughter."

His hands tightened on the steering wheel. I pictured Paula in my mind, and then Bethie. Then my own wife, for some reason, but it was a little harder to bring her image into focus.

Until it was time to go to the bank we sat around waiting for the phone to ring. The whisperer had told Anse there wouldn't be any more calls, but what guarantee was that?

He mostly talked about Paula, maybe to keep from talking about Bethie. It bothered me some, the turn the conversation was taking, but I don't guess I let it show.

When the phone finally did ring it was McVeigh at the bank, saying the money was ready. Anse took the new plaid suitcase and got in his car, and I followed him down there in my own car. He parked in the bank's lot. I found a spot on the street. It was a little close to a fireplug, but I was behind the wheel with the motor running and didn't figure I had much to worry about from Wally's boys in blue.

He was in the bank a long time. I kept looking at my watch and every few hours another minute would pass. Then he came out of the bank's front door and the suitcase looked heavier than when he'd gone in there. He came straight to the car and went around to the back. I'd left the trunk unlocked and he tossed the suitcase inside and slammed it shut.

He got in beside me and I drove. "I feel like a bank robber," he said. "I come out with the money and you've got the motor running."

My car picked that moment to backfire. "Some getaway car," I said.

I kept an eye on the rearview mirror. I'd suggested taking my car just in case anybody was watching him. McVeigh might have acted on suspicions, I'd told Anse, and might say something to law enforcement people without saying anything to us. It wouldn't do to be tailed to the overpass where the exchange was supposed to take place. If the kidnappers spotted a tail they might panic and kill Bethie.

Of course I didn't believe for a moment she was still alive. But you play these things by the book. What else can you do?

No one was following us. I cut the engine when we got to the designated spot. It was an overpass, and a good spot for a drop. A person could be waiting below, hidden from view, and he could pick up the suitcase and get out of there on foot and nobody up above could do anything about it.

The engine coughed and coughed and sputtered and finally cut out. Anse told me I ought to get it fixed. I didn't bother saying that nobody seemed to be able to fix it. "Just sit here," I told him. "I'll take care of it."

I got out of the car, went around to the trunk. He was watching as I carried the plaid suitcase and sent it sailing over the rail. I heard the car door open, and then he was standing beside me, trying to see where it had landed. I pointed to the spot but he couldn't see it, and I'm not sure there was anything to see.

"I can't look down from heights," he said.

"Nothing to look at anyway."

We got back in the car. I dropped him at the bank, and on the way there he asked if the kidnappers would keep their end of the bargain. "They said she'd be delivered to the house within the next four hours," he said. "But would they take the chance of delivering her to the house?"

"Probably not," I told him. "Easiest thing would be to drive her into the middle of one town or another and just let her out of the car. Somebody'll find her and call you right off. Bethie knows her phone number, doesn't she?"

"Of course she does."

"Best thing is for you to be at home and wait for a call."

"You'll come over, Lou, won't you?"

I said I would. He went to get his car from the lot and I drove to my house to check the mail. It didn't take me too long to get to his place, and we sat around waiting for a call I knew would never come.

Because it was pretty clear somebody local had taken her. An out-of-towner wouldn't have known what a perfect spot that overpass was for dropping a suitcase of ransom money. An out-of-towner wouldn't have sent Anse to a specific luggage shop to buy a specific suitcase. An out-of-towner probably wouldn't have known how to spot Bethie Pollard in the first place.

And a local person wouldn't dare leave her alive, because she was old enough and bright enough to tell people who had taken her. It stood to reason that she'd been killed right away, as soon as she'd been snatched, and that her corpse had been covered with fresh earth before the ransom note had been delivered to Anson's mailbox.

After I don't know how long he said, "I don't like it, Lou. We should have heard something by now."

"Could be they're playing it cagey."

"What do you mean?"

"Could be they're watching that dropped suitcase, waiting to make sure it's not staked out."

He started. "Staked out?"

"Well, say you'd gone and alerted the Bureau. What they might have done is staked out the area of the drop and just watched and waited to see who picked up the suitcase. Now a kidnapper might decide to play it just as cagey his own self. Maybe they'll wait twenty-four hours before they make their move."

"God."

"Or maybe they picked it up before it so much as bounced, say, but they want to hold onto Bethie long enough to be sure the bills aren't in sequence and there's no electronic bug in the suitcase."

"Or maybe they're not going to release her, Lou."

"You don't want to think about that, Anse."

"No," he said. "I don't want to think about it."

He started in on the bourbon then, and I was relieved to see him do it. I figured he needed it. To tell the truth, I had a thirst for it myself right about then. The plain fact is that sitting and waiting is the hardest thing I know about, especially when you're waiting for something that's not going to happen.

I was about ready to make an excuse and go on home when the doorbell rang. "Maybe that's her now," he said. "Maybe they waited until dark." But there was a hollow tone in his voice, as if to say he didn't believe it himself.

"I'll get it," I told him. "You stay where you are."

There were two men at the door. They were almost my height, dressed alike in business suits, and holding guns, nasty little black things. First thought I had was they were robbers, and what crossed my mind was how bad Anse's luck had turned.

Then one of them said, "FBI," and showed me an ID I didn't have time to read. "Let's go inside," he said, and we did.

Anse had a glass in his hand. His face didn't look a whole lot different from before. If he was surprised he didn't much show it.

One of them said, "Mr. Pollard? We kept the drop site under

careful observation for three full hours. In that time no one approached the suitcase. The only persons entering the culvert were two boys approximately ten years old, and they never went near the suitcase."

"Ten years old," Anse said.

"After three hours Agent Boudreau and I went down into the culvert and examined the suitcase. The only contents were dummy packages like this one." He showed a banded stack of bills, then riffled it to reveal that only the top and bottom were currency. The rest of the stack consisted of newspaper cut the size of bills.

"I guess your stakeout wasn't such a much," I said. "Anse, why didn't you tell me you decided to call the Bureau after all?"

"Jim McVeigh called them," he said. "They were there when I went to get the money. I didn't know anything about it until then."

"Well, either we beat 'em to the drop site or they don't know much about staking a place out. You get people who aren't local and it's easy for them to make a mistake, I guess. The kidnappers just went and switched suitcases on you. You saw a suitcase still lying in the weeds and you figured nobody'd come by yet, but it looks like you were wrong." I took a breath and let it out slow. "Maybe they saw you there after they told Anse not to go to the cops. Maybe that's why Bethie's not home yet."

"That's not why," one of them said. Boudreau, I guess his name was. "We were there to see you fling that case over the railing. I had it under observation through high-powered field glasses from the moment it landed and I didn't take my eyes off it until we went and had a look at it."

Must have been tiring, I thought, staring through binoculars for three full hours.

"Nobody touched the suitcase," the other one said. "There was a rip in the side from when it landed. It was the same suitcase."

"That proves a lot, a rip in the side of a suitcase."

"There was a switch," Boudreau said. "You made it. You had a second suitcase in the trunk of your car, underneath the blankets

217

and junk you carry around. Mr. Pollard here put the suitcase full of money in your trunk. Then you got the other case out of the trunk and threw it over the side."

"Her father taught her not to go with strangers," the other said. I never did get his name. "But you weren't a stranger, were you? You were a friend of the family. The sheriff, the man who lectured on safety procedures. She got in your car without a second thought, didn't she?"

"Anse," I said, "tell them they're crazy, will you?"

He didn't say anything.

Boudreau said, "We found the money, Mr. Pollard. That's what took so long. We wanted to find it before confronting him. He'd taken up some floorboards and stashed the money under them, still in the suitcase it was packed in. We didn't turn up any evidence of your daughter's presence. He may never have taken her anywhere near his house."

"This is all crazy," I said, but it was as if they didn't hear me.

"We think he killed her immediately upon picking her up," Boudreau went on. "He'd have to do that. She knew him, after all. His only chance to get away with it lay in murdering her."

My mind filled with that picture again. Bethie's crumpled body lying on the ground in that patch of woods the other side of Little Cross Creek. And a big man turning the damp earth with a spade. I could feel a soreness in my shoulders from the digging.

I should have dug that hole the day before. Having to do it with Bethie lying there, that was a misery. Better by far to have it dug ahead of time and just drop her in and shovel on the lid, but you can't plan everything right.

Not that I ever had much chance of getting away with it, now that I looked at it straight on. I'd had this picture of myself down in the Florida sun with more money than God's rich uncle, but I don't guess I ever really thought it would happen that way. I suppose all I wanted was to take a few things away from Anson Pollard.

I sort of tuned out for a while there. Then one of them—I'm not even sure which one—was reading me my rights. I just stood there, not looking at anybody, least of all at Anse. And not listening too close to what they were saying.

Then they were asking me where the body was, and talking about checking the stores to find out when I'd bought the duplicate suitcase, and asking other questions that would build the case against me. I sort of pulled myself together and said that somebody was evidently trying real hard to frame me and I couldn't understand why but in the meantime I wasn't going to answer any questions without a lawyer present.

Not that I expected it would do me much good. But you have to make an effort, you have to play the hand out. What else can you do? You go through the motions, that's all.

# THIS CRAZY BUSINESS OF OURS

THE ELEVATOR, SWIFT and silent as a garotte, whisked the young man eighteen stories skyward to Wilson Colliard's penthouse. The doors opened to reveal Colliard himself. He wore a cashmere smoking jacket the color of vintage port. His flannel slacks and broadcloth shirt were a matching oyster white. They could have been chosen to match his hair, which had been expensively barbered in a leonine mane. His eyes, beneath sharply defined white brows, were as blue and as bottomless as the Caribbean, upon the shores of which he had acquired his radiant tan. He wore doeskin slippers upon his small feet and a smile upon his thinnish lips, and in his right hand he held an automatic pistol of German origin, the precise manufacturer and calibre of which need not concern us.

"My abject apologies," Colliard said. "Of course you're Michael Haig. I regret the gun, Mr. Haig, even as I regret the necessity for it. It's inconsistent greeting a guest with gun in hand and bidding him welcome, but I assure you that you are welcome indeed. Come in, come in. Ah, yes." The doors swept silently shut behind Haig. "This thing," Colliard said distastefully, looking down at the gun in his hand. "But of course you understand."

"Of course, Mr. Colliard."

"This crazy business of ours. Always the chance, isn't there, that you might turn out to be other than the admiring youngster you're purported to be. And surely there's a tradition of that sort of thing, isn't there? Just look at the Old West. Young gunfighter out to make a name for himself, so he goes up against the old gunfighter. Quickest way to acquire a reputation, isn't it? Why, it's a veritable cliché in the world of Western movies, and I daresay they do the same thing in gangster films and who knows what else. Now I don't for the moment think that's your game, you see, but I've learned over the years never to take an unnecessary chance. And I've learned that most chances *are* unnecessary. So if you don't mind a frisk—"

"Of course not."

"You'll have to assume an undignified posture, I'm afraid. Over that way, if you don't mind. Now reach forward with both hands and touch the wall. Excellent. Now walk backwards a step and another step, that's right, very good, yes. You'll hardly make any abrupt moves now, will you? Undignified, as I said, but utilitarian beyond doubt."

The old man's hand moved expertly over the young man's body, patting and brushing here and there, making quite certain that no weapon was concealed beneath the dark pinstripe suit, no gun wedged under the waistband of the trousers, no knife strapped to calf or forearm. The search was quick but quite thorough, and at its conclusion Wilson Colliard sighed with satisfaction and returned his own weapon to a shoulder holster where it reposed without marring in the least the smooth lines of the smoking jacket. "There we are," he said. "Once again, my apologies. Now all that's out of the way and I have the opportunity to make you welcome. I have a very nice cocktail sherry which I think you might like. It's bone dry with a very nutty taste to it. Or perhaps you might care for something stronger?"

"The sherry sounds fine."

Colliard led his guest through rooms furnished as impeccably as he himself was dressed. He seated Michael Haig in one of a pair of green leather tub chairs on opposite sides of a small marble cocktail table. While he set about filling two glasses from a cut-glass decanter, the younger man gazed out the window.

222

"Quite a view," he said.

"Central Park does look best when you're a good ways above it. But then so many things do. It's a great pleasure for me, sitting at this window."

"I can imagine."

"You can see for miles on a clear day. Pity there aren't more of them. When I was your age the air was clearer, but then at your age I could never have afforded an apartment anything like this one." The older man took a chair for himself, placed the two glasses of sherry on the table. "Well, well," he said. "So you're Michael Haig. The most promising young assassin in a great many years."

"You honor me."

"I merely echo what I've been given to understand. Your reputation precedes you."

"If I have a reputation, I'm sure it's a modest one. But you, sir. You're a legend."

"That union leader was one of yours, wasn't he? Head of the rubber workers or whatever he was? Nice bit of business the way you managed that decoy operation. And then you had to shoot downhill at a moving target. Very interesting the way you put all of that together."

Haig bared his bright white teeth in a smile that gave his otherwise unremarkable face a foxlike cast. "I patterned that piece of work on a job that went down twenty years ago. An Ecuadorian minister of foreign affairs, I think it was."

"Ah."

"One of yours, I think."

"Ah."

"Imitation, I assure you, is definitely the sincerest form of flattery in this case. If I do have a reputation, sir, I owe not a little of it to you."

"How kind of you to say so," Colliard said. His fingers curled around the stem of his glass. "The occasion would seem to call for a toast, but what sort of toast? No point in honoring the memory of those we've put in the ground. They're dead and gone. I never think about them. I've found it's best not to."

"I agree."

"We could drink to reputations and to legends."

"Fine."

"Or we could just drink to the line of work we're in. It's a crazy business, Lord knows, but it has its points."

They raised their glasses and drank.

"When I was young," Colliard was saying, "I drank whiskey on occasion. A highball or two in the evening, say. And I often had a martini before dinner. Not when I was working, of course. I've never had alcohol in any form when I was on a job. But between jobs I'd have spirits now and then. But I stopped that altogether."

"Why was that?"

"I decided that they are damaging. I'm not talking about what they might do to one's liver so much as what they do to one's brain. I think they dull one's edge like a file drawn across a knife blade. Wine's another matter entirely. In moderation, of course."

"Of course."

"But I'm rambling, Michael. You don't want to hear all of this. I've been talking for an hour now."

"And I've been hanging on every word, sir. This is the sort of thing I want to hear."

"You're just taking this all in and filing it all away, aren't you?"

"Yes, I am," Haig admitted. "Everything you can tell me about the way you operate and... and even the way you live, your whole style. If there were fan clubs in our profession I guess I'd be the president of yours."

"You flatter me."

"It's not flattery, sir. And it's not entirely unselfish, believe me." Haig lowered his eyes. He had long lashes, the older man noted, and his hands, one of them now in repose upon the little marble table, were possessed of a certain sensitivity. The fellow had no flair, but then he was young, unfinished. He himself had been relatively undefined at that age.

"I know I can learn from you," Michael Haig went on. "I've already learned a good deal from you, you know. Oh, it's hard to separate hard fact from legend, but I've picked up a lot from what I've heard about your career. Even though we've never met before, what I've known about you has helped form my whole attitude toward our profession."

"Really."

"Yes. Some months ago I had a problem, or at least it seemed like a problem to me. The, uh, the target was a woman."

"The client's wife?"

"Yes. You don't know the case?"

Colliard smiled, shook his head. "It's almost always the client's wife," he said. "But do continue. I gather this was the first time you had a woman for a target?"

"Yes, it was."

"And I gather further that it bothered you?"

Haig frowned at the question. "I *think* it bothered me," he said. "The idea of it seemed to bother me. I certainly wasn't afraid that I couldn't do it. If you pull a trigger, why should it matter to you what's standing in front of you? But, oh, I had difficulty with self-image, I guess you might say. It's one thing putting the touch to some powerful man who ought to be able to look out for himself and another thing entirely doing the same to a defenseless woman."

"The weaker sex," Colliard murmured.

"But then I asked myself, 'What about Wilson Colliard? How would he feel about a situation like this?' And that straightened me out, because I knew you'd killed women in your career, and I suppose what I told myself was that if it was all right for you to do, well, it was all right for me."

"And you went ahead and fulfilled the assignment."

"Yes."

"With no difficulty?"

"None." Michael Haig smiled, and Colliard felt there was pride in the smile. Proud as a puppy, he thought, and every bit as eager. "I killed her with a knife," he said. "Made it look like a burglary."

"And it felt no different than if she had been a man?"

"No different at all. There was that thrilling moment when I

225

did it, that sensation that's always there, but it was no different from the way it always was."

Then a shadow flickered on the younger's man face, and Colliard, amused, left him wondering for a moment before rescuing him. "Yes," he said, "that little shiver of delight and triumph and something more. It's always there for me, too, Michael. In case you were wondering."

"I was, sir."

"The best people always get a thrill out of it, Michael. We don't do it for the thrill, of course. We do it for the money. But there's a touch of excitement in the act and it would be puerile to deny it. Don't bother worrying about it."

"I don't know that I was worried, exactly. But thank you, sir."

Colliard smiled. Now of whom did this young man remind him? The eagerness, the sincerity—God, the almost painful sincerity. It all held a sense of recognition, but recognition of whom? His own younger self? The son he had never sired? Those were the standard echoes one got, weren't they?

Yet he didn't really think he'd been very much like Michael Haig in his own younger days, not really. Had there been a veteran hand at the game whom he'd idolized? Certainly not. Could he ever, at his most callow, have been capable of playing the role Haig was playing in this conversation? No. God, no.

Nor would he have wanted a son like this youth, or indeed any sort of son at all. Women were a pleasure, certainly, like good food and good wine, like anything beautiful and luxurious and costly. But they were to be enjoyed and discarded. One didn't want to *own* one, and one surely wouldn't care to breed with them, to produce offspring, to litter the landscape with Xerox copies of oneself.

And yet he could not deny that he was enjoying this afternoon. The younger man's company was refreshing in its way, there was no denying that, and the idolatry he provided was pleasant food for the ego.

And it was not as if he had any pressing engagements.

"So you'd like to hear me talk about...what? My life and times? My distinguished career?"

"I'd like that very much."

"Anecdotes and bits of advice? The perspective gained through years at the top of this crazy business? All that sort of thing?"

"All of that. And anything else you'd care to tell me."

Wilson Colliard considered for a moment, then rose to his feet. "I'm going to smoke a cigar," he announced. "I allow myself one or two a day. They're Havanas, not terribly hard to get if you know someone. I acquired a taste for them, oh, it must be twenty years ago. I did a job of work down there, you see. But I suppose you know the story."

"I don't, and I'd love to hear it."

"Perhaps you will. Perhaps you will, Michael. But first may I bring a cigar for you?"

Michael Haig accepted the cigar. Somehow this did not surprise Wilson Colliard in the least.

As the afternoon wore on, Colliard found himself increasingly at ease in the role of reminiscent sage. Never before had he trotted out his memories like this for the entertainment and education of another. Oh, in recent years he had become increasingly inclined to sit at this window and look back over the years, but this had heretofore been a silent and solitary pursuit. It was quite a different matter to be giving voice to one's memories and to have another person on hand, worshipful and attentive, to utter appropriate syllables and draw out one's own recollections. Why, he was telling young Haig things he hadn't even bothered to think about in years, and in so doing he was making mental connections and developing perceptions he'd never had before.

With the cigars extinguished and fresh glasses of sherry poured, Colliard leaned back and said, "Now how far are we with our Assassin's Credo, Michael? Point the first—minimize risk. And point the second—seize the moment, strike while the iron is hot, all those banalities. Is that all we've established so far? It's certainly taken me a great many words to hammer out those two points. You know, I think the third principle is more important than either of them."

"And what is that, sir?"

"Look to your reputation."

"Ah."

"Reputation," Colliard said. "It's all one has going for oneself in this business, Michael. We have no bankable assets, you and I. We have only our reputations. And what reputations we possess are underground matters. We can't hire public relations men or press agents to give us standing. We have to depend wholly upon word of mouth. We must make ourselves known to those who might be inclined to engage our services, and they have to be supremely confident of our skill, our reliability, our discretion."

"Yes."

"We are paid in advance, Michael. Our clients must be able to take it for granted that once a fee has been passed to us the target is as good as dead. And, because the client himself is a party to criminal homicide, he must be assured that whatever fate befalls the assassin, the client will not be publicly involved. Skill, reliability, discretion. Reputation, Michael. It's everything to us."

They were silent for a moment. Wilson Colliard aimed his eyes out the window at the expanse of green far below. But his gaze was not focused on the park. He was looking off into the middle distance, seeing across time.

Tentatively Haig said, "I suppose if a man does good work, sooner or later he develops a good reputation."

"Sooner or later."

"You make it sound as though there's a better way to go about it."

"Oh, there is," Colliard agreed. "Sometimes circumstances are such that you can be your own advertising man, your own press agent, your own public relations bureau. Now and then you will find yourself with the opportunity to act with a certain flair that captures the public imagination so dramatically, so vividly, that it will go on to serve as the very cornerstone of your professional reputation for the remainder of your life. When such a chance comes to you, Michael, you have to take hold of it."

"I think—"

"Yes?"

"I think I know the case you mean, sir."

"It's quite possible that you do."

"I was wondering if you would mention it. I almost brought it up myself. I don't know how many times I've heard the story. It's at the very heart of the legend of Wilson Colliard."

"Indeed. 'The Legend of Wilson Colliard.'"

"But you *are* a legend, sir. And the story—I hope you'll tell me just what did and didn't happen. I've heard several versions and it's hard to know where the truth leaves off."

Colliard smiled indulgently. "Suppose you tell me what you've heard. If I'm to tell you the truth it wouldn't hurt me to know first how the legend goes. If the legend's better than the truth I'd probably be well advised to leave well enough alone."

"Well, from what I've heard, you accepted two assignments at about the same time. A businessman in New Jersey, I believe in Camden—"

"Trenton, actually," Colliard said. "Not that it makes any substantial difference. Neither city has ever been possessed of anything you might be inclined to call charm. Of course, this was some time ago and the urban blight was less pronounced then, but even so, both Trenton and Camden were towns no one ever went to without a good reason. My client manufactured bicycle tires. The business is long gone now, of course. I believe some bicycle manufacturer bought up the firm and absorbed it. My client's name—well, names don't really matter, do they?"

"And he wanted you to murder his wife."

"Indeed he did. Men so often do. If they want their mistresses killed they're apt to perform the deed on their own, but they call a professional when they want an instant divorce."

"And before you could conclude the assignment, a woman hired you to kill her husband."

"It's an interesting thing," Colliard said. "When a woman wants her husband done away with she's very much apt to hire help, but what's odd is she more often than not engages the services of a rank amateur. The newspapers are full of that sort of thing. Typically the woman works it all out with her lover, who's likely to be some rough-diamond type out of a James M.

229

Cain novel. And the paramour knows someone who went to jail once for passing bad checks, and the bad-check artist knows somebody who served time for assault, and ultimately an exceedingly sloppy operation is mounted, and either the woman is swindled out of a couple of thousand dollars by a man who hasn't the slightest intention of killing anybody or else the husband is indeed killed and the police have everybody in custody before the body's had time to go cold. Interesting how often women operate in that fashion."

"Well, after you'd accepted both assignments, and of course you'd been paid in front by both clients—"

"A matter of personal policy."

"—Then you discovered that your two clients were husband and wife, and each had engaged you to murder the other."

"And what did I do?"

"According to what I've heard, the husband hired you first, and so the first thing you did was murder the wife."

Wilson Colliard nodded, smiling gently at a memory. "The husband had to go to Chicago on business. We scheduled the affair for that time. I called him at his hotel there to make very certain that he was indeed out of town. Then I went to his home. He and his wife shared an enormous Victorian pile of a house in the heart of Trenton. It was still a decent neighborhood at the time. By now the old house has probably been partitioned into a half dozen apartments. But that's off the point, isn't it? I went there and did what I was supposed to do. Made it look like a burglary, left some signs of forced entry, overturned dresser drawers and added a few professional flourishes. I killed the bitch with a knife from her very own kitchen. I thought that was a nice touch."

"And of course the police figured it as a burglary."

"Of course they did. A burglary for gain followed by a murder on impulse. There was never the slightest suspicion of my client. He was rid of a wife and home free."

The younger man was breathing more quickly and his face was slightly flushed. "And then," he said.

"Yes?"

230

"Then you killed him."

"Indeed. Why would I do a thing like that?"

"Because the wife had hired you and once you accepted a fee the target was as good as dead. Of course you didn't have to kill the man. The only person who knew you'd been hired to kill him was the woman who hired you, and she was already dead. You could have kept the fee she paid you and done nothing to earn it and no one would ever have known the difference. But you were true to the ethics of the profession, true to your own personal ethics, and so you killed him all the same."

"I waited almost a month," Colliard said. "I didn't want his death to look like murder, and I didn't even want it to take place in Trenton, so I waited until he made another trip, this time a short one to Philadelphia. I followed him there, stole a car off the street, dogged his footsteps until they led off a curb, and then performed vehicular homicide. He turned in my direction just as the car was about to remove him from this life, and do you know, I can still see the expression on his face. I don't know whether he recognized my face through the windshield or whether he simply recognized that he was about to be struck down and killed. Facial expressions at such times are distressingly ambiguous, you see. Be that as it may, the car did the job and I had no trouble making a clean getaway."

"So it really happened that way," Haig said, eyes shining. "And then your reputation was made. Everyone knew that when Colliard took an assignment the target was a dead man."

"Yes. They all knew."

"So the legend is true."

"'The Legend of Wilson Colliard,'" Colliard intoned. "It is an effective legend, isn't it? And now do you see what I meant when I said a man can see to the growth of his own reputation?"

"I certainly do. But isn't it really just a question of being true to your professional standards and ethics? Oh, I can see how you must have functioned as your own press agent and all that, because you would have had to be the source of the legend. Only the man and the woman knew they'd hired you, and even they didn't know that you were hired by both of them, so the story could never have gotten out if you hadn't done something to spread it in the first place. But as far as what you did, well, that was a matter of behaving professionally."

"Do you think so?" Colliard raised his prominent white eyebrows. "Don't you think it might have been more professional to keep the woman's fee and not kill her husband? After all, she was in the grave and was thus certain to remain silent. The only reason to kill her husband was for publicity purposes. Otherwise, Michael, I'd have been better advised to adhere to the first principle of minimizing risk. But by performing the second murder I assured myself of a reputation."

"Of course," Haig said. "You're absolutely right. I should have realized that."

Colliard made a tent of his fingertips. "Ah, Michael," he said, "there's more to it then you could possibly realize. It's interesting that the legend is incomplete. You know, I think this is really one of those rare occasions wherein the truth is more dramatic than the legend."

"How do you mean?"

"This crazy business of ours. Wheels within wheels, complexities underlying complexities. I wonder, Michael, if you have a sufficiently Byzantine mind to distinguish yourself in your chosen profession."

"I don't understand."

"The woman never hired me."

Michael Haig stared.

"Never hired me, never knew of my existence as far as I know. She and I didn't set eyes one upon the other until the night I stuck a carbon-steel Sabatier chef's knife between her ribs. For all I know the poor woman adored her husband and never would have harmed him for the world."

"But—"

"So I killed her and went on my way, Michael, and then about a month later I happened to be in Philadelphia for reasons I can't at the moment recall, not that they matter, and whom did I chance to see emerging from Bookbinder's after a presumably satisfying lunch than the Bicycle Tire King of Trenton. Do you know, the mind is capable of extraordinary quantum leaps. All at once I saw the whole thing plain, saw just the shape the entire legend would take. All I had to do was kill the fool and my place in my profession was assured. It was the sort of thing people would talk about forever, and everything they said could only redound to my benefit. I followed him, I stole a car, and—" he spread his hands "—and the rest is history. Or legend, if you prefer."

"That's... that's incredible."

"I saw an opportunity and I grasped it before it could get away."

"You just killed him for—"

"For the benefit that could not help but accrue to my reputation. Killed him without a fee, you might say, but there's no question but that his death paid me more handsomely in the long run than any murder I ever undertook for immediate gain. Overnight I became the standard of the profession. I stood head and shoulders above the competition as far as potential clients were concerned. I had an edge over men with infinitely more distinguished careers, men who had far more years in the business than I. And what gave me this advantage? An elementary hit-and-run killing of a former client, an act that but for the ensuing publicity would have been pointless beyond belief. Remarkable, isn't it?"

"It's better than the legend," Michael Haig said. There was a film of perspiration on his upper lip and he wiped at it with his forefinger. "Better than the legend. If people knew what you actually did—"

"I think it's ever so much better that they don't, Michael. Oh, if I were to write memoirs for posthumous publication it's the sort of material I'd be inclined to include, but I'm not the sort to write my memoirs, I'm afraid. No, I think I'd rather let the legend go on as it stands. It wouldn't do me much good if my public knew that Wilson Colliard was a man who once killed one of his clients for no reason at all. My reputation has been carefully designed to build a client's confidence and that's the sort of revelation that might have the opposite effect entirely."

"I don't know what to say."

"Then don't say anything at all," Colliard advised. "But let me just pour us each one final tot of sherry."

"I've had quite a bit already."

"It's very light stuff," Colliard said. "One more won't hurt you." And, returning with the filled glasses, he added, "We ought to drink to legends. May the truth never interfere with them."

The younger man took a sip. Then, when he saw his host toss off his drink in a single swallow, he imitated his example and drank off the rest of his own sherry. Wilson Colliard nodded, satisfied with the way things had gone. He could scarcely recall a more pleasant afternoon.

"Minimize your risks," he said. "Seize the moment. And look to your professional reputation."

"The three points of the Assassin's Credo," Haig said.

"Three of the four points."

"Oh?" The younger man grinned in anticipation. "You mean there's a fourth point?"

"Oh, yes." Colliard studied him, paying close attention to his guest's eyes. "A fourth point."

"Are you going to tell me what it is?"

"Squash the competition."

"Oh?"

"When it's convenient," Colliard said. "And when it's useful. There's no point doing anything about the bunglers. But when someone turns up who's talented and resourceful and not without a sense of the dramatic, and when you have the opportunity to wipe him out, why, it's just good business to do so. There are only so many really top jobs available every year, you know, and one doesn't want them spread too thin. Of course when you eliminate a competitor you don't noise it around. That sort of thing's kept secret. But there have been eight times over the years when I've had a chance to put the fourth principle into play."

"And you've seized the opportunity?"

"I could hardly do otherwise, could I?" Colliard smiled. "You're number nine, Michael. That last glass of sherry had poison in it, I'm afraid. You can probably feel the numbness spreading. It already shows in your eyes. No, don't even try to get up. You

234

won't be able to accomplish anything. Don't blame yourself. You were doomed from the start, poor boy. I shouldn't have agreed to see you this afternoon if I hadn't decided to, uh, purge you from the ranks."

The younger man's face was a study in horror. Colliard eyed him equably. Already he was beginning to feel that familiar sensation, the excitement, the thrill.

"You were quite good," he said charitably. "For as long as you lasted you were quite good indeed. Otherwise I'd not have bothered with you. Oh, Michael, it's a crazy business, isn't it? Believe me, lad, you're lucky to be getting out of it."

# AND MILES TO GO BEFORE I SLEEP

WHEN THE BULLETS struck, my first thought was that someone had raced up behind me to give me an abrupt shove. An instant later I registered the sound of the gunshots, and then there was fire in my side, burning pain, and the impact had lifted me off my feet and sent me sprawling at the edge of the lawn in front of my house.

I noticed the smell of the grass. Fresh, cut the night before and with the dew still on it.

I can recall fragments of the ambulance ride as if it took place in some dim dream. I worried at the impropriety of running the siren so early in the morning.

They'll wake half the town, I thought.

Another time, I heard one of the white-coated attendants say something about a red blanket. My mind leaped to recall the blanket that lay on my bed when I was a boy almost forty years ago. It was plaid, mostly red with some green in it. Was that what they were talking about?

These bits of awareness came one after another, like fast cuts in a film. There was no sensation of time passing between them.

I was in a hospital room. The operating room, I suppose. I was spread out on a long white table while a masked and green-gowned doctor probed a wound in the left side of my chest. I

237

must have been under anesthetic—there was a mask on my face with a tube connected to it. And I believe my eyes were closed, Nevertheless, I was aware of what was happening, and I could see.

I don't know how to explain this.

There was a sensation I was able to identify as pain, although it didn't actually hurt me. Then I felt as though my side were a bottle and a cork were being drawn from it. It popped free. The doctor held up a misshapen bullet for examination. I watched it fall in slow motion from his forceps, landing with a plinking sound in a metal pan.

"Other's too close to the heart," I heard him say. "Can't get a grip on it. Don't dare touch it, way it's positioned. Kill him if it moves."

*Cut.*

Same place, an indefinite period of time later. A nurse saying, "Oh, God, he's going," and then all of them talking at once.

Then I was out of my body.

It just happened, just like that. One moment I was in my dying body on the table and a moment later I was floating somewhere beneath the ceiling. I could look down and see myself on the table and the doctors and nurses standing around me.

I'm dead, I thought.

I was very busy trying to decide how I felt about it. It didn't hurt. I had always thought it would hurt, that it would be awful. But it wasn't so terrible.

So this is death, I thought.

And it was odd seeing myself, my body, lying there. I thought, you were a good body. I'm all right, I don't need you, but you were a good body.

Then I was gone from that room. There was a rush of light that became brighter and brighter, and I was sucked through a long tunnel at a furious speed, and then I was in a world of light and in the presence of a Being of light.

This is hard to explain.

I don't know if the Being was a man or a woman. Maybe it was both, maybe it changed back and forth. I don't know. He was all in white, and He was light and was surrounded by light.

And in the distance behind Him were my father and my mother and my grandparents. People who had gone before me, and they were holding out their hands to me and beaming at me with faces radiant with light and love.

I went to the Being, I was drawn to Him, and He held out His arm and said, "Behold your life."

And I looked, and I could behold my entire life. I don't know how to say what I saw. It was as if my whole life had happened at once and someone had taken a photograph of it and I was looking at that photograph. I could see in it everything that I remembered in my life and everything that I had forgotten, and it was all happening at once and I was seeing it happen. And I would see something bad that I'd done and think, I'm sorry about that. And I would see something good and be glad about it.

And at the end I woke and had breakfast and left the house to walk to work and a car passed by and a gun came out the window. There were two shots and I fell and the ambulance came and all the rest of it.

And I thought, Who killed me?

The Being said, "You must find out the answer."

I thought, I don't care, it doesn't matter.

He said, "You must go back and find the answer."

I thought, No, I don't want to go back.

All of the brilliant light began to fade. I reached out toward it because I didn't want to go back, I didn't want to be alive again. But it all continued to fade.

Then I was back in my body again.

"We almost lost you," the nurse said. Her smile was professional but the light in her eyes showed she meant it. "Your heart actually stopped on the operating table. You really had us scared there."

"I'm sorry," I said.

She thought that was funny. "The doctor was only able to remove one of the two bullets that were in you. So you've still got a chunk of lead in your chest. He sewed you up and put a drain in the wound, but obviously you won't be able to walk around like that. In fact it's important for you to lie absolutely still or the bullet might shift in position. It's right alongside your heart, you see."

It might shift even if I didn't move, I thought. But she knew better than to tell me that.

"In four or five days we'll have you scheduled for another operation," she went on. "By then the bullet may move of its own accord to a more accessible position. If not, there are surgical techniques that can be employed." She told me some of the extraordinary things surgeons could do. I didn't pay attention.

After she left the room, I rolled back and forth on the bed, shifting my body as jerkily as I could. But the bullet did not change its position in my chest.

I was afraid of that.

I stayed in the hospital that night. No one came to see me during visiting hours, and I thought that was strange. I asked the nurse and was told I was in intensive care and could not have visitors.

I lost control of myself. I shouted that she was crazy. How could I learn who did it if I couldn't see anyone?

"The police will see you as soon as it's allowed," she said. She was terribly earnest. "Believe me," she said, "it's for your own protection. They want to ask you a million questions, naturally, but it would be bad for your health to let you get all excited."

Silly bitch, I thought. And almost put the thought into words.

Then I remembered the picture of my life and the pleasant and unpleasant things I had done and how they all had looked in the picture.

I smiled. "Sorry I lost control," I said. "But if they didn't want me to get excited they shouldn't have given me such a beautiful nurse."

She went out beaming.

I didn't sleep. It did not seem to be necessary.
I lay in bed wondering who had killed me.

My wife? We'd married young, then grown apart. Of course she hadn't shot at me because she'd been in bed asleep when I left the house that morning. But she might have a lover. Or she could have hired someone to pull the trigger for her.

My partner? Monty and I had turned a handful of borrowed capital into a million-dollar business. But I was better than Monty at holding onto money. He spent it, gambled it away, paid it out in divorce settlements. Profits were off lately. Had he been helping himself to funds and cooking the books? And did he then decide to cover his thefts the easy way?

My girl? Peg had a decent apartment, a closet full of clothes. Not a bad deal. But for awhile I'd let her think I'd divorce Julia when the kids were grown, and now she and I both knew better. She'd seemed to adjust to the situation, but had the resentment festered inside her?

My children?

The thought was painful. Mark had gone to work for me after college. The arrangement didn't last long. He'd been too headstrong, while I'd been unwilling to give him the responsibility he wanted. Now he was talking about going into business for himself. But he lacked the capital.

If I died, he'd have all he needed.

Debbie was married and expecting a child. First she'd lived with another young man, one of whom I hadn't approved, and then she'd married Scott, who was hard-working and earnest and ambitious. Was the marriage bad for her, and did she blame me for costing her the other boy? Or did Scott's ambition prompt him to make Debbie an heiress?

These were painful thoughts.

Someone else? But who and why?

Some days ago I'd cut off another motorist at a traffic circle. I remembered the sound of his horn, his face glimpsed in my rearview mirror, red, ferocious. Had he copied down my license plate, determined my address, lain in ambush to gun me down?

It made no sense. But it did not make sense for anyone to kill me.

Julia? Monty? Peg? Mark? Debbie? Scott?

A stranger?

I lay there wondering and did not truly care. Someone had killed me and I was supposed to be dead. But I was not permitted to be dead until I knew the answer to the question.

Maybe the police would find it for me.

They didn't.

I saw two policemen the following day. I was still in intensive care, still denied visitors, but an exception was made for the police. They were very courteous and spoke in hushed voices. They had no leads whatsoever in their investigation and just wanted to know if I could suggest a single possible suspect.

I told them I couldn't.

My nurse turned white as paper.

"You're not supposed to be out of bed! You're not even supposed to move! What do you think you're doing?"

I was up and dressed. There was no pain. As an experiment, I'd been palming the pain pills they issued me every four hours, hiding them in the bedclothes instead of swallowing them. As I'd anticipated, I did not feel any pain.

The area of the wound was numb, as though that part of me had been excised altogether. But nothing hurt. I could feel the slug that was still in me and could tell that it remained in position. It did not hurt me, however.

She went on jabbering away at me. I remembered the picture of my life and avoided giving her a sharp answer.

"I'm going home," I said.

"Don't talk nonsense."

"You have no authority over me," I told her. "I'm legally entitled to take responsibility for my own life."

"For your own death, you mean."

"If it comes to that. You can't hold me here against my will. You can't operate on me without my consent."

"If you don't have that operation, you'll die."

"Everyone dies."

242

"I don't understand," she said, and her eyes were wide and filled with sorrow, and my heart went out to her.

"Don't worry about me," I said gently. "I know what I'm doing. And there's nothing anyone can do."

"They wouldn't even let me see you," Julia was saying. "And now you're home."

"It was a fast recovery."

"Shouldn't you be in bed?"

"The exercise is supposed to be good for me," I said. I looked at her, and for a moment I saw her as she'd appeared in parts of the picture of my life. As a bride. As a young mother.

"You know, you're a beautiful woman," I said.

She colored.

"I suppose we got married too young," I said. "We each had a lot of growing to do. And the business took too much of my time over the years. And I'm afraid I haven't been a very good husband."

"You weren't so bad."

"I'm glad we got married," I said. "And I'm glad we stayed together. And that you were here for me to come home to."

She started to cry. I held her until she stopped. Then, her face to my chest, she said, "At the hospital, waiting, I realized for the first time what it would mean for me to lose you. I thought we'd stopped loving each other a long time ago. I know you've had other women. For that matter, I've had lovers from time to time. I don't know if you knew that."

"It's not important."

"No," she said, "it's not important. I'm glad we got married, darling. And I'm glad you're going to be all right."

Monty said, "You had everybody worried there, kid. But what do you think you're doing down here? You're supposed to be home in bed."

"I'm supposed to get exercise. Besides, if I don't come down here how do I know you won't steal the firm into bankruptcy?"

My tone was light, but he flushed deeply. "You just hit a nerve," he said.

"What's the matter?"

"When they were busy cutting the bullet out of you, all I could think was you'd die thinking I was a thief."

"I don't know what you're talking about."

He lowered his eyes. "I was borrowing partnership funds," he said. "I was in a bind because of my own stupidity and I didn't want to admit it to you, so I dipped into the till. It was a temporary thing, a case of the shorts. I got everything straightened out before that clown took a shot at you. They know who it was yet?"

"Not yet."

"The night before you were shot, I stayed late and covered things. I wasn't going to say anything, and then I wondered if you'd been suspicious, and I decided I'd tell you about it first thing in the morning. Then it looked as though I wasn't going to get the chance. You didn't suspect anything?"

"I thought our cash position was light. But after all these years I certainly wasn't afraid of you stealing from me."

"All those years," he echoed, and I was seeing the picture of my life again. All the work Monty and I had put in side by side. The laughs we'd shared, the bad times we'd survived.

We looked at each other, and a great deal of feeling passed between us. Then he drew a breath and clapped me on the shoulder. "Well, that's enough about old times," he said gruffly. "Somebody's got to do a little work around here."

"I'm glad you're here," Peg said. "I couldn't even go to the hospital. All I could do was call every hour and ask anonymously for a report on your condition. Critical condition, that's what they said. Over and over."

"It must have been rough."

"It did something to me and for me," she said. "It made me realize that I've cheated myself out of a life. And I was the one who did it. You didn't do it to me."

"I told you I'd leave Julia."

"Oh, that was just a game we both played. I never really expected you to leave her. No, it's been my fault, dear. I settled into a nice secure life. But when you were on the critical list I decided my life was on the critical list, too, and that it was time I took some responsibility for it."

"Meaning?"

"Meaning it's good you came over tonight and not this after-noon, because you wouldn't have found me at home. I've got a job. It's not much, but it's enough to pay the rent. You see, I've decided it's time I started paying my own rent. In the fall I'll start night classes at the university."

"I see."

"You're not angry?"

"Angry? I'm happy for you."

"I don't regret what we've been to each other. I was a lost little girl with a screwed-up life and you made me feel loved and cared for. But I'm a big girl now. I'll still see you, if you want to see me, but from here on in I pay my own way."

"No more checks?"

"No more checks. I mean it."

I remembered some of our times together, seeing them as I had seen them in the picture of my life. I was filled with desire. I went and took her in my arms.

She said, "But is it safe? Won't it be dangerous for you?"

"The doctor said it'll do me good."

Her eyes sparkled. "Well, if it's just what the doctor ordered—" And she led me to the bedroom.

Afterward I wished I could have died in Peg's bed. Almost immediately I realized that would have been bad for her and bad for Julia.

Anyway, I hadn't yet done what I'd come back to do.

Later, while Julia slept, I lay awake in the darkness. I thought, This is crazy. I'm no detective. I'm a businessman. I died and You won't let me stay dead. Why can't I be dead?

I got out of bed, went downstairs and laid out the cards for a game of solitaire. I toasted a slice of bread and made myself a cup of tea.

I won the game of solitaire. It was a hard variety, one I could normally win once in fifty or a hundred times.

I thought. It's not Julia, it's not Monty, it's not Peg. All of them have love for me.

I felt good about that.

But who killed me? Who was left of my list?

I didn't feel good about that.


The following morning I was finishing my breakfast when Mark rang the bell. Julia went to the door and let him in. He came into the kitchen and got himself a cup of coffee from the pot on the stove.

"I was at the hospital," he said. "Night and day, but they wouldn't let any of us see you. I was there."

"Your mother told me."

"Then I had to leave town the day before yesterday and I just got back this morning. I had to meet with some men." A smile flickered on his face. He looked just like his mother when he smiled.

"I've got the financing," he said. "I'm in business."

"That's wonderful."

"I know you wanted me to follow in your footseps, dad. But I couldn't be happy having my future handed to me that way. I wanted to make it on my own."

"You're my son. I was the same myself."

"When I asked you for a loan—"

"I've been thinking about that," I said, remembering the scene as I'd witnessed it in the picture of my life. "I resented your independence and I envied your youth. I was wrong to turn you down."

"You were *right* to turn me down." That smile again, just like his mother. "I wanted to make it on my own, and then I turned around and asked for help from you. I'm just glad you knew better than to give me what I was weak enough to ask for. I

246

realized that almost immediately, but I was too proud to say anything, and then some madman shot you and—well, I'm glad everything turned out all right, dad."

"Yes," I said. "So am I."

Not Mark, then.

Not Debbie either. I always knew that, and knew it with utter certainty when she cried out "Oh, daddy!" and rushed to me and threw herself into my arms. "I'm so glad," she kept saying. "I was so worried."

"Calm down," I told her. "I don't want my grandchild born with a nervous condition."

"Don't worry about your grandchild. You're grandchild's going to be just fine."

"And how about my daughter?"

"Your daughter's just fine. Do you want to know something? These past few days, wow, I've really learned a lot during these past few days."

"So have I."

"How close I am to you, for one thing. Waiting at the hospital, there was a time when I thought, God, he's gone. I just had this feeling. And then I shook my head and said, no, it was nonsense, you were all right. And you know what they told us afterward? Your heart stopped during the operation, and it must have happened right when I got that feeling. I *knew*, and then I knew again when it resumed beating."

When I looked at my son I saw his mother's smile. When I looked at Debbie I saw myself.

"And another thing I learned, and that's how much people need each other. People were so good to us! So many people called me, asked about you. Even Philip called, can you imagine? He just wanted to let me know that I should call on him if there was anything he could do."

"What could he possibly do?"

"I have no idea. It was funny hearing from him, though. I hadn't heard his voice since we were living together. But it was nice of him to call, wasn't it?"

I nodded. "It must have made you wonder what might have been."

"What it made me wonder was how I ever thought Philip and I were made for each other. Scott was with me every minute, you know, except when he went down to give blood for you—"

"He gave blood for me?"

"Didn't mother tell you? You and Scott are the same blood type. It's one of the rarer types and you both have it. Maybe that's why I fell in love with him."

"Not a bad reason."

"He was with me all the time, you know, and by the time you were out of danger I began to realize how close Scott and I have grown, how much I love him. And then when I heard Philip's voice I thought what kid stuff that relationship of ours had been. I know you never approved."

"It wasn't my business to approve or disapprove."

"Maybe not. But I know you approve of Scott, and that's important to me."

I went home.

I thought, What do You want from me? It's not my son-in-law. You don't try to kill a man and then donate blood for a transfusion. Nobody would do a thing like that.

The person I cut off at the traffic circle? But that was insane. And how would I know him anyway? I wouldn't know where to start looking for him.

Some other enemy? But I had no enemies.

Julia said, "The doctor called again. He still doesn't see how you could check yourself out of the hospital. But he called to say he wants to schedule you for surgery."

Not yet, I told her. Not until I'm ready.

"When will you be ready?"

When I feel right about it, I told her.

She called him back, relayed the message. "He's very nice,"

248

she reported. "He says any delay is hazardous, so you should let him schedule as soon as you possibly can. If you have something to attend to he says he can understand that, but try not to let it drag on too long."

I was glad he was a sympathetic and understanding man, and that she liked him. He might be a comfort to her later when she needed someone around to lean on.

Something clicked.

I called Debbie.

"Just the one telephone call," she said, puzzled. "He said he knew you never liked him but he always respected you and he knew what an influence you were in my life. And that I should feel free to call on him if I needed someone to turn to. It was nice of him, that's what I told myself at the time, but there was something creepy about the conversation."

And what had she told him?

"That it was nice to hear from him, and that, you know, my husband and I would be fine. Sort of stressing that I was married, but in a nice way. Why?"

The police were very dubious. Ancient history, they said. The boy had lived with my daughter a while ago, parted amicably, never made any trouble. Had he ever threatened me? Had we ever fought?

He's the one, I said. Watch him, I said. Keep an eye on him.

So they assigned men to watch Philip, and on the fourth day the surveillance paid off. They caught him tucking a bomb beneath the hood of a car. The car belonged to my son-in-law, Scott.

"He thought you were standing between them. When she said she was happily married, well, he shifted his sights to the husband."

There had always been something about Philip that I had not liked. Something creepy, as Debbie put it. Perhaps he'll get treatment now. In any event, he'll be unable to harm anyone.

Is that why I was permitted to return? So that I could prevent Philip from harming Scott?

Perhaps that was the purpose. The conversations with Julia, with Monty, with Peg, with Mark and Debbie, those were fringe benefits.

Or perhaps it was the other way around.

All right.

They've prepared me for surgery. The doctor, understanding as ever, called again. This time I let him schedule me, and I came here and let them prepare me. And I've prepared myself.

All right.

I'm ready now.

# OUT
# THE
# WINDOW

THERE WAS NOTHING special about her last day. She seemed a little jittery, preoccupied with something or with nothing at all. But this was nothing new for Paula.

She was never much of a waitress in the three months she spent at Armstrong's. She'd forget some orders and mix up others, and when you wanted the check or another round of drinks you could go crazy trying to attract her attention. There were days when she walked through her shift like a ghost through walls, and it was as though she had perfected some arcane technique of astral projection, sending her mind out for a walk while her long lean body went on serving food and drinks and wiping down empty tables.

She did make an effort, though. She damn well tried. She could always manage a smile. Sometimes it was the brave smile of the walking wounded and other times it was a tight-jawed, brittle grin with a couple tabs of amphetamine behind it, but you take what you can to get through the days and any smile is better than none at all. She knew most of Armstrong's regulars by name and her greeting always made you feel as though you'd come home. When that's all the home you have, you tend to appreciate that sort of thing.

And if the career wasn't perfect for her, well, it certainly hadn't been what she'd had in mind when she came to New York in the first place. You no more set out to be a waitress in a Ninth Avenue gin mill than you intentionally become an ex-cop coasting through the months on bourbon and coffee. We have that sort of greatness thrust upon us. When you're as young as Paula Wittlauer you hang in there, knowing things are going to get better. When you're my age you just hope they don't get too much worse.

She worked the early shift, noon to eight, Tuesday through Saturday. Trina came on at six so there were two girls on the floor during the dinner rush. At eight Paula would go wherever she went and Trina would keep on bringing cups of coffee and glasses of bourbon for another six hours or so.

Paula's last day was a Thursday in late September. The heat of the summer was starting to break up. There was a cooling rain that morning and the sun never did show its face. I wandered in around four in the afternoon with a copy of the *Post* and read through it while I had my first drink of the day. At eight o'clock I was talking with a couple of nurses from Roosevelt Hospital who wanted to grouse about a resident surgeon with a Messiah complex. I was making sympathetic noises when Paula swept past our table and told me to have a good evening.

I said, "You too, kid." Did I look up? Did we smile at each other? Hell, I don't remember.

"See you tomorrow, Matt."

"Right," I said. "God willing."

But He evidently wasn't. Around three Justin closed up and I went around the block to my hotel. It didn't take long for the coffee and bourbon to cancel each other out. I got into bed and slept.

My hotel is on Fifty-seventh Street between Eighth and Ninth. It's on the uptown side of the block and my window is on the street side looking south. I can see the World Trade Center at the tip of Manhattan from my window.

I can also see Paula's building. It's on the other side of Fifty-seventh Street a hundred yards or so to the east, a towering high-rise that, had it been directly across from me, would have blocked my view of the trade center.

She lived on the seventeenth floor. Sometime after four she went out a high window. She swung out past the sidewalk and landed in the street a few feet from the curb, touching down between a couple of parked cars.

In high school physics they teach you that falling bodies accelerate at a speed of thirty-two feet per second. So she would have fallen thirty-two feet in the first second, another sixty-four feet the next second, then ninety-six feet in the third. Since she fell something like two hundred feet, I don't suppose she could have spent more than four seconds in the actual act of falling.

It must have seemed a lot longer than that.

I got up around ten, ten-thirty. When I stopped at the desk for my mail Vinnie told me they'd had a jumper across the street during the night. "A dame," he said, which is a word you don't hear much anymore. "She went out without a stitch on. You could catch your death that way."

I looked at him.

"Landed in the street, just missed somebody's Caddy. How'd you like to find something like that for a hood ornament? I wonder if your insurance would cover that. What do you call it, act of God?" He came out from behind the desk and walked with me to the door. "Over there," he said, pointing. "The florist's van there is covering the spot where she flopped. Nothing to see anyway. They scooped her up with a spatula and a sponge and then they hosed it all down. By the time I came on duty there wasn't a trace left."

"Who was she?"

"Who knows?"

I had things to do that morning, and as I did them I thought from time to time of the jumper. They're not that rare and they usually do the deed in the hours before dawn. They say it's always darkest then.

Sometime in the early afternoon I was passing Armstrong's

and stopped in for a short one. I stood at the bar and looked around to say hello to Paula but she wasn't there. A doughy redhead named Rita was taking her shift.

Dean was behind the bar. I asked him where Paula was. "She skipping school today?"

"You didn't hear?"

"Jimmy fired her?"

He shook his head, and before I could venture any further guesses he told me.

I drank my drink. I had an appointment to see somebody about something, but suddenly it ceased to seem important. I put a dime in the phone and cancelled my appointment and came back and had another drink. My hand was trembling slightly when I picked up the glass. It was a little steadier when I set it down.

I crossed Ninth Avenue and sat in St. Paul's for a while. Ten, twenty minutes. Something like that. I lit a candle for Paula and a few other candles for a few other corpses, and I sat there and thought about life and death and high windows. Around the time I left the police force I discovered that churches were very good places for thinking about that sort of thing.

After a while I walked over to her building and stood on the pavement in front of it. The florist's truck had moved on and I examined the street where she'd landed. There was, as Vinnie had assured me, no trace of what had happened. I tilted my head back and looked up, wondering what window she might have fallen from, and then I looked down at the pavement and then up again, and a sudden rush of vertigo made my head spin. In the course of all this I managed to attract the attention of the building's doorman and he came out to the curb anxious to talk about the former tenant. He was a black man about my age and he looked as proud of his uniform as the guy in the Marine Corps recruiting poster. It was a good-looking uniform, shades of brown, epaulets, gleaming brass buttons.

"Terrible thing," he said. "A young girl like that with her whole life ahead of her."

"Did you know her well?"

He shook his head. "She would give me a smile, always say hello, always call me by name. Always in a hurry, rushing in, rushing out again. You wouldn't think she had a care in the world. But you never know."

"You never do."

"She lived on the seventeenth floor. I wouldn't live that high above the ground if you gave me the place rent-free."

"Heights bother you?"

I don't know if he heard the question. "I live up one flight of stairs. That's just fine for me. No elevator and no, no high window." His brow clouded and he looked on the verge of saying something else, but then someone started to enter his building's lobby and he moved to intercept him. I looked up again, trying to count windows to the seventeenth floor, but the vertigo returned and I gave it up.


"Are you Matthew Scudder?"

I looked up. The girl who'd asked the question was very young, with long straight brown hair and enormous light brown eyes. Her face was open and defenseless and her lower lip was quivering. I said I was Matthew Scudder and pointed at the chair opposite mine. She remained on her feet.

"I'm Ruth Wittlauer," she said.

The name didn't register until she said, "Paula's sister." Then I nodded and studied her face for signs of a family resemblance. If they were there I couldn't find them. It was ten in the evening and Paula Wittlauer had been dead for eighteen hours and her sister was standing expectantly before me, her face a curious blend of determination and uncertainty.

I said, "I'm sorry. Won't you sit down? And will you have something to drink?"

"I don't drink."

"Coffee?"

"I've been drinking coffee all day. I'm shaky from all the damn coffee. Do I *have* to order something?"

She was on the edge, all right. I said, "No, of course not. You don't have to order anything." And I caught Trina's eye and warned her off and she nodded shortly and let us alone. I sipped my own coffee and watched Ruth Wittlauer over the brim of the cup.

"You knew my sister, Mr. Scudder."

"In a superficial way, as a customer knows a waitress."

"The police say she killed herself."

"And you don't think so?"

"I know she didn't."

I watched her eyes while she spoke and I was willing to believe she meant what she said. She didn't believe that Paula went out the window of her own accord, not for a moment. Of course, that didn't mean she was right.

"What do you think happened?"

"She was murdered." She made the statement quite matter-of-factly. "I know she was murdered. I think I know who did it."

"Who?"

"Cary McCloud."

"I don't know him."

"But it may have been somebody else," she went on. She lit a cigarette, smoked for a few moments in silence. "I'm pretty sure it was Cary," she said.

"Why?"

"They were living together." She frowned, as if in recognition of the fact that cohabitation was small evidence of murder. "He could do it," she said carefully. "That's why I think he did. I don't think just anyone could commit murder. In the heat of the moment, sure, I guess people fly off the handle, but to do it deliberately and throw someone out of a, out of a, to just deliberately throw someone out of a——"

I put my hand on top of hers. She had long small-boned hands and her skin was cool and dry to the touch. I thought she was going to cry or break or something but she didn't. It was just not going to be possible for her to say the word *window* and she would stall every time she came to it.

"What do the police say?"

"Suicide. They say she killed herself." She drew on the cigarette. "But they don't know her, they never knew her. If Paula

256

wanted to kill herself she would have taken pills. She liked pills."

"I figured she took ups."

"Ups, tranquilizers, ludes, barbiturates. And she liked grass and she liked to drink." She lowered her eyes. My hand was still on top of hers and she looked at our two hands and I removed mine. "I don't do any of those things. I drink coffee, that's my one vice, and I don't even do that much because it makes me jittery. It's the coffee that's making me nervous tonight. Not...all of this."

"Okay."

"She was twenty-four. I'm twenty. Baby sister, square baby sister, except that was always how she *wanted* me to be. She did all these things and at the same time she told me not to do them, that it was a bad scene. I think she kept me straight. I really do. Not so much because of what she was saying as that I looked at the way she was living and what it was doing to her and I didn't want that for myself. I thought it was crazy, what she was doing to herself, but at the same time I guess I worshipped her, she was always my heroine. I loved her, God, I really did, I'm just starting to realize how much, and she's dead and he killed her, I *know* he killed her, I just know it."

After a while I asked her what she wanted me to do.

"You're a detective."

"Not in an official sense. I used to be a cop."

"Could you...find out what happened?"

"I don't know."

"I tried talking to the police. It was like talking to the wall. I can't just turn around and do nothing. Do you understand me?"

"I think so. Suppose I look into it and it still looks like suicide?"

"She didn't kill herself."

"Well, suppose I wind up thinking that she did."

She thought it over. "I still wouldn't have to believe it."

"No," I agreed. "We get to choose what we believe."

"I have some money." She put her purse on the table. "I'm the straight sister, I have an office job, I save money. I have five hundred dollars with me."

"That's too much to carry in this neighborhood."

"Is it enough to hire you?"

I didn't want to take her money. She had five hundred dollars and a dead sister, and parting with one wouldn't bring the other back to life. I'd have worked for nothing but that wouldn't have been good because neither of us would have taken it seriously enough.

And I have rent to pay and two sons to support, and Armstrong's charges for the coffee and the bourbon. I took four fifty-dollar bills from her and told her I'd do my best to earn them.

After Paula Wittlauer hit the pavement, a black-and-white from the Eighteenth Precinct caught the squeal and took charge of the case. One of the cops in the car was a guy named Guzik. I hadn't known him when I was on the force but we'd met since then. I didn't like him and I don't think he cared for me either, but he was reasonably honest and had struck me as competent. I got him on the phone the next morning and offered to buy him a lunch.

We met at an Italian place on Fifty-sixth Street. He had veal and peppers and a couple glasses of red wine. I wasn't hungry but I made myself eat a small steak.

Between bites of veal he said, "The kid sister, huh? I talked to her, you know. She's so clean and so pretty it could break your heart if you let it. And of course she don't want to believe sis did the Dutch act. I asked is she Catholic because then there's the religious angle but that wasn't it. Anyway your average priest'll stretch a point. They're the best lawyers going, the hell, two thousand years of practice, they oughta be good. I took that attitude myself. I said, 'Look, there's all these pills. Let's say your sister had herself some pills and drank a little wine and smoked a little pot and then she went to the window for some fresh air. So she got a little dizzy and maybe she blacked out and most likely she never knew what was happening.' Because there's no question of insurance, Matt, so if she wants to think it's an accident I'm not gonna shout suicide in her ear. But that's what it says in the file."

"You close it out?"

"Sure. No question."

"She thinks murder."

He nodded. "Tell me something I don't know. She says this McCloud killed sis. McCloud's the boyfriend. Thing is he was at an after-hours club at Fifty-third and Twelfth about the time sis was going skydiving."

"You confirm that?"

He shrugged. "It ain't airtight. He was in and out of the place, he coulda doubled back and all, but there was the whole business with the door."

"What business?"

"She didn't tell you? Paula Wittlauer's apartment was locked and the chain bolt was on. The super unlocked the door for us but we had to send him back to the basement for a bolt cutter so's we could get through the chain bolt. You can only fasten the chain bolt from inside and you can only open the door a few inches with it on, so either Wittlauer launched her own self out the window or she was shoved out by Plastic Man, and then he went and slithered out the door without unhooking the chain bolt."

"Or the killer never left the apartment."

"Huh?"

"Did you search the apartment after the super came back and cut the chain for you?"

"We looked around, of course. There was an open window, there was a pile of clothes next to it. You know she went out naked, don't you?"

"Uh-huh."

"There was no burly killer crouching in the shrubbery, if that's what you're getting at."

"You checked the place carefully?"

"We did our job."

"Uh-huh. Look under the bed?"

"It was a platform bed. No crawl space under it."

"Closets?"

He drank some wine, put the glass down hard, glared at me. "What the hell are you getting at? You got reason to believe there was somebody in the apartment when we went in there?"

"Just exploring the possibilities."

"Jesus. You honestly think somebody's gonna be stupid enough to stay in the apartment after shoving her out of it? She musta been on the street ten minutes before we hit the building. If somebody did kill her, which never happened, but if they did they coulda been halfway to Texas by the time we hit the door, and don't that make more sense than jumping in the closet and hiding behind the coats?"

"Unless the killer didn't want to pass the doorman."

"So he's still got the whole building to hide in. Just the one man on the front door is the only security the building's got, anyway, and what does he amount to? And suppose he hides in the apartment and we happen to spot him. Then where is he? With his neck in the noose, that's where he is."

"Except you didn't spot him."

"Because he wasn't there, and when I start seeing little men who aren't there is when I put in my papers and quit the department."

There was an unvoiced challenge in his words. I had quit the department, but not because I'd seen little men. One night some years ago I broke up a bar holdup and went into the street after the pair who'd killed the bartender. One of my shots went wide and a little girl died, and after that I didn't see little men or hear voices, not exactly, but I did leave my wife and kids and quit the force and start drinking on a more serious level. But maybe it all would have happened just that way even if I'd never killed Estrellita Rivera. People go through changes and life does the damnedest things to us all.

"It was just a thought," I said. "The sister thinks it's murder so I was looking for a way for her to be right."

"Forget it."

"I suppose. I wonder why she did it."

"Do they even need a reason? I went in the bathroom and she had a medicine cabinet like a drugstore. Ups, downs, sideways.

260

Maybe she was so stoned she thought she could fly. That would explain her being naked. You don't fly with your clothes on. Everybody knows that."

I nodded. "They find drugs in her system?"

"Drugs in her...oh, Jesus, Matt. She came down seventeen flights and she came down fast."

"Under four seconds."

"Huh?"

"Nothing," I said. I didn't bother telling him about high school physics and falling bodies. "No autopsy?"

"Of course not. You've seen jumpers. You were in the department a lot of years, you know what a person looks like after a drop like that. You want to be technical, there coulda been a bullet in her and nobody was gonna go and look for it. Cause of death was falling from a great height. That's what it says and that's what it was, and don't ask me was she stoned or was she pregnant or any of those questions because who the hell knows and who the hell cares, right?"

"How'd you even know it was her?"

"We got a positive ID from the sister."

I shook my head. "I mean how did you know what apartment to go to? She was naked so she didn't have any identification on her. Did the doorman recognize her?"

"You kidding? He wouldn't go close enough to look. He was alongside the building throwing up a few pints of cheap wine. He couldn't have identified his own ass."

"Then how'd you know who she was?"

"The window." I looked at him. "Hers was the only window that was open more than a couple of inches, Matt. Plus her lights were on. That made it easy."

"I didn't think of that."

"Yeah, well, I was there, and we just looked up and there was an open window and a light behind it, and that was the first place we went to. You'da thought of it if you were there."

"I suppose."

He finished his wine, burped delicately against the back of his hand. "It's suicide," he said. "You can tell the sister as much."

"I will. Okay if I look at the apartment?"

"Wittlauer's apartment? We didn't seal it, if that's what you mean. You oughta be able to con the super out of a key."

"Ruth Wittlauer gave me a key."

"Then there you go. There's no department seal on the door. You want to look around?"

"So I can tell the sister I was there."

"Yeah. Maybe you'll come across a suicide note. That's what I was looking for, a note. You turn up something like that and it clears up doubts for the friends and relatives. If it was up to me I'd get a law passed. No suicide without a note."

"Be hard to enforce."

"Simple," he said. "If you don't leave a note you gotta come back and be alive again." He laughed. "That'd start 'em scribbling away. Count on it."

The doorman was the same man I'd talked to the day before. It never occurred to him to ask me my business. I rode up in the elevator and walked along the corridor to 17G. The key Ruth Wittlauer had given me opened the door. There was just the one lock. That's the way it usually is in high-rises. A doorman, however slipshod he may be, endows tenants with a sense of security. The residents of unserviced walk-ups affix three or four extra locks to their doors and still cower behind them.

The apartment had an unfinished air about it, and I sensed that Paula had lived there for a few months without ever making the place her own. There were no rugs on the wood parquet floor. The walls were decorated with a few unframed posters held up by scraps of red Mystik tape. The apartment was an L-shaped studio with a platform bed occupying the foot of the L. There were newspapers and magazines scattered around the place but no books. I noticed copies of Variety and Rolling Stone and People and the Village Voice.

The television set was a tiny Sony perched on top of a chest of drawers. There was no stereo, but there were a few dozen records, mostly classical with a sprinkling of folk music, Pete

Seeger and Joan Baez and Dave Van Ronk. There was a dust-free rectangle on top of the dresser next to the Sony.

I looked through the drawers and closets. A lot of Paula's clothes. I recognized some of the outfits, or thought I did.

Someone had closed the window. There were two windows that opened, one in the sleeping alcove, the other in the living room section, but a row of undisturbed potted plants in front of the bedroom window made it evident she'd gone out of the other one. I wondered why anyone had bothered to close it. In case of rain, I supposed. That was only sensible. But I suspect the gesture must have been less calculated than that, a reflexive act akin to tugging a sheet over the face of a corpse.

I went into the bathroom. A killer could have hidden in the stall shower. If there'd been a killer.

Why was I still thinking in terms of a killer?

I checked the medicine cabinet. There were little tubes and vials of cosmetics, though only a handful compared with the array on one of the bedside tables. Here were containers of aspirin and other headache remedies, a tube of antibiotic ointment, several prescriptions and nonprescription hay fever preparations, a cardboard packet of Band-aids, a roll of adhesive tape, a box of gauze pads. Some Q-tips, a hairbrush, a couple of combs. A toothbrush in the holder.

There were no footprints on the floor of the stall shower. Of course he could have been barefoot. Or he could have run water and washed away the traces of his presence before he left.

I went over and examined the window sill. I hadn't asked Guzik if they'd dusted for prints and I was reasonably certain no one had bothered. I wouldn't have taken the trouble in their position. I couldn't learn anything looking at the sill. I opened the window a foot or so and stuck my head out, but when I looked down the vertigo was extremely unpleasant and I drew my head back inside at once. I left the window open, though. The room could stand a change of air.

There were four folding chairs in the room, two of them closed and leaning against a wall, one near the bed, the fourth alongside the window. They were royal blue and made of high-impact plastic. The one by the window had her clothes piled on it. I went through the stack. She'd placed them deliberately on the chair but hadn't bothered folding them.

You never know what suicides will do. One man will put on a tuxedo before blowing his brains out. Another one will take off everything. Naked I came into the world and naked will I go out of it, something like that.

A skirt. Beneath it a pair of panty hose. Then a blouse, and under it a bra with two small, lightly padded cups, I put the clothing back as I had found it, feeling like a violator of the dead.

The bed was unmade. I sat on the edge of it and looked across the room at a poster of Mick Jagger. I don't know how long I sat there. Ten minutes, maybe.

On the way out I looked at the chain bolt. I hadn't even noticed it when I came in. The chain had been neatly severed. Half of it was still in the slot on the door while the other half hung from its mounting on the jamb. I closed the door and fitted the two halves together, then released them and let them dangle. Then I touched their ends together again. I unhooked the end of the chain from the slot and went to the bathroom for the roll of adhesive tape. I brought the tape back with me, tore off a piece and used it to fasten the chain back together again. Then I let myself out of the apartment and tried to engage the chain bolt from outside, but the tape slipped whenever I put any pressure on it.

I went inside again and studied the chain bolt. I decided I was behaving erratically, that Paula Wittlauer had gone out the window of her own accord. I looked at the window sill again. The light dusting of soot didn't tell me anything one way or the other. New York's air is filthy and the accumulation of soot could have been deposited in a couple of hours, even with the window shut. It didn't mean anything.

I looked at the heap of clothes on the chair, and I looked again at the chain bolt, and I rode the elevator to the basement and found either the superintendent or one of his assistants. I asked to borrow a screwdriver. He gave me a long screwdriver with an amber plastic grip. He didn't ask me who I was or what I wanted it for.

I returned to Paula Wittlauer's apartment and removed the chain bolt from its moorings on the door and jamb. I left the building and walked around the corner to a hardware store on Ninth Avenue. They had a good selection of chain bolts but I wanted one identical to the one I'd removed and I had to walk down Ninth Avenue as far as Fiftieth Street and check four stores before I found what I was looking for.

Back in Paula's apartment I mounted the new chain bolt, using the holes in which the original had been mounted. I tightened the screws with the super's screwdriver and stood out in the corridor and played with the chain. My hands are large and not terribly skillful, but even so I was able to lock and unlock the chain bolt from outside the apartment.

I don't know who put it up, Paula or a previous tenant or someone on the building staff, but that chain bolt had been as much protection as the Sanitized wrapper on a motel toilet seat. As evidence that Paula'd been alone when she went out the window, well, it wasn't worth a thing.

I replaced the original chain bolt, put the new one in my pocket, returned to the elevator and gave back the screwdriver. The man I returned it to seemed surprised to get it back.


It took me a couple of hours to find Cary McCloud. I'd learned that he tended bar evenings at a club in the West Village called The Spider's Web. I got down there around five. The guy behind the bar had knobby wrists and an underslung jaw and he wasn't Cary McCloud. "He don't come on till eight," he told me, "and he's off tonight anyway." I asked where I could find McCloud. "Sometimes he's here afternoons but he ain't been in today. As far as where you could look for him, that I couldn't tell you."

A lot of people couldn't tell me but eventually I ran across someone who could. You can quit the police force but you can't stop looking and sounding like a cop, and while that's a hindrance in some situations it's a help in others. Ultimately I found a man in a bar down the block from The Spider's Web who'd learned it was best to cooperate with the police if it didn't cost you anything. He gave me an address on Barrow Street and told me which bell to ring.

I went to the building but I rang several other bells until somebody buzzed me through the downstairs door. I didn't want Cary to know he had company coming. I climbed two flights of stairs to the apartment he was supposed to be occupying. The bell downstairs hadn't had his name on it. It hadn't had any name at all.

Loud rock music was coming through his door. I stood in front of it for a minute, then hammered on it loud enough to make myself heard over the electric guitars. After a moment the music dropped in volume. I pounded on the door again and a male voice asked who I was.

I said, "Police. Open up." That's a misdemeanor but I didn't expect to get in trouble for it.

"What's it about?"

"Open up, McCloud."

"Oh, Jesus," he said. He sounded tired, aggravated. "How did you find me, anyway? Give me a minute, huh? I want to put some clothes on."

Sometimes that's what they say while they're putting a clip into an automatic. Then they pump a handful of shots through the door and into you if you're still standing behind it. But his voice didn't have that kind of edge to it and I couldn't summon up enough anxiety to get out of the way. Instead I put my ear against the door and heard whispering within. I couldn't make out what they were whispering about or get any sense of the person who was with him. The music was down in volume but there was still enough of it to cover their conversation.

The door opened. He was tall and thin, with hollow cheeks and prominent eyebrows and a worn, wasted look to him. He must have been in his early thirties and he didn't really look much older than that but you sensed that in another ten years he'd look twenty years older. If he lived that long. He wore patched jeans and a T-shirt with The Spider's Web silkscreened on it. Beneath the legend there was a sketch of a web. A macho

266

spider stood at one end of it, grinning, extending two of his eight arms to welcome a hesitant girlish fly.

He noticed me noticing the shirt and managed a grin. "Place where I work," he said.

"I know."

"So come into my parlor. It ain't much but it's home."

I followed him inside, drew the door shut after me. The room was about fifteen feet square and held nothing you could call furniture. There was a mattress on the floor in one corner and a couple of cardboard cartons alongside it. The music was coming from a stereo, turntable and tuner and two speakers all in a row along the far wall. There was a closed door over on the right. I figured it led to the bathroom, and that there was a woman on the other side of it.

"I guess this is about Paula," he said. I nodded. "I been over this with you guys," he said. "I was nowhere near there when it happened. The last I saw her was five, six hours before she killed herself. I was working at the Web and she came down and sat at the bar. I gave her a couple of drinks and she split."

"And you went on working."

"Until I closed up. I kicked everybody out a little after three and it was close to four by the time I had the place swept up and the garbage on the street and the window gates locked. Then I came over here and picked up Sunny and we went up to the place on Fifty-third."

"And you got there when?"

"Hell, I don't know. I wear a watch but I don't look at it every damn minute. I suppose it took five minutes to walk here and then Sunny and I hopped right in a cab and we were at Patsy's in ten minutes at the outside, that's the after-hours place, I told you people all of this, I really wish you would talk to each other and leave me the hell alone."

"Why doesn't Sunny come out and tell me about it?" I nodded at the bathroom door. "Maybe she can remember the time a little more clearly."

"Sunny? She stepped out a little while ago."

"She's not in the bathroom?"

"Nope. Nobody's in the bathroom."

"Mind if I see for myself?"

"Not if you can show me a warrant."

We looked at each other. I told him I figured I could take his word for it. He said he could always be trusted to tell the truth. I said I sensed as much about him.

He said, "What's the hassle, huh? I know you guys got forms to fill out, but why not give me a break? She killed herself and I wasn't anywhere near her when it happened."

He could have been. The times were vague, and whoever Sunny turned out to be, the odds were good that she'd have no more time sense than a koala bear. There were any number of ways he could have found a few minutes to go up to Fifty-seventh Street and heave Paula out a window, but it didn't add up that way and he just didn't feel like a killer to me. I knew what Ruth meant and I agreed with her that he was capable of murder but I don't think he'd been capable of this particular murder.

I said, "When did you go back to the apartment?"

"Who said I did?"

"You picked up your clothes, Cary."

"That was yesterday afternoon. The hell, I needed my clothes and stuff."

"How long were you living there?"

He hedged. "I wasn't exactly living there."

"Where were you exactly living?"

"I wasn't exactly living anywhere. I kept most of my stuff at Paula's place and I stayed with her most of the time but it wasn't as serious as actual living together. We were both too loose for anything like that. Anyway, the thing with Paula, it was pretty much winding itself down. She was a little too crazy for me." He smiled with his mouth. "They have to be a little crazy," he said, "but when they're too crazy it gets to be too much of a hassle."

Oh, he could have killed her. He could kill anyone if he had to, if someone was making too much of a hassle. But if he were to kill cleverly, faking the suicide in such an artful fashion, fastening the chain bolt on his way out, he'd pick a time when he had a solid alibi. He was not the sort to be so precise and so slipshod all at the same time.

"So you went and picked up your stuff."

"Right."

"Including the stereo and records."

"The stereo was mine. The records, I left the folk music and the classical shit because that belonged to Paula. I just took my records."

"And the stereo."

"Right."

"You got a bill of sale for it, I suppose."

"Who keeps that crap?"

"What if I said Paula kept the bill of sale? What if I said it was in with her papers and cancelled checks?"

"You're fishing."

"You sure of that?"

"Nope. But if you did say that, I suppose I'd say the stereo was a gift from her to me. You're not really gonna charge me with stealing a stereo, are you?"

"Why should I? Robbing the dead's a sacred tradition. You took the drugs, too, didn't you? Her medicine cabinet used to look like a drugstore but there was nothing stronger than Excedrin when I took a look. That's why Sunny's in the bathroom. If I hit the door all the pretty little pills go down the toilet."

"I guess you can think that if you want."

"And I can come back with a warrant if I want."

"That's the idea."

"I ought to rap on the door just to do you out of the drugs but it doesn't seem worth the trouble. That's Paula Wittlauer's stereo. I suppose it's worth a couple hundred dollars. And you're not her heir. Unplug that thing and wrap it up, McCloud. I'm taking it with me."

"The hell you are."

"The hell I'm not."

"You want to take anything but your own ass out of here, you come back with a warrant. Then we'll talk about it."

"I don't need a warrant."

"You can't—"

"I don't need a warrant because I'm not a cop. I'm a detective, McCloud, I'm private, and I'm working for Ruth Wittlauer, and that's who's getting the stereo. I don't know if she wants it or not, but that's her problem. She doesn't want Paula's pills so you can pop them yourself or give them to your girl friend. You can shove 'em up your ass for all I care. But I'm walking out of here with that stereo and I'll walk through you if I have to, and don't think I wouldn't enjoy it."

"You're not even a cop."

"Right."

"You got no authority at all." He spoke in tones of wonder. "You said you were a cop."

"You can always sue me."

"You can't take that stereo. You can't even be in this room."

"That's right." I was itching for him. I could feel my blood in my veins. "I'm bigger than you," I said, "and I'm a whole lot harder, and I'd get a certain amount of satisfaction in beating the crap out of you. I don't like you. It bothers me that you didn't kill her because somebody did and it would be a pleasure to hang it on you. But you didn't do it. Unplug the stereo and pack it up so I can carry it or I'm going to take you apart."

I meant it and he realized as much. He thought about taking a shot at me and he decided it wasn't worth it. Maybe it wasn't all that much of a stereo. While he was unhooking it I dumped a carton of his clothes on the floor and we packed the stereo in it. On my way out the door he said he could always go to the cops and tell them what I'd done.

"I don't think you want to do that," I said.

"You said somebody killed her."

"That's right."

"You just making noise?"

"No."

"You're serious?" I nodded. "She didn't kill herself? I thought it was open and shut, from what the cops said. It's interesting. In a way, I guess you could say it's a load off my mind."

270

"How do you figure that?"

He shrugged. "I thought, you know, maybe she was upset it wasn't working out between us. At the Web the vibes were on the heavy side, if you follow me. Our thing was falling apart and I was seeing Sunny and she was seeing other guys and I thought maybe that was what did it for her. I suppose I blamed myself, like."

"I can see it was eating away at you."

"I just said it was on my mind."

I didn't say anything.

"Man," he said, "*nothing* eats away at me. You let things get to you that way and it's death."

I shouldered the carton and headed on down the stairs.

Ruth Wittlauer had supplied me with an Irving Place address and a GRamercy 5 telephone number. I called the number and didn't get an answer, so I walked over to Hudson and caught a northbound cab. There were no messages for me at the hotel desk. I put Paula's stereo in my room, tried Ruth's number again, then walked over to the Eighteenth Precinct. Guzik had gone off duty but the desk man told me to try a restaurant around the corner, and I found him there drinking draft Heinekens with another cop named Birnbaum. I sat at their table and ordered bourbon for myself and another round for the two of them.

I said, "I have a favor to ask. I'd like you to seal Paula Wittlauer's apartment."

"We closed that out," Guzik reminded me.

"I know, and the boyfriend closed out the dead girl's stereo." I told him how I'd reclaimed the unit from Cary McCloud. "I'm working for Ruth, Paula's sister. The least I can do is make sure she gets what's coming to her. She's not up to cleaning out the apartment now and it's rented through the first of October. McCloud's got a key and God knows how many other people have keys. If you slap a seal on the door it'd keep the grave robbers away."

"I guess we can do that. Tomorrow all right?"

"Tonight would be better."

"What's there to steal? You got the stereo out of there and I didn't see anything else around that was worth much."

"Things have a sentimental value."

He eyed me, frowned. "I'll make a phone call," he said. He went to the booth in the back and I jawed with Birnbaum until he came back and told me it was all taken care of.

I said, "Another thing I was wondering. You must have had a photographer on the scene. Somebody to take pictures of the body and all that."

"Sure. That's routine."

"Did he go up to the apartment while he was at it? Take a roll of interior shots?"

"Yeah. Why?"

"I thought maybe I could have a look at them."

"What for?"

"You never know. The reason I knew it was Paula's stereo in McCloud's apartment was I could see the pattern in the dust on top of the dresser where it had been. If you've got interior pictures maybe I'll see something else that's not there anymore and I can lean on McCloud a little and recover it for my client."

"And that's why you'd like to see the pictures."

"Right."

He gave me a look. "That door was bolted from the inside, Matt. With a chain bolt."

"I know."

"And there was no one in the apartment when we went in there."

"I know that, too."

"You're still barking up the murder tree, aren't you? Jesus, the case is closed and the reason it's closed is the ditzy broad killed herself. What are you making waves for?"

"I'm not. I just wanted to see the pictures."

"To see if somebody stole her diaphragm or something."

"Something like that." I drank what remained of my drink.

"You need a new hat anyway, Guzik. The weather's turning and a fellow like you needs a hat for fall."

"If I had the price of a hat, maybe I'd go out and get one."

"You got it," I said.

He nodded and we told Birnbaum we wouldn't be long. I walked with Guzik around the corner to the Eighteenth. On the way I palmed him two tens and a five, twenty-five dollars, the price of a hat in police parlance. He made the bills disappear.

I waited at his desk while he pulled the Paula Wittlauer file. There were about a dozen black-and-white prints, eight by tens, high-contrast glossies. Perhaps half of them showed Paula's corpse from various angles. I had no interest in these but I made myself look at them as a sort of reinforcement, so I wouldn't forget what I was doing on the case.

The other pictures were interior shots of the L-shaped apartment. I noted the wide-open window, the dresser with the stereo sitting on it, the chair with her clothing piled haphazardly upon it. I separated the interior pictures from the ones showing the corpse and told Guzik I wanted to keep them for the time being. He didn't mind.

He cocked his head and looked at me. "You got something, Matt?"

"Nothing worth talking about."

"If you ever do, I'll want to hear about it."

"Sure."

"You like the life you're leading? Working private, scuffling around?"

"It seems to suit me."

He thought it over, nodded. Then he started for the stairs and I followed after him.

Later that evening I managed to reach Ruth Wittlauer. I bundled the stereo into a cab and took it to her place. She lived in a well-kept brownstone a block and a half from Gramercy Park. Her apartment was inexpensively furnished but the pieces looked to have been chosen with care. The place was clean and neat. Her clock radio was tuned to an FM station that was playing chamber music. She had coffee made and I accepted a cup and sipped it while I told her about recovering the stereo from Cary McCloud.

"I wasn't sure whether you could use it," I said, "but I couldn't see any reason why he should keep it. You can always sell it."

"No, I'll keep it. I just have a twenty-dollar record player that I bought on Fourteenth Street. Paula's stereo cost a couple of hundred dollars." She managed a smile. "So you've already more than earned what I gave you. Did he kill her?"

"No."

"You're sure of that?"

I nodded. "He'd kill if he had a reason but I don't think he did. And if he did kill her he'd never have taken the stereo or the drugs, and he wouldn't have acted the way he did. There was never a moment when I had the feeling that he'd killed her. And you have to follow your instincts in this kind of situation. Once they point things out to you, then you can usually find the facts to go with them."

"And you're sure my sister killed herself?"

"No. I'm pretty sure someone gave her a hand."

Her eyes widened.

I said, "It's mostly intuition. But there are a few facts to support it." I told her about the chain bolt, how it had proved to the police that Paula'd killed herself, how my experiment had shown it could have been fastened from the corridor. Ruth got very excited at this but I explained that it didn't prove anything in and of itself, only that suicide remained a theoretical possibility.

Then I showed her the pictures I'd obtained from Guzik. I selected one shot which showed the chair with Paula's clothing without showing too much of the window. I didn't want to make Ruth look at the window.

"The chair," I said, pointing to it. "I noticed this when I was in your sister's apartment. I wanted to see a photograph taken at the time to make sure things hadn't been rearranged by the cops or McCloud or somebody else. But that clothing's exactly the way it was when I saw it."

"I don't understand."

"The supposition is that Paula got undressed, put her clothes on the chair, then went to the window and jumped." Her lip was trembling but she was holding herself together and I went right on talking. "Or she'd taken her clothes off earlier and maybe she took a shower or a nap and then came back and jumped. But look at the chair. She didn't fold her clothes neatly, she didn't put them away. And she didn't just drop them on the floor, either. I'm no authority on the way women get undressed but I don't think many people would do it that way."

Ruth nodded. Her face was thoughtful.

"That wouldn't mean very much by itself. If she were upset or stoned or confused she might have thrown things on the chair as she took them off. But that's not what happened. The order of the clothing is all wrong. The bra's underneath the blouse, the panty hose is underneath the skirt. She took her bra off after she took her blouse off, obviously, so it should have wound up on top of the blouse, not under it."

"Of course."

I held up a hand. "It's nothing like proof, Ruth. There are any number of other explanations. Maybe she knocked the stuff onto the floor and then picked it up and the order of the garments got switched around. Maybe one of the cops went through the clothing before the photographer came around with his camera. I don't really have anything terribly strong to go on."

"But you think she was murdered."

"Yes, I guess I do."

"That's what I thought all along. Of course I had a reason to think so."

"Maybe I've got one, too. I don't know."

"What are you going to do now?"

"I think I'll poke around a little. I don't know much about Paula's life. I'll have to learn more if I'm going to find out who killed her. But it's up to you to decide whether you want me to stay with it."

"Of course I do. Why wouldn't I?"

"Because it probably won't lead anywhere. Suppose she was

upset after her conversation with McCloud and she picked up a stranger and took him home with her and he killed her. If that's the case we'll never know who he was."

"You're going to stay with it, aren't you?"

"I suppose I want to."

"It'll be complicated, though. It'll take you some time. I suppose you'll want more money." Her gaze was very direct. "I gave you two hundred dollars. I have three hundred more that I can afford to pay. I don't mind paying it, Mr. Scudder. I already got... I got my money's worth for the first two hundred, didn't I? The stereo. When the three hundred runs out, well, you can tell me if you think it's worth staying with the case. I couldn't afford more cash right away, but I could arrange to pay you later on or something like that."

I shook my head. "It won't come to more than that," I said. "No matter how much time I spend on it. And you keep the three hundred for the time being, all right? I'll take it from you later on. If I need it, and if I've earned it."

"That doesn't seem right."

"It seems right to me," I said. "And don't make the mistake of thinking I'm being charitable."

"But your time's valuable."

I shook my head. "Not to me it isn't."

I spent the next five days picking the scabs off Paula Wittlauer's life. It kept turning out to be a waste of time but the time's always gone before you realize you've wasted it. And I'd been telling the truth when I said my time wasn't valuable. I had nothing better to do, and my peeks into the corners of Paula's world kept me busy.

Her life involved more than a saloon on Ninth Avenue and an apartment on Fifty-seventh Street, more than serving drinks and sharing a bed with Cary McCloud. She did other things. She went one evening a week to group therapy on West Seventy-ninth Street. She took voice lessons every Tuesday morning on Amsterdam Avenue. She had an ex-boyfriend she saw once in a while. She hung out in a couple of bars in the neighborhood and a couple of others in the Village. She did this, she did that, she went here, she went there, and I kept busy dragging myself around town and talking to all sorts of people, and I managed to learn quite a bit about the person she'd been and the life she'd led without learning anything at all about the person who'd put her on the pavement.

At the same time, I tried to track her movements on the final night of her life. She'd evidently gone more or less directly to The Spider's Web after finishing her shift at Armstrong's. Maybe she'd stopped at her apartment for a shower and a change of clothes, but without further ado she'd headed downtown. Somewhere around ten she left the Web, and I traced her from there to a couple of other Village bars. She hadn't stayed at either of them long, taking a quick drink or two and moving on. She'd left alone as far as anyone seemed to remember. This didn't prove a thing because she could have stopped elsewhere before continuing uptown, or she could have picked someone up on the street, which I'd learned was something she'd done more than once in her young life. She could have found her killer loitering on a street corner or she could have phoned him and arranged to meet him at her apartment.

Her apartment. The doormen changed off at midnight, but it was impossible to determine whether she'd returned before or after the changing of the guard. She'd lived there, she was a regular tenant, and when she entered or left the building it was not a noteworthy occasion. It was something she did every night, so when she came home for the final time the man at the door had no reason to know it was the final time and thus no reason to take mental notes.

Had she come in alone or with a companion? No one could say, which did suggest that she'd come in alone. If she'd been with someone her entrance would have been a shade more memorable. But this also proved nothing, because I stood on the other side of Fifty-seventh Street one night and watched the doorway of her building, and the doorman didn't take the pride in his position that the afternoon doorman had shown. He was away from the door almost as often as he was on it. She could have walked in flanked by six Turkish sailors and there was a chance no one would have seen her.

The doorman who'd been on duty when she went out the window was a rheumy-eyed Irishman with liver-spotted hands. He hadn't actually seen her land. He'd been in the lobby, keeping himself out of the wind, and then he came rushing out when he heard the impact of the body on the street.

He couldn't get over the sound she made.

"All of a sudden there was this noise," he said. "Just out of the blue there was this noise and it must be it's my imagination but I swear I felt it in my feet. I swear she shook the earth. I had no idea what it was, and then I came rushing out, and Jesus God, there she was."

"Didn't you hear a scream?"

"Street was empty just then. This side, anyway. Nobody around to scream."

"Didn't *she* scream on the way down?"

"Did somebody say she screamed? I never heard it."

Do people scream as they fall? They generally do in films and on television. During my days on the force I saw several of them after they jumped, and by the time I got to them there were no screams echoing in the air. And a few times I'd been on hand while they talked someone in off a ledge, but in each instance the talking was successful and I didn't have to watch a falling body accelerate according to the immutable laws of physics.

Could you get much of a scream out in four seconds?

I stood in the street where she'd fallen and I looked up toward her window. I counted off four seconds in my mind. A voice shrieked in my brain. It was Thursday night, actually Friday morning, one o'clock. Time I got myself around the corner to Armstrong's, because in another couple of hours Justin would be closing for the night and I'd want to be drunk enough to sleep.

And an hour or so after that she'd be one week dead.

I'd worked myself into a reasonably bleak mood by the time I got to Armstrong's. I skipped the coffee and crawled straight into the bourbon bottle, and before long it began to do what it was

supposed to do. It blurred the corners of the mind so I couldn't
see the bad dark things that lurked there.

When Trina finished for the night she joined me and I bought
her a couple of drinks. I don't remember what we talked about.
Some but by no means all of our conversation touched upon
Paula Wittlauer. Trina hadn't known Paula terribly well—their
contact had been largely limited to the two hours a day when
their shifts overlapped—but she knew a little about the sort of
life Paula had been leading. There'd been a year or two when
her own life had not been terribly different from Paula's. Now
she had things more or less under control, and maybe there would
have come a time when Paula would have taken charge of her
life, but that was something we'd never know now.

I suppose it was close to three when I walked Trina home.
Our conversation had turned thoughtful and reflective. On the
street she said it was a lousy night for being alone. I thought of
high windows and evil shapes in dark corners and took her hand
in mine.

She lives on Fifty-sixth between Ninth and Tenth. While we
waited for the light to change at Fifty-seventh Street I looked over
at Paula's building. We were far enough away to look at the high
floors. Only a couple of windows were lighted.

That was when I got it.

I've never understood how people think of things, how little
perceptions trigger greater insights. Thoughts just seem to come
to me. I had it now, and something clicked within me and a
source of tension unwound itself.

I said something to that effect to Trina.

"You know who killed her?"

"Not exactly," I said. "But I know how to find out. And it can
wait until tomorrow."

The light changed and we crossed the street.

She was still sleeping when I left. I got out of bed and dressed
in silence, then let myself out of her apartment. I had some
coffee and a toasted English muffin at the Red Flame. Then I

went across the street to Paula's building. I started on the tenth floor and worked my way up, checking the three or four possible apartments on each floor. A lot of people weren't home. I worked my way clear to the top floor, the twenty-fourth, and by the time I was done I had three possibles listed in my notebook and a list of over a dozen apartments I'd have to check that evening.

At eight-thirty that night I rang the bell of Apartment 21G. It was directly in line with Paula's apartment and four flights above it. The man who answered the bell wore a pair of Lee corduroy slacks and a shirt with a blue vertical stripe on a white background. His socks were dark blue and he wasn't wearing shoes.

I said, "I want to talk with you about Paula Wittlauer."

His face fell apart and I forgot my three possibles forever because he was the man I wanted. He just stood there. I pushed the door open and stepped forward and he moved back automatically to make room for me. I drew the door shut after me and walked around him, crossing the room to the window. There wasn't a speck of dust or soot on the sill. It was immaculate, as well-scrubbed as Lady Macbeth's hands.

I turned to him. His name was Lane Posmantur and I suppose he was around forty, thickening at the waist, his dark hair starting to go thin on top. His glasses were thick and it was hard to read his eyes through them but it didn't matter. I didn't need to see his eyes.

"She went out this window," I said. "Didn't she?"

"I don't know what you're talking about."

"Do you want to know what triggered it for me, Mr. Posmantur? I was thinking of all the things nobody noticed. No one saw her enter the building. Neither doorman remembered it because it wasn't something they'd be likely to remember. Nobody saw her go out the window. The cops had to look for an open window in order to know who the hell she was. They backtracked her from the window she fell out of.

"And nobody saw the killer leave the building. Now that's the one thing that would have been noticed, and that's the point that occurred to me. It wasn't that significant by itself but it made me dig a little deeper. The doorman was alert once her body hit

the street. He'd remember who went in or out of the building
from that point on. So it occurred to me that maybe the killer
was still inside the building, and then I got the idea that she was
killed by someone who *lived* in the building, and from that point
on it was just a question of finding you because all of a sudden
it all made sense."

I told him about the clothes on the chair. "She didn't take
them off and pile them up like that. Her killer put her clothes
like that, and he dumped them on the chair so that it would look
as though she undressed in her apartment, and so that it would
be assumed she'd gone out of her own window.

"But she went out of your window, didn't she?"

He looked at me. After a moment he said he thought he'd
better sit down. He went to an armchair and sat in it. I stayed
on my feet.

I said, "She came here. I guess she took off her clothes and
you went to bed with her. Is that right?"

He hesitated, then nodded.

"What made you decide to kill her?"

"I didn't."

I looked at him. He looked away, then met my gaze, then
avoided my eyes again. "Tell me about it," I suggested. He looked
away again and a minute went by and then he started to talk.

It was about what I'd figured. She was living with Cary McCloud
but she and Lane Posmantur would get together now and then
for a quickie. He was a lab technician at Roosevelt and he brought
home drugs from time to time and perhaps that was part of his
attraction for her. She'd turned up that night a little after two
and they went to bed. She was really flying, he said, and he'd
been taking pills himself, it was something he'd begun doing
lately, maybe seeing her had something to do with it.

They went to bed and did the dirty deed, and then maybe
they slept for an hour, something like that, and then she was
awake and coming unglued, getting really hysterical, and he tried
to settle her down and he gave her a couple of slaps to bring her
around, except they didn't bring her around, and she was staggering and she tripped over the coffee table and fell funny, and

by the time he sorted himself out and went to her she was lying with her head at a crazy angle and he knew her neck was broken and when he tried for a pulse there was no pulse to be found.

"All I could think of was she was dead in my apartment and full of drugs and I was in trouble."

"So you put her out the window."

"I was going to take her back to her own apartment. I started to dress her but it was impossible. And even with her clothes on I couldn't risk running into somebody in the hallway or on the elevator. It was crazy.

"I left her here and went to her apartment. I thought maybe Cary would help me. I rang the bell and nobody answered and I used her key and the chain bolt was on. Then I remembered she used to fasten it from outside. She'd showed me how she could do that. I tried with mine but it was installed properly and there's not enough play in the chain. I unhooked her bolt and went inside.

"Then I got the idea. I went back to my apartment and got her clothes and I rushed back and put them on her chair. I opened her window wide. On my way out the door I put her lights on and hooked the chain bolt again.

"I came back here to my own apartment. I took her pulse again and she was dead, she hadn't moved or anything, and I couldn't do anything for her, all I could do was stay out of it, and I, I turned off the lights here, and I opened my own window and dragged her body over to it, and, oh, God in heaven, God, I almost couldn't make myself do it but it was an accident that she was dead and I was so damned *afraid*—"

"And you dropped her out and closed the window." He nodded. "And if her neck was broken it was something that happened in the fall. And whatever drugs were in her system was just something she'd taken by herself, and they'd never do an autopsy anyway. And you were home free."

"I didn't hurt her," he said. "I was just protecting myself."

"Do you really believe that, Lane?"

"What do you mean?"

"You're not a doctor. Maybe she was dead when you threw her out the window. Maybe she wasn't."

"There was no pulse!"

"You couldn't find a pulse. That doesn't mean there wasn't any. Did you try artificial respiration? Do you know if there was any brain activity? No, of course not. All you know was that you looked for a pulse and you couldn't find one."

"Her neck was broken."

"Maybe. How many broken necks have you had occasion to diagnose? And people sometimes break their necks and live anyway. The point is that you couldn't have known she was dead and you were too worried about your own skin to do what you should have done. You should have phoned for an ambulance. You know that's what you should have done and you knew it at the time but you wanted to stay out of it. I've known junkies who left their buddies to die of overdoses because they didn't want to get involved. You went them one better. You put her out a window and let her fall twenty-one stories so that you wouldn't get involved, and for all you know she was alive when you let go of her."

"No," he said. "No. She was dead."

I'd told Ruth Wittlauer she could wind up believing whatever she wanted. People believe what they want to believe. It was just as true for Lane Posmantur.

"Maybe she was dead," I said. "Maybe that's your fault, too."

"What do you mean?"

"You said you slapped her to bring her around. What kind of a slap, Lane?"

"I just tapped her on the face."

"Just a brisk slap to straighten her out."

"That's right."

"Oh, hell, Lane. Who knows how hard you hit her? Who knows whether you may not have given her a shove? She wasn't the only one on pills. You said she was flying. Well, I think maybe you were doing a little flying yourself. And you'd been sleepy and you were groggy and she was buzzing around the room and being a general pain in the ass, and you gave her a slap and a shove and another slap and another shove and—"

"No!"

"And she fell down."

"It was an accident."

"It always is."

"I didn't hurt her. I liked her. She was a good kid, we got on fine, I didn't hurt her, I—"

"Put your shoes on, Lane."

"What for?"

"I'm taking you to the police station. It's a few blocks from here, not very far at all."

"Am I under arrest?"

"I'm not a policeman." I'd never gotten around to saying who I was and he'd never thought to ask. "My name's Scudder, I'm working for Paula's sister. I suppose you're under citizen's arrest. I want you to come to the precinct house with me. There's a cop named Guzik there and you can talk to him."

"I don't have to say anything," he said. He thought for a moment. "You're not a cop."

"No."

"What I said to you doesn't mean a thing." He took a breath, straightened up a little in his chair. "You can't prove a thing," he said. "Not a thing."

"Maybe I can and maybe I can't. You probably left prints in Paula's apartment. I had them seal the place a while ago and maybe they'll find traces of your presence. I don't know if Paula left any prints here or not. You probably scrubbed them up. But there may be neighbors who know you were sleeping with her, and someone may have noticed you scampering back and forth between the apartments that night, and it's even possible a neighbor heard the two of you struggling in here just before she went out the window. When the cops know what to look for, Lane, they usually find it sooner or later. It's knowing what you're after that's the hard part.

"But that's not even the point. Put your shoes on, Lane. That's right. Now we're going to go see Guzik, that's his name, and he's going to advise you of your rights. He'll tell you that you have a right to remain silent, and that's the truth, Lane, that's a right that you have. And if you remain silent and if you get a decent lawyer and do what he tells you I think you can beat this charge, Lane. I really do."

"Why are you telling me this?"

"Why?" I was starting to feel tired, drained, but I kept on with it. "Because the worst thing you could do is remain silent, Lane. Believe me, that's the worst thing you could do. If you're smart you'll tell Guzik everything you remember. You'll make a complete voluntary statement and you'll read it over when they type it up and you'll sign your name on the bottom.

"Because you're not really a killer, Lane. It doesn't come easily to you. If Cary McCloud had killed her he'd never lose a night's sleep over it. But you're not a psychopath. You were drugged and half-crazy and terrified and you did something wrong and it's eating you up. Your face fell apart the minute I walked in here tonight. You could play it cute and beat this charge, Lane, but all you'd wind up doing is beating yourself.

"Because you live on a high floor, Lane, and the ground's only four seconds away. And if you squirm off the hook you'll never get it out of your head, you'll never be able to mark it Paid in Full, and one day or night you'll open the window and you'll go out of it, Lane. You'll remember the sound her body made when she hit the street—"

"No!"

I took his arm. "Come on," I said. "We'll go see Guzik."

Tough, Suspenseful Novels by
Edgar Award-winning Author

# LAWRENCE BLOCK

## FEATURING MATTHEW SCUDDER

### THE DEVIL KNOWS YOU'RE DEAD
72023-X/ $5.99 US/ $6.99 Can

### A DANCE AT THE SLAUGHTERHOUSE
71374-8/ $4.99 US/ $5.99 Can

### A TICKET TO THE BONEYARD
70994-5/ $4.99 US/ $5.99 Can

### OUT ON THE CUTTING EDGE
70993-7/ $4.95 US/ $5.95 Can

### THE SINS OF THE FATHERS
76363-X/ $4.99 US/ $5.99 Can

### TIME TO MURDER AND CREATE
76365-6/ $4.99 US/ $5.99 Can

### A STAB IN THE DARK
71574-0/ $4.99 US/ $5.99 Can

### IN THE MIDST OF DEATH
76362-1/ $4.99 US/ $5.99 Can

### EIGHT MILLION WAYS TO DIE
71573-2/ $4.99 US/ $5.99 Can

### A WALK AMONG THE TOMBSTONES
71375-6/ $4.99 US/ $5.99 Can